CHASING PACQUIAO

CHASING PACQUIAO

ROD PULIDO

VIKING

VIKING
An imprint of Penguin Random House LLC, New York

First published in the United States of America by Viking,
an imprint of Penguin Random House LLC, 2023

Visit us online at PenguinRandomHouse.com.

Library of Congress Cataloging-in-Publication Data is available.

Printed in the United States of America

ISBN 9780593526736

1   3   5   7   9   10   8   6   4   2

BVG

Design by Opal Roengchai

Text set in Athelas

For Alex.
Love who you are, because you are amazing.
—Dad

Please be aware this story contains homophobic language and scenes of graphic violence.

CHASING PACQUIAO

ROUND 1

Whenever I text Brandon from school, I almost feel like a super-hero. Not that there's anything super heroic about texting my boyfriend, but it puts me in danger of exposing my secret identity.

I also get to flex my poetry powers. My thumbs hover over my phone like two asps about to strike. A flurry of tapping follows. I read the text over, and, with a groan, delete it from existence. For the past few days, this has been my pattern: *write, groan, delete, repeat.* Bran deserves more—especially today—but I don't have a hell of a lot of options. Or time. A few more tries and the piece is more or less complete:

> *Like the Bat-Signal at night*
> *I'll come running when you call*
> *You are my one and only*
> *Just like Nick Fury's eyeball*

I count the number of syllables, making sure there are twenty-eight total. Four lines, seven syllables each. The structure of the Filipino poetry form tanaga.

"Aw, comic book fanboys in love. Happy anniversary, B!" Rosie, a strikingly pretty Latina and my best bud, plops onto the seat beside me and brushes back her dyed-orange drapes of hair.

"Announce it over the loudspeaker, why don't ya?" I whisper. With a sigh, I tap send, and the text flies out into the ether. At the surrounding lunch tables, the usual goes down: chatting, eating, littering. Thankfully, nobody seems to have noticed Rosie's characteristic outburst.

"Sorry, mi amigo." She lowers her voice to a near-acceptable level. "Hey, I made you something to mark the occasion. *Relax*. I didn't use your names."

She pulls a black picture frame from her bag and sets it between us on the table. My breath catches. It's a painting of a dark purple heart set against a backdrop of blue and black swirls. Written across the heart in calligraphy are the initials B + B. It's incredibly detailed, gorgeous, thoughtful. Before I can thank Rosie, someone else cuts in.

"Who's B-plus-B?"

Shit. Right off, I know the owner of the shrill voice: Charlotte Wilkes—the nosiest girl in school, possibly all of MacArthur Park. A one-teen TMZ.

She whips her platinum-blond hair over her shoulder and takes a seat across from us without being invited. "What, your nerdy ass finally nab a girlfriend, Bobby?"

My stomach clenches, but I'm ready for her question. Been ready for months, practicing my answer out loud ad nauseam in front of the bathroom mirror, in the shower, probably even in my sleep. "I actually do have a girlfriend. She's homeschooled, she's a total geek, and she's cute."

The key to selling a good lie is to cloak it in layers of truth.

Charlotte leans in closer. "Uh-huh. So what's the name of this cute geek of a girlfriend nobody's ever seen or heard of?"

"Brandy."

She squints, game for the challenge. "Where'd you meet?"

"Where else do geeks meet? The comic shop." Also the truth.

"Right. Got a pic of her? Let's see." She grabs for my cell, but I slip it into my pocket. Okay, I wasn't ready for that one. My phone has a few selfies of Brandon and me; no way can I let her see them.

"Um, we don't—she doesn't like taking pics." My eyes dip slightly. "She's kind of shy."

Charlotte smirks. "Sure she is."

"Hey, chica," Rosie says, "back off with the interrogation."

"Yeah," I say, "don't you have a Gossipers Anonymous meeting to get to?"

"Whatever." Charlotte's distracted by a gathering at the center of the quad, and she dashes toward the commotion.

Air shoots from my mouth. *Close one.* The knot in my stomach starts to loosen, but it quickly tightens again. In the middle of the crowd, a giant student repeatedly pummels a smaller boy with spiky blond hair. Freshman, from the looks of it.

"Fuck that little faggot up!" somebody yells.

I wince at the slur, even though hearing it at school has become a regular occurrence. There are some words I never want to get used to.

Onlookers cheer, while others barely take notice, numb to the routine. He floors the boy with a punch to his jaw, making him spit blood. Possibly a tooth. Before any teachers arrive, the bell clangs off-key, and the larger boy disappears through the stream of bodies.

Rosie sighs. "Another peaceful day at Westlake High."

As a few students help the battered boy to his feet, blood spills from his lips—a graphic reminder of why my secret identity can never get out.

I rise and shove the frame Rosie made into my backpack. The gift really is amazing; Rosie's so thoughtful. Just wish she'd been thoughtful enough to give it to me anywhere but school.

At the end of the day, I hop on my bike—a cherry-red seven-speed—and tear off campus like I stole something. Back in 2008, when I was only nine years old, Dad gave me this bike right before he died. He'd used it every day to get to his job at the laundromat. Without this bike, our family would not have eaten. As he lay withering away in bed, the cancer shredding his stomach, he said he wished he could have given me more. That memory slips into my thoughts every time I go for a ride.

I pedal over cracked concrete, past brick walls decorated with various gang tags, then hang a right onto the obstacle course of chaos known as Alvarado Street. A red SUV swerves and nearly clips me. The driver blasts his horn—'cause it's *my* fault he texts and drives. They say driving in L.A. will make even the most chill person freak out. I wouldn't know, but somehow I doubt it's as terrifying as biking through it. I wouldn't risk the trip without a good reason.

Brandon Elpusan is better than a good reason.

The shadows of the 101 Freeway swallow me as I ride under

the overpass, through the shanty tent town. My body slumps at the sight of so many families who are even poorer than Mom and me living on the street. A few blocks later, I cut into the hilly residentials of Silver Lake, where the streets are cleaner, the homes larger, the graffiti nonexistent. Silver Lake sits barely three miles from MacArthur Park, but it's a whole other world. A richer, whiter one. More than just the 101 divides the two neighborhoods.

Five minutes later, I coast up to the Villain's Lair, my favorite comic book shop in L.A. Six months ago to the day, I met Brandon here. He'd just started working as a cashier after school, and we hit it off right away. We talked for nearly an hour that first day and had a highly informative discussion regarding the age-old question: *Why don't the Hulk's pants rip when he transforms?* We decided on gamma-irradiated stretchy pants.

I chain up my bike and open the glass door. Posters of iconic heroes dominate the walls—Wonder Woman, Teen Titans, the Avengers—along with lesser-known characters like Deena Pilgrim and Savage Dragon. I breathe in the familiar scent of lemon air freshener and new comic books, and the stress of the school day fades away.

Bran leans over the cashier counter, sporting a *Dawn of the Dead* tee, the sleeves tight against his lean arms. Like me, he's Filipino, but his brown complexion is a shade lighter—probably because he spends so much time indoors at the Lair. The boy could use more sun, but other than that, he's perfect.

He brushes back his dark bangs and greets me with a dimpled smile that makes my palms sweat. "Welcome to the Villain's Lair. May I help you?"

I grin back. "Hope so. I'm looking for a dope gift for that special geek in my life."

He furrows his brow in that cute way he does. "Right. Well, we just got in some super-cool hardcover editions: *All-Star Superman*, *Powers: Who Killed Retro Girl?*, *Civil War*."

"Hmm, hardcovers?" I chuckle. "He's not *that* special."

"Really now? Okay, you know what makes the best gift? Poetry. Writing your own, I mean. It's personal and shows you put real thought into it, instead of just being lazy and buying something off the shelf."

"That's what I keep saying!" I lean in closer. "So what'd you get me?"

"Bought you something off the shelf." Bran gives me a grin that makes my earlobes warm and pulls a flat rectangular package from behind the counter. "Happy anniversary, B."

It's obviously a comic book, but which one? Out of all the millions of comics in the world, what single issue did he pick to mark our big day? My fingertips tingle. I tear off the wrapping paper to reveal *Alpha Flight*, issue #106.

I've read it before as a reprint, so I immediately recognize the issue. Alpha Flight is Marvel Comics's designated Canadian superhero team—they're basically the D-list Avengers with maple leaves across their chests. On the cover, in mid-scream, is the mutant speedster Northstar. Issue 106 deals with him saving an abandoned baby who has AIDS, and ends with Northstar coming out as Marvel's first gay superhero. Landmark stuff.

I bite my lip, crossing my arms so I don't fling myself into Brandon's. The first out queer superhero—it's perfect. Still, a nagging thought wiggles into the back of my brain: *Is he trying to tell me something?* He's out to his family and friends—has been for a couple years. Me? Besides Brandon, exactly two people know: Rosie and my mom.

"Thanks, Bran. This is incredibly sweet."

"Of course," Brandon says. "And I really love the poem, B. It's a Marvel/DC epic crossover in four lines." He means it. And he doesn't seem to mind that I'm so dirt poor I can't afford a real gift. He tries to take my hand, but a stranger walks up to the counter with his purchases. I back away and let Bran ring up the customer.

Bran's boss, Larry, the owner and manager of the Lair, is pretty laid back and always lets me hang out—as long as I help out around the store. While Bran works, I stock shelves, chat with the regulars, and try to stay out of the way.

A few hours later, closing time arrives. Bran activates the store alarm and hits the lights, and I follow him to the front entrance.

I want to do something to mark the moment, to show Bran what I have yet to say in words. *What the hell, the store is empty.* Before he can open the door, I take his hand, lean in, and kiss him. Softly at first. He flinches in surprise because I'm never affectionate in public, but then he pulls me close. Adrenaline courses through me, and my chest heaves. Is that his pulse thumping or mine? Even in the dim light coming inside from the streetlamp, I see him blush. It's catching; my cheeks flush.

Bran's lips split into a grin. "Now that was a good present. So what did you think of mine?" I follow him out to the deserted sidewalk. The night is gorgeous, as smoggy, starless Los Angeles nights go.

Bran tries to take my hand, but I stuff it inside my pocket.

"You mean the comic book hinting that I should just announce my complete gayness to the world already? Not too subtle is what I think."

"Dude, I should be able to hold my boyfriend's hand when we go for a walk."

"Easy for you to say in the queer haven of Silver Lake. Not gonna fly in my hood."

"Come on. It's not that different from here. People are just people."

I stare at Bran. Sometimes I can't believe he's so naive about certain things. "Yeah, well, you don't go to War Zone High, where there's a fight every other day. And what if someone from my school sees us? What's my motto?"

He sighs. "Self-preservation."

"And it's a damn good one." I climb onto my bike and almost ride off, but a tugging in my chest stops me. I can't stand the thought of leaving on a bad note, especially today. "Give me time, all right?"

He breaks eye contact and sighs, but eventually nods. "You know, you said the same exact thing back on our three-month anniversary."

His words make me wince. *How much more time will I need? And how much longer will he continue to wait for me?* The questions linger like the cold breeze on my neck as I pedal away.

Despite nearly dozing off during the ride, I make it home okay. To say our apartment is small would be charitable. It's basically two bedrooms the size of walk-in closets, a tiny kitchen with a used restaurant table for two, and a living room furnished with a dingy couch Mom found on the curb five years ago. It's sparse, but it's home. Right now, it's an empty home. As usual, Mom won't be back from waitressing until well after midnight.

I down a plate of leftover rice and chicken adobo for dinner while trying not to fall asleep. I accidentally bite into one of the tiny black peppers, and it gives me a much-needed jolt. After eating, I wade through twenty problems of algebra homework, then belly flop into bed beneath a poster of my childhood hero, boxing champ Manny "Pacman" Pacquiao. It's the only thing decorating my walls.

As sleep begins to overtake me, the final thoughts that sprinkle my mind are of Brandon. How his scent reminds me of comic books and long bike rides. How he brushes back his bangs like a curtain, revealing the shine and warmth in his eyes. How I would do almost anything for him—except, it would seem, come out.

My eyelids blink open to the wail of the alarm. The clock reads 7:24 a.m.

And I'm late.

I rush through my morning routine at triple speed, skipping breakfast and a shower. On my way out, I pass Mom, asleep on the couch, her uniform a map of condiment stains. Another late night of waiting tables for her. I'd love to actually speak to her, but she needs her rest. I peck her on the forehead and let her snooze.

My favorite time to bike through the neighborhood is in the

early morning. The air is cool, and fewer cars are on the road. My mind wanders to Rosie and her gift, then to Brandon and that kiss. *Damn.*

Pretty sure I love him. I should've said it. It was the perfect time to say it.

I pop a mini wheelie up the curb and speed into the school lot. Without coming to a full stop, I hop off my bike and guide it into the rack.

At the west double-door entrance, the metal detector wand declares me weaponless, and I pass through with five minutes to spare. Enough time to unload my books at my locker.

Up ahead, a crowd clogs up traffic—probably another point-less fight. I break through the gathering and stop short. My heart booms like a bass drum in my chest. Scrawled across my locker door in bright red letters are the words: BOBBY AGBAYANI IS A FUCKING FAGGOT!

I read the slur again and again, my pulse clicking like a metronome on high speed. Sweat forms across my forehead as I try to process how this could have happened.

"This is bullshit," I say through clenched teeth.

Heads turn from the graffiti over to me. They're all wondering if it's true. Most have already made up their minds. Their expressions say, *Of course it is. Knew it the whole time.*

My skin burns. Wish I could crawl into my locker and slam the door behind me forever. I rack my brain. I have to do something, anything, to fix this—or I am dead.

"Who wrote this?" I say, struggling not to yell. The crowd stares without answering. Any one of them could be the perp.

Giggles come from the back: Charlotte and her clique of gossip mongers.

"You do this?" I snap.

She throws me major side-eye. "Oh, don't be accusing me of shit, Bobby. You the one everyone's wondering about."

"So, you a gayboy or what?" someone yells from the back.

I scan the crowd of faces, some smug, a few sympathetic. All want an answer straight from my lips. I remember my rehearsed lie. It's the only thing that can save me now.

Screw it.

"Yeah, I have a *boyfriend*. He's homeschooled, he's a total geek, and he's *damn* hot."

ROUND 2

The crowd's in an uproar as I plod away. *What in the name of Thor, God of Thunder, did I just do?*

I'm actually out.

Like, completely.

This was not the plan. Not that there was a plan. But I was robbed of the decision, the choice of the how and the when.

"Told you," Charlotte says. "Boy's a total butt pirate."

Some dude makes a crack—something about packing fudge. Hilarious. If you're going to be a homophobic douchebag, at least be original about it.

My eyelid flutters out of control like a strobe light. Some anonymous asshole just drew a huge target on my forehead—in a place where people love to take shots. On the plus side, Brandon will be happy. So there's that. Maybe I'd laugh if my jaw would stop chattering.

When I enter algebra class, Rosie rushes up to me. "Hey, you okay?" The first bell hasn't even rung, and she's already heard the news. Hooray for texting.

"Not here," I tell her.

I hurry to my seat and hide behind my propped-up binder until class starts. Unfortunately, Eric Ocampo, a Pinoy kid who sits directly behind me, doesn't catch my dire need for privacy.

When we were in third grade, we'd have playdates at the park, even a few sleepovers. That was before Eric turned into a meth head. Now he's just another screwed-up kid who peeks over my shoulder for the answers. Which is doubly annoying because his breath reeks like burnt plastic.

"Ay, pare, that was messed up," Eric says, using the Filipino word for friend. He nudges my arm. "What they wrote on your locker?"

"Yep." I manage.

"Ay, I got your back, bruh." He holds out a fist over my shoulder.

A sigh slips through my lips, but I bump his fist with my own. "Good to know."

"I know you ain't bakla."

The Tagalog gay slur is another gut punch to my psyche. I shut my eyes and pretend I'm sipping an ube milkshake on a Hawaiian beach, far from the special hell that has become my life.

Eric leans over my shoulder, and his breath makes me gag. "Ay, you do the homework? What you get for the first page?"

I try to follow along with Mrs. Jennings's lesson, but instead of the numbers on the board, my mind dwells on the scarlet letters across my locker. By second period, the word will have spread over the entire school—but that doesn't mean I have to leave the damn announcement up.

After Jennings finishes her lesson, I raise my hand and ask to use the restroom. She usually frowns on bathroom breaks, but I'm part of the minority that actually does her assignments.

On my way out, Rosie raises her brow at me. I look past her.

The halls are empty, quieter than a morgue at midnight. Appropriate, since I feel like I'm a pallbearer at my own funeral. I hurry by my locker without looking at it and exit the building. The morning light splits the clouds and hits me in the eyes. I shield my face and hurry across the quad to Mr. Hopkins's office near the basketball gym.

The door is open, and classical music filters out from a beat-up boom box. I peek my head in. Every kind of cleaning solution assaults my nostrils. Hopkins sits at his desk, filling out paperwork. He's a short, thin white man known for the raggedy Lakers cap perpetually attached to his noggin.

I knock. "Hello? Mr. Hopkins? Um, someone wrote all over my locker. Will you clean it up? Please?"

"Good morning." He rises, extends his hand. "I'd love to help you, um . . ."

"Bobby." We shake hands; his grip is firm, but not imposing.

"Bobby, I'd love to help, but I need to get down to the boys' restroom and clean up some graffiti. Write your locker number down, and I'll try to get to it tomorrow."

Tomorrow? Hell no, that is not going to fly. "You sure you can't get to it now? What they wrote is, um, pretty messed up."

"Sorry, son, but someone wrote, 'Principal Peterson, your lunch is served' right above the toilet. In huge block letters. So, you can imagine that kind of takes priority."

I try to stifle a laugh with my hand, but I'm not entirely successful.

Hopkins turns off the music, tips his hat to me. "You have yourself a good day."

Have yourself a good day? This guy has to be the most polite janitor ever. Does he hold open the toilet-stall door for you too?

Hopkins pushes a cart full of cleaning supplies outside the Dutch door and shuts the bottom half.

Splinters line the top edge of the door, which would make a suitable deterrent to most trespassers. Unfortunately, I'm more desperate than most.

Hopkins continues down the path toward the gymnasium, humming the classical piece. I wait until he rounds the corner, then climb over the door, which earns me a lovely splinter in the tip of my right index finger. Perfect. I ignore the throbbing pain and grab an abrasive sponge and an all-purpose cleaner off the shelf.

Back at my locker, I picture the vandal in my firing sights and shoot the hateful words with the spray setting on wide. I scrub the message, putting my elbow and all my built-up hostility into it. Neither the ink nor my anger fades. *Damn it.* Whoever did this sure picked the right marker for the job.

I spray the door again. Rosie rounds the corner, clutching a bathroom pass.

"Figured you'd be here. Jennings was ready to call the office. Lucky for you she said I could wrangle you in." She puts her hand on my shoulder. "You okay?"

I shrug, continue scrubbing. "Yeah, I planned to post a coming-out notice on the school website anyway. Something short, tasteful. This just saves me the hassle."

She leans against the lockers. "What happened? How'd it get out?"

"*What happened?* You gave me that frame at school, and Charlotte figured it all out and shifted her mouth into overdrive."

"Hold up. You're blaming this on me?"

"You got a better explanation?"

"Yeah, maybe you aren't as slick as you think you are. Maybe somebody realized you don't talk about girls' asses like other dudes, or when we're talking you actually look at my eyes, not my boobs."

Rosie might have a point, but no way am I going to admit it. Not when she's acting salty.

"Or maybe nobody's noticed I don't stare at your boobs 'cause your boobs aren't as great as you think."

Her mouth drops open. "Not cool, Agbayani." Rosie storms off down the hall.

Okay, she didn't deserve that, and I probably shouldn't have pissed off my only real friend right about now. Sometimes I can be such a d-hole.

Yep, *best day ever.*

I scrub harder and wish I could erase "faggot" not only from my locker but from the vocabulary of the entire world. Not that it would do any good. Somebody somewhere would come up with another evil word to replace it.

The bell rings, and students filter out into the halls. The graffiti has slightly faded, but the words still linger, ghostlike. The stares and murmurs begin again. I open my locker, toss the cleaner and sponge inside, and dash back to class.

When I get back to algebra, the room's filling up with the

next period. Mrs. Jennings arches her brow at me but says nothing. I probably just used up all my good-student cred with her. Can't worry about that now. I jot down tonight's homework from the board, grab my backpack, and rush to my next class.

At lunch, I hide out at a back table in the library, secluded near the stacks. The library, like most of the school's facilities, is barely functional. It boasts two archaic computers that take the better part of an hour to load, plus three stacks of bookshelves lined with outdated reference materials and moldy textbooks. The library is less a place of research and study and more a lunchtime refuge for the outcasts of Westlake High—of which I'm apparently now a member.

My name floats through the room in not-so-guarded whispers. The shade is palpable. At a table of lowly freshmen, one kid stares at me, says something to a couple of his friends, and the whole lot cracks up. Yes, even here among the Westlake High pariahs, I'm the object of scrutiny and ridicule.

Tonight's homework has piled up after four periods. But instead of tackling quadratic equations, I work on a tanaga for Rosie. Hopefully it'll get her to forgive me. After a false start in which I fail to find a word that rhymes with "douche nozzle," the four lines are complete.

I'm sorry I was evil
Like Loki and Magneto
If you would please forgive me
I'll buy you a burrito

Okay, so I'm no Lin-Manuel Miranda, but it'll do. I rhymed a Mexican fast-food staple with a megalomaniac mutant. That has to count for something. I punch send and break out my Algebra II textbook.

Fifteen minutes later, Rosie hasn't replied. Guess she's making me sweat it out. Ugh. Can't say I blame her.

"What kind of a burrito? And don't say no pinche Taco Bell." Rosie looms in front of me, arms folded.

"El Charro's veggie burrito with bell peppers, rice, and guac?"

"Extra guac."

"Of course."

"And my boobs?"

I can't withhold a smirk. "Oh, *so* spectacular. I can feel the gay slipping away just looking at them."

"Okay then." She grabs a seat beside me and pulls out her algebra book.

For the remainder of lunch, we go through the homework. Rosie isn't the best at math, so I explain a few problems to her. I've been her unofficial math tutor since we first started hanging out in junior high. I've always felt safer with Rosie, so it's more than a fair trade-off. Hanging with her is probably why people didn't mess with me before. The prettiest girl in school won't date you if you punk her best friend.

As I explain a problem, Rosie's attention wanes and she drops her pencil in between the pages of her textbook.

"What's up?" I ask.

She averts her eyes before answering. "Sorry for being my

usual loudmouth self. Do you really think it was Charlotte who outed you?"

"I don't know. Forget about it. Shouldn't have blamed you." I scan the room. A couple of students eye me; their smirks make my face flush. "Anyway, knowing this school, it could've been anyone."

ROUND 3

During sixth-period English, Mrs. Cisneros talks about the theme of religion in *Animal Farm*. She says Sugarcandy Mountain represents the afterlife and is used to pacify the farm animals so they'll continue to toil away and not revolt. Seems fairly obvious to me, especially since the raven who spouts the Sugarcandy Mountain gospel is named Moses. My stomach grumbles throughout the lecture. I wouldn't mind gobbling up a mountain of candy.

When school lets out, I hang back and talk to Mrs. C so I don't have to deal with any drama in the overcrowded halls. I ask if the pig Old Major represents Vladimir Lenin, and she lights up like Thor's hammer. Teachers are so predictable, always starved for an interested student.

I glance at the clock. Nearly twenty minutes have passed since the bell rang. Should be plenty. I say bye and escape into the deserted halls. I'd picked up all my books during lunch, so I don't need to stop by my locker. The less I see of it, the better.

I exit the building and make my way over to the main bike rack. The school grounds are quiet, peaceful. Maybe from now on I'll stay late every day. I unlock my seven-speed and guide it toward the parking lot. A group of rowdy upperclassmen are hanging out by the exit, so I make a detour and head to the soc-cer field instead.

The field's grass is unkempt—green and thriving in the middle, yellow and dead near the goals. The open expanse is peaceful and gives me a sliver of hope that I can get through this unwanted turn in my life.

I stop suddenly. My first thought when I see them is that Rosie was right: I'm not as slick as I think I am. I should have left with everyone else.

When there were witnesses.

On the bleachers sits one of the more notorious crews at Westlake High, led by Rex "T-Rex" Banta, a Filipino, five-foot-ten mass of muscle with an immaculately combed pompadour. He's totally aping Bruno Mars's signature hair and might even pass for his evil twin—if Bruno had bad acne like Rex does from injecting too many steroids. With him is his younger and much smaller brother, Eddie, along with Jorge, a skinny Mexi-can kid with a shaved head.

The brothers play Pusoy Dos, a Filipino card game, while Jorge sits off to the side, flipping a balisong knife. Even yards away, I can tell the blade is real, not a trainer. My skin chills. Jorge has a few decent moves, but it doesn't sit well with me that he's using a Pinoy weapon. Especially when there's a strong possibility he could use it on me.

"Pusoy!" Eddie slams down his last card and cackles. "That's three in a row, bruh."

Rex shakes his head, gathering the stray cards. "You keep getting all the twos. Shuffle that shit right this time."

I almost turn around and head back toward the school, but

Eddie sees me and jumps down to the grass, deck of cards in hand.

"Check it out," Eddie says, strolling over to me. "The little faggot himself. All by his little faggot self." He flicks the card edges. "'Sup, faggot."

Rex rises. He looks ten feet tall standing on the lowest bleacher seat. He hops off, and the metal creaks as if sighing. "Ay, bruh, don't you know you can't say 'faggot' no more? That shit's politically incorrect."

"Aw, for real? My bad."

"Yeah, they wanna be called 'queer' now. Ain't that right, queer boy?"

Sweat trickles down my neck and forms a puddle at the small of my back. I climb on my bike and try to pedal away, but Eddie grabs the handlebars and blocks my path. No avoiding a confrontation now, and nobody is coming to help me. We're too far out from the main building.

"Where you going, queer boy?" Eddie flings a playing card at my face, grazing my cheek.

My pulse pounds at my temple. My legs quiver. "Hey, guys, I just wanna get home, okay?"

"Ay, lemme ask you something on the real, pare." Rex wanders over to a spot a few feet behind his brother. "You're Pinoy. Catholic, yeah?"

I shrug. "I guess."

"You know what the Bible says about homosexuality, right? *You shall not lie with a male as with a woman; it is an abomination.* So what you gotta say about that?"

"I dunno. Not all that into the Bible."

"Well, you should be, pare. It's the straight-up word of God. Shit'll save your soul." Great, another homophobe who uses religion to justify bigotry. He studies me for a moment like I'm some alien species, then turns to his brother. "All right, let him go, Eddie."

"Got a sweet bike there, pare," Eddie says to me, ignoring his brother. "I could use a nice ride. Help a Pinoy brother out." He flashes a yellow overbite. I want to put my fist through each of his stained teeth. If it were just him, I probably would.

My arms tremble. My grip tightens around the handlebars, and I think of Dad. He didn't give in to the pain; I sure as hell am not giving in to these assholes. "You're never getting my bike."

Rex studies me. "You got a big sack on you, dude. I respect that." He chews his lip. "Leave the bike, and you can walk away."

"You heard him," Eddie says. "Off, bitch."

In one motion, I jerk the handlebars up and slam the front tire into Eddie's stomach. He topples to the ground, and the deck of cards scatters.

"Eddie!" Rex runs up and drives a punch into my gut. I cry out and crumple to the grass, taking the bike with me. The pedal stabs my thigh, sending a shooting pain through my leg.

"Damn bakla," Rex says. "Let's kick his ass. Jorge! What you waiting for, gago? Get over here!"

"No," I mumble, bracing for the knife strike. It doesn't come. Instead, a flurry of kicks connect with my side and face; each feels like a hammer blow. One bursts my lip, and my mouth fills with hot blood. My gag reflex kicks in, and I cough it up. I cover my head with my arms and roll up like a pill bug.

"Okay," Rex says, "little dude's had enough."

Eddie gets in one more kick. "Don't ever touch me, you fucking fag!"

Rex stoops down so our noses are barely a foot apart. His breath feels like a hand dryer on my face. "Remember this, bakla boy. I was gonna let you walk, but nobody messes with my little bro—especially not no stupid-ass faggot don't know where to stick his titi."

I try to grab Rex's arm, but my muscles won't cooperate. "Don't take my bike . . . please."

"Hey, what are you doing?" a woman's voice calls from far off. "Get away from him!"

"Shit," Rex says. "Teacher lady coming."

Through the blur, I make out Eddie and Jorge sprinting away. Ahead of them, Rex tears away on my bike—my last connection to Dad. My head falls to the grass. I clamp my eyes shut to block the tears welling up, but they break through. The thrashing of grass alerts me to a newcomer.

"Easy, Bobby," Mrs. Cisneros says. She puts a hand on my shoulder, and I flinch at the contact. "Can you move?"

I blink at her and nod. She helps me take off my backpack and lifts me up. If it didn't hurt too much to speak, I'd thank her for chasing them off.

Mrs. C helps me over to the bleachers and takes out a tissue, puts it to my mouth. "Hold here," she says. The muscles in my arm flare with pain, but I follow her instructions.

"Was it Rex and his gang?"

The image of Rex, Eddie, and Jorge taunting me, humiliating me, plays in my head. Before I can think it through, I nod—and immediately regret it.

Mrs. Cisneros turns a shade redder. "So sick of all these punks getting away with shit like this."

Wow, she actually cursed. She's seriously pissed. Not good. If Mrs. C reports Rex and his crew, maybe they'll get suspended for a few days, possibly a week. But that would only encourage them to kick my ass again.

I groan and manage to say, "Can we just forget this ever happened?"

"What are you talking about?"

"It's not a big deal. Really, I'm okay."

She regards me for a moment. "It's my responsibility to report this, Bobby. I can't just let this go."

Great. She's not going to budge on this. I rise to my feet slowly. "Whatever."

I just want to get home.

ROUND 4

Mrs. Cisneros offers to take me to the hospital. If she weren't a teacher, I'd probably reply, *Thanks. On the way, can we stop by my mansion and pick up my gold-plated flip-flops?* Instead, I ask her to just take me home. We don't have insurance. There's no way Mom could afford a trip to the ER—plus they'd definitely notify her about what happened.

Mrs. C drives me home in her clunky pickup truck, and every time she hits a bump or a pothole—which is often—it feels like my brain is doing backflips. Thankfully, the ride isn't too long.

I climb the stairs to our apartment and discover a new kind of agony. With each step, my arms and thighs shiver. My whole body feels like it's about to vibrate apart. Instead of carrying my backpack, I drag it behind me.

I manage to stumble through the living room and into the kitchen, where I grab a bag of frozen broccoli from the freezer. My jaw clenches when I place the bag against my cheek, and I let out a moan. I search the pantry for painkillers, but we're out. Mom must be getting her migraines again.

The bathroom is only a few yards away, but the walk feels like a hundred. The stranger staring back at me in the mirror looks vaguely familiar. My lip has puffed up, and my left eye is a grotesque shade of purple—not unlike a rotten eggplant. No way can I let Mom see me like this. What I wouldn't give for Deadpool's healing factor.

I mentally cross my fingers and turn on the bathtub faucet. More often than not, only cold water pours out. This time I get lucky. Guess I was bound to sometime today. Never have I been more thankful for lukewarm water.

While I sit and soak, I try to clear my mind, but my thoughts can't outrun the day's events. My chest heaves, and I succumb to the turmoil that racks my body and spirit. Tears stream down my face and sting my cracked lips.

With a splash, I jolt awake. Must've dozed off. Darkness slips through the window blinds, and the water is frigid. I grab a towel and flee from the tub, shivering.

I have every intention of doing my homework, but I fall into bed without even brushing my teeth. I probably couldn't even hold the pencil or the toothbrush anyway.

Before I nod off, I remember to pull the covers up close to my head and cover my bruises. Usually Mom won't disturb me if I'm already asleep when she gets home. Hopefully she'll stick to the routine.

The alarm screams like a hungry, neglected baby. I blink, rub the gunk from my eyes out of reflex, and flinch when I brush the swelling. I bang the alarm off. Apparently it's been ringing for hours, because the clock reads 10:16 a.m. I'm over *two hours* late for school. Looks like Mom didn't notice my bruises, since she went to work without waking me.

I should get up.

Have to get up.

God, it hurts just breathing.

Screw it. Today's Friday, and I'm a straight A student. Yeah, not getting up.

I let the temporary refuge of sleep reclaim me.

"Are you sick, anak?" Mom asks, calling me the Filipino word for son. "The attendance office called and said you weren't at school."

Moonlight outlines her image. It's nighttime. I turn my back to her and grunt, "Yeah, yeah. Bad cold."

"You need anything? Food? Juice?"

"No." I fake a cough, which sends a shock of pain through my core. "Just need to rest."

She squeezes my shoulder, and it feels like she's tearing it off. I bite back a scream, force it down with a shot of bile.

Finally she says, "Okay, dear. Drink a lot of water, okay? I'll be working late again tomorrow. Text if you need anything."

I nod from under the covers. Even that slight movement hurts. "Thanks, Mom."

"Oh. And happy anniversary to you and Brandon."

She's a couple days late, but she remembered. The thought that she might remember never occurred to me, which makes me even more grateful that she did. A smile starts to form on my lips, but a jolt of pain stops all movement. I don't attempt to turn my head to watch her go. The light from the hallway shrinks to a sliver as Mom leaves the door open a smidge.

My phone buzzes somewhere like the incessant chirp of a cricket. I blink the sleep away and search for my cell on my night table and desk. Finally, I find it in my pants on the floor. According to the screen, it's Saturday afternoon. I've been in bed over thirty-six hours.

Brandon has sent me texts—a dozen of them. Same with Rosie. Both are wondering what's going on and where I am. They're worried. And neither even knows about my epic ass-kicking.

They both ask if I'm still going tonight. Tonight? Crap, to-night is Brandon's dad's birthday, and they're having a big family party at their house. How can I go like this?

I might not have a choice. Bran's mom likes me—some might even say *adores*. His dad? Yeah, not so much. Mr. Elpusan isn't necessarily homophobic—at least, according to Brandon. Rosie's theory is he just doesn't want his son dating someone from the "other side of the tracks." Or, in my case, the other side of the freeway. Every misstep is a point against me.

I shoot a text to Bran and Rosie telling them I'm fine and to pick me up for the party at six. Might as well update them to-gether. It'll save me the trouble of repeating myself.

"What the hell?" Brandon says. "Say that again?"

He hovers over me in my living room, arms folded, Rosie

beside him. I sit up on the couch, hugging my knees, feeling like a seven-year-old being scolded by overprotective parents.

"I said someone outed me at school, I got jumped, and my bike was jacked."

"And you didn't tell me any of this?"

"Why didn't you call us, Bobby?" Rosie chimes in.

"Well, I thought about it, but talking's a little hard when your lip's the size of a beach ball. And telling your friends that you got beaten to a bloody pulp? Not something you spill over text. But please, continue making me feel shittier than I already do."

Damn, get out of the water—snark attack. The words are barely out, and I already regret them. Sometimes I can't help myself.

With a sigh, Bran's shoulders slump, and he plops down next to me. "Sorry. I just . . . I want to know what's happening with you. I want to be there for you."

Rosie sits on the other side of me. "What he said, minus the lovesick goo-goo eyes."

"Shut up, please." Bran squeezes my still-tender shoulder. "You were right, B. I . . . I don't know what it's like for you at school. I shouldn't have pushed."

"Not your fault what happened." I take Bran's hand. He may be a little overprotective, but I'll take that over the opposite extreme. "It's okay."

"No, it's not. None of this is okay." Bran grinds his teeth; the sound grates on my ears. "What are you going to do?"

"I'm gonna take my bike back, that's what."

"Seriously?" Rosie grimaces. "That's a good way to earn another beatdown."

"It's just a bike, B," Brandon says.

I drop his hand, stand up, and pace. "No, it's not."

"Why? What's so special about it?"

"That was my dad's bike. He rode it to work every morning. It was the last thing he gave me—right before he died."

They absorb my words in silence.

"Okay, we get it," Bran says. "It's important to you. But it's not more important than staying safe."

"You don't understand! Every day my memories of my dad get blurrier. Sometimes I have trouble just picturing his face. That bike is all I have left of him, Bran!"

Rosie rises and wraps me in a hug. "Don't stress, okay? We'll figure this out."

I really don't see how, but I take a full breath and try to calm myself. "Yeah, okay."

"All right," she continues. "Let's call operation bike retrieval problem number two. Problem one is protecting yourself. Eventually Rex or some other Neanderthal homophobe is gonna come at you again. When they do, use this." She pulls out a small canister from her bag.

I groan. "Pepper spray? Come on, really?"

"Hey, this right here? This stuff works. One spray, and I guarantee you T-Rex will be crying like the first day of kindygarten."

"I am not using pepper spray, Rosie. That is beyond weak."

Rosie shakes her head and turns to Bran. "Will you talk to your man, please?"

"Come on, B," Brandon says. "Keep it on you just in case. You have to protect yourself."

This is not going well. I take a desperate stab. "You know, carrying that would just play into the stereotype that gay guys can't fight."

"But you *can't* fight," Rosie says. She grins and makes a half-assed attempt to cover it with a trio of fingers.

My face flushes hot. "Yeah? Well . . . what about that time I kicked Toby Jenkins's ass?"

Rosie frowns. "That was in second grade, and all you did was push him down and make him scrape his knee."

"Little weasel had it coming. He knew there were no tag-backs."

"I don't like the idea of you trying to trade punches with a whole crew," Brandon says. "Take the pepper spray, B. For me, okay?"

I grab the can out of Rosie's hand. "God, I feel like a grade A wuss."

She pats me on the shoulder. "Well, Robert, better to feel like a wuss than feel another beatdown."

She means well, and she's kind of right. Ugh. I hate it when Rosie's right. It usually means things are about to get worse. I pocket the spray with no intention of ever using it.

I scowl, which shoots a wave of pain from my lips to my eye. "Maybe I shouldn't go to the party looking like this. Not the best impression for your parents."

"What?" Bran blinks at me. "You said you'd come. We haven't hung out in a while."

"B, I look like I took an adamantium claw to the face."

"Am I going to have to bust out the Guilt-a-Tron?"

"Come on, Bran."

His eyebrows shoot up, and his lips curl inward in a reverse pucker. In a robotic voice, he says, "Do not. Disappoint. Guilt-a-Tron. Guilt-a-Tron. Will make you feel. Guilt."

Rosie shudders. "God . . . *nerds*. Make it stop."

I straighten my back, lift my chin. "Guilt-a-Tron's not gonna work, B. Nope, not this time." A mechanical-like whimper escapes Bran's pouting lips. "All right, all right." I punctuate my defeat with a sigh. "Let's go."

Bran springs up from the couch. "Yay!"

ROUND 5

Brandon drives us to the party in his Dragon Fire Red BMW 320i—the kind of ride that screams tourist to the hardened MacArthur Park locals. It's a gorgeous machine with a sunroof and twenty-inch chrome rims. Not your stereotypical rice rocket. A boyfriend with a luxury car is a definite plus, but sometimes all of Bran's swanky stuff reminds me how little Mom and I have.

"Hey," Rosie says from the back seat, "when are you gonna let me get behind the wheel of this sweet ride?"

"What?" Brandon frowns. "No way are you qualified to drive this ultimate synthesis of luxury and machinery."

"Why, because I'm a girl? Dude, don't be sexist."

"Tell her, B."

"He won't let me drive, either," I say.

Bran shifts gears. "Not until you learn to drive stick, he said without sexual innuendo."

"Ew," Rosie says. "Please put on some music now so I can forget the image you just put in my brain."

The best part of Bran's ride is his dope sound system and even doper playlist. He punches up one of our favorite tracks, "Fallin' Down" by the fierce Filipina rapper Ruby Ibarra.

"Aw, that's my jam," Rosie says, and we bob our heads and

rap along to Ruby's sick flow. I flub a line, but Rosie nails every syllable with the swag of a battle-tested emcee.

The hook hits, and I check my features in the visor mirror. After I woke up, I applied another cold compress—this time a bag of frozen carrots—to my bruises. The marks are a bright shade of purple, but they look better than they did yesterday. Still, not a great look for dinner with your boyfriend's family.

When we walk in, the place is quiet, which isn't surprising. Brandon's extended family is always on Filipino time, so they probably won't arrive for another hour.

Compared to my tiny apartment, Bran's house looks like a mansion. Whenever I step through the front door, I enter a world I've only seen in movies or television.

The rooms are spacious and filled with furnishings straight out of a Pier 1 catalog. Their living room alone is larger than our entire apartment, and it's centered around an ornate marble fireplace that dwarfs our lone bathroom. Above the mantel hangs a framed family portrait of Brandon and his parents in Filipino formal wear; Bran looks dapper in an embroidered long-sleeved barong tagalog. The photograph is beautiful, but it only makes me wish Dad, Mom, and I could have taken our own family portrait before he passed.

A beautiful capiz-shell chandelier hangs in the far corner like a cascading waterfall. All this luxury is paid for by Mr. Elpusan's dentistry practice, which is one of the most success- ful in Silver Lake. Whenever I catch Bran's father giving me a disapproving glance, I wonder whether he's judging not only my personal character, but the condition of my teeth. I've never been to a dentist—it's an expense Mom has never been able to afford—but I relate when people say that they dread going to see one. For completely different reasons.

The scent of rich peanut butter filters out from the kitchen. Mrs. Elpusan is cooking my favorite Pinoy entrée, kare-kare, a dish of oxtail, crisp string beans, and a thick peanut butter sauce. Oh my God, it smells like peanut-buttery heaven.

She's busily frying lumpia at the stove but stops everything when we stroll into the kitchen.

"Bobby! Rosie! How are you?" She's all warmth and positive energy until she sees my bruises. "What happened? Are you okay? Do you need some ice?"

My cheeks go warm, and I dip my chin. "No, Tita, I'm fine. Thank you. Just got into a little, uh, disagreement at school is all."

"A disagreement?" Mr. Elpusan enters from the living room, wearing a USC sweater over a collared shirt, his gait slow and measured like his voice. "That's not what we called it back in my day." He throws a smirk that does little to mask his dislike of me. "Bobby, I hope you're not getting into too much trouble over there in the hood."

Bran winces. "Really, Dad? 'The hood?'"

"Hi, Mr. Elpusan. Happy birthday, sir. No, it was nothing, really."

He eyes me like I'm a cockroach invading his home. "If you say so." As he turns from me to Rosie, his expression makes a complete one-eighty, from disapproval to delight. "Hello again, Rosie. Glad you could make it."

Rosie shows off her parent-winning charm. "Thanks, Mr.

Elpusan. You know I wouldn't miss me some Filipino home cooking. Happy thirtieth birthday!"

Mr. Elpusan laughs and gives Rosie a hug.

Happy thirtieth birthday? Really? Bran's dad is turning forty-six, and his salt-and-pepper hair is more salt than pepper. And since when does she love Filipino food? She's a vegetarian! Ugh. I love Rosie, but sometimes she's so extra, not to mention disgustingly lovable. Obviously Mr. Elpusan would much rather have her dating Bran than me—whether he's a homophobe or not.

"We're going to hang out upstairs until everyone gets here," Bran tells his parents and leads us upstairs.

Bran's room is practically overflowing with geek memorabilia. Some freebies from the shop, but most are bought and paid for. Teen Titans maquettes crowd his desk, bobbleheads of every Avenger populate his bookshelf, and a Whilce Portacio–drawn X-Men poster hangs above his bed. While I'm completely envious, I can't hate. I'd cover my room with geek merchandise, too, if I had cash to burn.

Most of the room, though, is covered with his main genre obsession: *zombies.* Movie posters of *28 Days Later* and *Shawn of the Dead* dominate the walls, and *The Walking Dead* trade paperbacks crowd his bookshelf, propped up by a zombie Wolverine bust. It's as if George Romero vomited all over his room.

Rosie sits at Bran's desk while he hovers over her shoulder. They're working on a joint comic book project, *Zombie Slayer Squad,* for an amateur creator contest at the Villain's Lair. Bran is writing the story, while Rosie handles the artwork.

I kick back on the bed and read a *New Mutants* back issue—or at least try to read while my friends struggle through a bout of creative differences.

"No, no, no, the splash page needs more red," Bran says. "We need entrails. Long, slimy, dangly entrails. Ooh, and maybe an undigested cheeseburger spilling out."

Rosie drops her pencil. "Dude, that's disgusting and not at all kid friendly."

"Kid friendly? It's a zombie book! With undead kid zombies!"

"Yeah, not with me drawing it."

I groan. "Enough with the zombie talk, *please*. I don't need to be reminded that I totally look like one right now."

"All right, all right." Bran pulls a DVD case from a shelf. "Hey, check it out." He holds up a bootleg copy of *Captain America: Civil War*.

"Dude," I say. "How'd you get a hold of a copy of *Civil War*? It's not even out until May."

"Hey, you know I have my ways." He pops the DVD into his flat-screen.

We sit down on the floor in front of the screen and settle back against Bran's bed with Rosie in the middle.

While we watch, Bran indulges in one of his favorite pastimes: breaking down the gay subtext. "It's not even really subtext!" he says. "It's totally blatant! Every dude in Captain America's life is competing for his love, and they're all mad jealous of each other. I mean, you can just feel the seething jealousy festering between Falcon and Bucky. And every time Falcon spreads his wings, he's saying, *'I'm ready to take flight with you, Cap. I'm ready to embrace our love.'*"

"Preach," I say, raising a fist. When Bran shifts into queer analyst geek mode—all passionate, his hands animated—he's pretty damn adorable. If Rosie weren't here and I weren't so beat up, I'd probably be all over him.

"Queer love triangle." Rosie gives a thumbs-up. "I like it."

"No, no, no!" Bran says. "There's also Iron Man, who shows up at the end to declare his love for Cap. Him opening his armor represents him coming out of his shell into a larger queer world. It's not a triangle but a beautiful gay square!"

"Damn, I love it when you talk queer and geeky," I say. I lean over Rosie and plant a kiss on Bran's cheek; the contact makes me wince. He pulls me closer, sending a shock of pain through my shoulder.

"Okay, this is a triangle I really don't need to be a part of." She frees herself from the pile and rises.

"Kids!" Bran's mom calls from the stairs. "Come down now! We're going to eat soon!"

Bran's face lights up, and we all bolt for the door.

The spread Mrs. Elpusan has laid out is drool inducing: pancit palabok, pork adobo, sinigang, and of course, kare-kare. I pile my plate with more than my fair share and with barely a twinge of guilt. Rarely do I ever get to enjoy such a feast, so you can be damn sure I am going to take advantage of it.

"You Pinoys are such meat eaters," Rosie says, frowning. Fortunately for her, the menu includes fresh lumpia stuffed with lettuce, carrots, and tofu.

At the dessert table, a plate of ube-filled sweet buns entices me. "Yes! Ube! Your mom knows me so well." I can't resist. I grab an extra plate and stack it high.

"Hey, that's not just for you, you know." Bran grabs a bun off my plate and bites into it. Besides comic books, the other passion Bran and I share is anything and everything ube related. "We're such purple yam stans."

"I prefer 'ube groupies.'"

We eat out on the patio with Bran's younger cousins, all elementary and junior high age. The conversation is fun, easy. They're all so close-knit. Makes me wonder what growing up with a large family would have been like.

In the corner there's an elaborate karaoke setup complete with video screen and dual microphones, because of course there is. Bran's Tita Betsy holds court with her rendition of the Tagalog love ballad "Nandito Ako," emoting hard like she's singing to the one that got away.

I feel the longing in every line, but not for a lost love the words supposedly convey. Well, not for a person, at least. My folks never taught me to speak Tagalog, mainly because their parents barely taught any to them. Like many American-born Pinoys, I know some words, but not enough to fully understand. Whenever I hear the melodic flow of the mother tongue, it feels like I'm missing a part of me that I may never recover.

Bran is so moved by the performance that he takes my hand. I let him. He's out to his extended family, which means I am, too, I guess. But that doesn't mean all of his relatives approve. At the table beside us, another of his aunts scowls at us and makes the sign of the cross. I wonder if she's praying for our souls or condemning us to hell. Either way, I don't need to put up with her bad vibe.

I squeeze Bran's hand. "Hey, can we go inside? Getting a little chilly out here," I say, staring back at the judgmental tita.

Bran nods, and we head inside. Cheers burst from the living room. A group of adults is crowded around the huge flat-screen watching a boxing match. I immediately recognize the fight because it was the first one I'd ever watched back when I was a little kid: Manny "Pacman" Pacquiao vs. "The Golden Boy" Oscar De La Hoya. Leave it to a gathering of Filipinos to cheer for a Pacquiao fight that's eight years old as if it were broadcasting live.

Brandon takes my hand. "Yeah, I don't want to watch this. Let's head back upstairs."

He's never been a boxing fan, and after my recent ass-beating, it's probably the last thing he wants to watch. But seeing my childhood hero feels too much like fate—even though I'm not sure I believe in fate.

"Can we check it out?" I make my way to an empty seat on the couch. Rosie and Bran follow but have to settle for a pair of chairs against the wall.

The fight is only in the second round, but Pacquiao is already controlling the pace. He's much too fast for the bigger, slower De La Hoya. Manny continuously circles Oscar, making him look like a statue. Over and over, his straight left splits Oscar's defense and pummels the Golden Boy's handsome features. But Oscar can't touch Manny. When he lunges with his jab, Pacman has already floated away.

Despite the sting, my mouth curls into a smile. After what that hulking menace Rex did to me, watching a smaller man best a larger one is exactly what I need. Living vicariously through Manny isn't much, but it'll do for now.

In the fifth round, a flurry of combinations from Pacman rocks De La Hoya. Manny presses the advantage, dancing on the balls of his feet and forcing Oscar back. At times, Oscar looks like an inert punching bag. A tilting tree caught in the hurricane that is Manny Pacquiao. The party guests cheer at the spectacle, but I start to sympathize with De La Hoya. I know what it feels like to be helpless against a punishing onslaught.

At the same time, I'm swept up in the excitement of a Pinoy warrior showcasing his unparalleled skills. Manny is the man. The GOAT. It can't be denied.

By the seventh round, Oscar's face is one big red welt. I wince and look away from the carnage. One commentator calls it "death by a thousand left hands." I wish the referee would put an end to the lopsided spectacle. After the eighth, Oscar confers with his corner and decides to stop it himself. Thankfully. He rises from his stool and embraces Manny in the center of the ring, congratulating him.

Pacquiao, gracious in victory, tells the legendary De La Hoya, "You're still my idol." I mouth the words along with him.

Someone switches the channel to a *New Girl* rerun and the crowd filters out for more food and bathroom breaks. I cut a path toward the front door and step outside into the night chill.

My mind replays images of Pacquiao dominating the bigger De La Hoya, humbling him. Oscar and Manny morph into Rex and me. If Manny can take the fight to a larger opponent, why can't I?

The memory of Rosie's words slams me back to reality: *But you can't fight.*

I shrug and look at the crescent moon as it knifes through the smoggy sky. "Who says I can't learn how?"

"Learn what?" Bran asks from behind me.

I turn to face him, this boy I care about more than any other, who makes me feel things inside that I decided long ago were right and true.

"Nothing. Just wondering what comes next." I take his hand, squeeze it. "Listen, I gotta head out."

"What? Right now?"

I release his hand. "Tell Rosie I'll see her at school."

"Hold up a minute, B. I'll drive you."

"No thanks. I want to run."

Bran's eyes go wide like I just sat on his copy of *The Walking Dead* #1. "What, all the way to MacArthur Park?"

With a shake of my head, I say, "Uh-uh. Farther."

My plan is still forming, so I don't tell him anything more. For now, I whirl around and dash down the street.

ROUND 6

My feet fly down the concrete hill as I pass out of the Silver Lake residentials. I let out a slow breath. Bran's neighborhood is clean and relatively safe, but I've never been comfortable there. MacArthur Park may have its problems, but it's still home.

My calves tighten, but I push through the pain. I sprint down Alvarado, which always seems more serene at night, despite the steady clog of cars and people. From out of the smoggy sky, the 101 overpass materializes, a mass of concrete and steel, bridging and dividing the people of Los Angeles.

Despite the stench, I slow my pace through the shantytown. My instinct is to turn away from the slumbering squatters, but I force myself to take them in. Mom and I could have ended up here. Easily.

A middle-aged woman, curled up on the pavement in a tattered sleeping bag, lifts her head and squints at me. Her long hair is matted, and her nose and cheeks are smudged with grime. Beside her rests a cardboard sign. Scrawled on it in red crayon: *Homeless Vet with 2 Kids. Please help.*

Damn. I'd give her money if I had any.

Even though it's a public street, I feel like I'm trespassing. I flee from the shadows and continue toward home at a near sprint.

While I run, the Pacquiao bout replays in my mind and it jars a memory of Dad and our special place. I haven't been there in years, and it's not too far off my path. At Beverly, I make a detour and sprint toward Unidad Park, into the heart of Historic Filipinotown—HiFi to the locals.

Toward the mural.

Along the way, I pass an old apartment building that's getting demolished. A chain-link fence with green slats surrounds it like a boa constrictor. My thighs burn and cramp. I thought I was in decent shape, but running through the dark unknown of Los Angeles is a whole other level of physical stress. I've gotten soft riding Dad's bike everywhere.

I hobble up to the small deserted park and peer through the barred fence. Painted across the building that stretches the length of the park is the Filipino history mural. When I was barely in grade school, Dad would bring me here, and in between games of tag and turns on the swing, he'd tell me the stories behind the pictures. Stories of oppression and rebellion, labor and struggle, triumph and loss.

The mural's official name in Tagalog is Gintong Kasaysayan, Gintong Pamana, which translates to *A Glorious History, A Golden Legacy*. Brown faces, both light and dark, stare at me, reassure me. Heroes who tell the story of Filipinos, both here in America and in the Philippines: Datu Lapu-Lapu, the tribal chieftain who fought against foreign invasion at the Battle of Mactan; Gabriela Silang, la Generala in the struggle against Spanish colonialism; Carlos Bulosan, author of *America Is in the Heart*; Larry Itliong and Philip Vera Cruz, the labor leaders who organized the Delano Grape Strike for better wages;

President Cory Aquino and the People Power Revolution for democracy in the Philippines. Even in the gloom of night, the huge portraits come alive.

I find the edge of the mural where Manny Pacquiao stands strong, a modern-day warrior armed with only a proud heart and taped fists.

And I remember.

Eight years ago—a few months after Dad had passed—Mom was struggling just to pay rent. We were on our own with no family to lend us a hand. Like me, Mom is an only child, and her parents died when I was a toddler. Dad's family wanted nothing to do with us. They still don't.

Food was scarce, smiles even more so. The holidays were days away, but we had no money for even the simplest celebration. Our Thanksgiving dinner was going to be Spam and rice, and if we saved up enough, maybe hot cocoa for dessert.

That was when Manny Pacquiao became my childhood hero—and not because he was a world-famous boxer.

I was nine years old, small for my age. Not just short, but malnourished. At dawn, Mom woke me and said we had to go to Lake Street Park, a good two-mile walk. When I asked why, she replied, "To see the champ."

Along with hundreds of others, we waited at the park for hours. I played on the jungle gym with the other kids, shot hoops, and laughed more than I had in a long time. Then a bright yellow truck rumbled into the parking lot, and Manny Pacquiao emerged, part superhero, part saint.

On that day, Manny and his people—including his long-time trainer, Freddie Roach—passed out five hundred free turkeys to the people of Historic Filipinotown. And like every one of his entrances to the ring, Manny engaged the crowd with an open heart and an infectious energy.

Manny himself handed me our turkey, tousled my hair, and said, "Happy Thanksgiving, champ."

I was too in awe to thank him; fortunately, Mom replied, "Salamat po, Manny!"

She let me carry our turkey all the way home, and it made me feel like the man of the house for the first time. I only had to stop to rest once.

Thanks to Manny, we had a delicious holiday feast. Mom roasted the turkey to a perfect golden brown and even splurged on stuffing. We had so many leftovers, I ate turkey sandwiches and turkey adobo for two straight weeks—and loved every bite.

After we washed dishes, Mom introduced me to tanaga poetry. Her own mother, Lola Tess—rest in peace—taught her the form when she was a little girl. That day, Mom wanted to pass it down to me. For years, she'd kept a notebook of all her poems, some of which she let me read. Other works—the ones to or about Dad—were too dear to her heart to share with anyone. Mom unlocked the power of words for me, as well as the beauty of brevity. In a mere twenty-eight syllables, she could tell an epic story of life and loss filled with humor and insight.

That night, I started a poetry book of my own in an unused composition book Mom had kept from her high school days. With her help, I wrote my first tanaga to Manny.

Thank you, Manny Pacquiao
For the holiday turkey
Would you like to come over
For some cake and beef jerky?

Not my best work, but I was just a kid. What the hell else rhymes with "turkey"? I don't even like beef jerky—tastes like salted plastic—but at least I got the number of syllables right. Mom and I clapped along to make sure there were seven in each line.

I will always remember that holiday and how Manny Pacquiao's generosity helped us at our lowest point.

Hopefully he can help me again.

ROUND 7

On Sunday morning, I get a 5:00 a.m. start before Mom rises. Today is Day 1 of the Bobby Agbayani Epic Makeover Plan, and I aim to *get shit done*.

First thing I need is the proper uniform. I search through all my drawers, through out-of-style shirts and sweaters, before I spot it hiding behind an old coat in my closet: my first and only Manny Pacquiao T-shirt. Mom had given it to me for Christmas a few years after that fateful turkey dinner. It may be a size too small with a small tear near the collar, but otherwise it's perfect.

In the bathroom, I slip on the shirt in front of the mirror and feel a shift. The faded red, blue, and yellow MP logo radiates out like a superhero emblem à la Superman's *S*. I stand up straighter, point my chin higher.

I'm ready. Ready for the new me.

Despite some lingering soreness, I power through a dozen push-ups and crunches. My plan is to add five to each total every other day. Without a set of dumbbells, I make do with a pair of gallon milk cartons filled with water. I knock out a set of ten curls, both arms.

The discoloring around my eye has faded, but not enough that Mom won't notice. The thought of her finding out about my injuries makes my stomach clench. She has enough to deal with at work. I experiment with some of her makeup to cover up the remaining bruise. It doesn't look perfect, but it should pass. Her eyesight isn't the greatest, and she can't afford glasses.

On my windowsill, I keep a cracked mug of spare change—coins I found at school and on the street. It's mostly pennies and nickels, but I do have a single dollar bill. I pour the contents out on my bed and count every cent. Then I do it again. Both times, I wince at the total, which comes to $3.76. The amount represents every penny I have in the world.

Hopefully it's enough for what I have planned.

For breakfast I boil three eggs for myself and scramble another two for Mom. I also fix her champorado; the chocolate rice's rich aroma fills the apartment and entices Mom out of her bedroom.

"You made breakfast?" she says as she trudges into the kitchen. "Okay, what horrible thing did you do?" She puts a hand to her mouth, gives a mock gasp. "Did you get an A-minus?"

One thing Mom never has to nag me to do is study. She had me when she was just sixteen—the same age I am now—so she didn't finish high school. "Don't be like me, anak," she always says. "Finish school so you can get a good job and move us out of this hellhole." No pressure.

"What, can't a son make breakfast for his mom?"

"Funny, I ask myself that every morning." She plops down at the table.

"Ha ha, my mom, the Ali Wong of MacArthur Park."

"I don't know who that is."

"Wow. Really?"

"I'm kidding. I'm thirty-two, not an FOB."

I wince. She's only joking about being "fresh off the boat," a recent immigrant, but I've had enough of people using derogatory labels—even if it is my own mother. I take a seat and keep my head down as we say prayers.

The sweet scent of champorado tempts me as steam rises from Mom's bowl. I stick to my eggs. No heavy carbs for me for a while, which will be tough since rice is our side dish for just about every meal.

"You getting enough sleep, anak? Eye's looking a little baggy there."

I nearly choke on my egg. "Yeah. I mean no, not really. Homework. Late nights, y'know?"

Her expression is unreadable, but she nods. "I do. So proud of my young scholar."

The eggs taste bland, but I scarf the last one down and rise. On my way out of the kitchen, I say, "I'm gonna hang out with Rosie today."

Technically a lie, yes, but if I have time later, I'll swing by her house. Maybe her dad will be cooking up one of his mouthwatering dishes that I'll deprive myself of enjoying. I'm now in training.

"Okay. Make sure you bike on the right-hand side, please."

Her words stab me in the gut. "Yeah," I mumble, and head out the front door. Eventually, I'll have to tell her about Dad's bike getting ripped off, but not right now. I need to keep moving.

* * *

My thighs ache from last night's run, but it's a good ache. Refreshing. The kind that tells you you're earning the new you. When I hit ground level, I stretch out the stiffness against the staircase railing.

As soon as I'm through the complex gate, I break into a steady run. The change in my pocket jangles around with each stride. In my head the beginning guitar riff of AC/DC's "Thunderstruck" plays, Manny Pacquiao's entrance music to the ring. Without a smartphone, I have to make do with my imagination and some off-key humming.

My destination is nearly three miles east. I have to venture all the way out to Echo Park because MacArthur Park has exactly zero boxing gyms.

I take my usual route up Alvarado, but instead of heading into the hills toward Bran's place, I hang a right at the car wash on Sunset. Since I'm no longer speeding through on my bike, the city feels closer, more intimate. The colors of the storefronts pop more, and the traffic sounds less angry. With the pavement beneath every stride, I'm more connected to the ground.

Fifteen minutes in, my breaths quicken to gasps. I no longer have the initial excitement and adrenaline rush of a first run to drive me. My side cramps. I slow to a trudge and fight the urge to stop altogether. Thankfully, my second wind saves me. I clench my jaw and jog on.

After a few turns onto side streets, the faded wood sign of the Jab Gym looms ahead. The redbrick building looks more like a firehouse than a gym. I've passed it many times on my treks into Echo Park, but having never been inside, I know next to nothing about it. So far it meets the first of my two criteria: it's within running distance. Hopefully it meets the second.

When I enter through the glass door, a wave of heat smacks me in the face and body odor assaults my sinuses. Directly inside, a dozen dust-covered trophies are on display in a glass case. Framed photos of boxers from bygone eras hang from brick walls. Across from the case, an unmanned check-in counter—the top of which is enclosed by metal mesh—looms over the lobby. Everything looks run-down and made from outdated materials, which, in my mind, is a plus. Maybe by some minor miracle, I'll be able to afford the membership fee.

I pass into the main section, dominated by two boxing rings on opposite sides of the room. Promotional posters from old fights plaster every inch of the walls. Individual stations are set up for heavy bags, speed bags, and weights. The place is quiet and, aside from a couple fighters and trainers, nearly empty. Is it due to the early hour or because they have few members?

A jolt runs through my core. I'm excited to get to work, to learn. Did Manny feel like this the first time he stepped into a gym? *Okay, don't get ahead of yourself.*

From behind me, a raspy voice says, "Can I help you, son?"

I turn around and find an older Black man behind the counter. His back and shoulders slump forward in a perpetual slouch, but his most distinguishing feature is an unkempt Afro streaked with gray at the sides that dominates his portly frame. The man could be anywhere from fifty to seventy. I can never tell with old people.

"Yeah. Hi. What are your membership rates?"

His chapped lips curl into a smile, and he taps his fingertips on the counter. "All right here."

Trying not to look too anxious, I walk over and peer down at the countertop. The prices for yearly and monthly membership, classes, and equipment rental are listed. I chew the inside of my cheek. My $3.76 isn't even enough to rent a pair of gloves for the day. "Um, you wouldn't happen to have any student rates, would you?"

"Sure do." He waves his palm over a lower column. The discount is about 5 percent—still out of my price range.

My plan's been derailed before it's even begun. I nearly retreat out the door. Instead, I glance around for anything to hold on to, to keep me in this place.

On the back wall I spot a HELP WANTED sign. I point at it and say, "What are you hiring for?"

The old guy sizes me up like he's deciding if he should even bother answering. "Work's part time. Four to eight on weeknights, nine to five on weekends. You mop up, empty spit buckets, and clean the head. All that fun stuff I'm too damn old to be doing. The pay is five bucks an hour, which you get in cash after each shift. Don't need to be messing with no W-2 nonsense."

I wince. I came here to learn how to defend myself, not join the custodial workforce. But if this is my only way in . . .

"Okay, can I start today?"

"Whoa, slow your roll there, son. There's protocols, an interview process, an application, references." The old guy digs around in a few drawers and ruffles through stacks of papers. This lasts a minute before he groans and stuffs them back in. "Screw it. You a criminal or a gangbanger?"

"What? No."

"Got any problem cleaning up blood, vomit, or a combination of both?"

"Uh, only if it's my own."

"Good answer. Welcome to the Jab Gym, kid."

We shake hands, and his callused grip feels like sandpaper. "Dope. I'm Bobby, by the way. Thank you, Mr.—"

"Good to meet you, Bobby. Call me Luke."

I almost ask, Skywalker or Cage? Thankfully I'm able to restrain my geek tendencies. "Cool," I say instead. I want to ask if employees can use the gym during off hours, but I hold off for now. Better prove myself first. "So what do you want me to do first?"

"Well, that depends. Do you like to ease in slowly or dive right in?" Luke grins right before he says the last part, revealing a missing incisor. I cringe at the impending horrors that await me.

May as well find out exactly what I've gotten myself into. "Point me toward the deep end," I say.

Luke cackles and says, "We got a lot of deep end here, kid. Question is, how long can you hold your breath?"

Okay, what the hell could he possibly mean by that? Something about it chills the back of my neck.

"Come on." Luke lets me behind the counter and leads me toward the back area where the lighting is dim.

Maybe I've read too many comic books with creepy villains, but I feel like I'm being led into a dungeon where unknown horrors await.

But whatever my new boss has in store, it can't be any scarier than Rex.

ROUND 8

Luke leads me down a faded lime-green hallway to the men's locker room. The place reeks of sweat and mold. Now I know what he meant about holding my breath. Unfortunately, I don't have the strongest lungs. The stench is so bad, I resort to pinching my nose.

Like the rest of the gym, it's small, functional, and looks like it hasn't been renovated since the '90s. A greenish-brown substance covers the faucets, most likely a combo of grime and rust. They probably haven't been cleaned in years. On the plus side, the restroom has only two urinals and toilets. Luke informs me one of them is continuously clogged. Wonderful.

He wheels in a rickety cart stocked with a host of cleaning supplies: disinfectants, brushes, abrasive sponges, brooms, mops. Inside the cart is a large trash container nearly filled to the brim.

"Say hello to Hank," Luke says, patting the cart.

"Hank? It has a name?"

"I've known this cart for over thirty years, longer than you been alive, kid. We've been through shit together—literally. I consider it a close friend. You don't think my friend deserves a name?"

"No, no. It's, uh, very worthy of a name. Hello, Hank." I

actually wave at the thing. And now I'm having second thoughts about my new job—or at least about my new boss.

"All right. I'll let you two get acquainted. After you take care of the stalls, you can sweep up." He exits.

Woo-hoo, let the not-fun begin. For the next hour and a half, I scrub every surface, scour the toilets inside and out, mop every inch of tile, and take the plunger to the clogged commode. Inside one of Hank's compartments, I find a can of lemon air freshener. I empty its contents, but it barely makes a difference.

All the while, I'm thinking I should be punching a bag, not punching the clock.

A few fighters come in to change into their gear, looking right through me. After washing his hands, one crumples his paper towel and shoots for the trash bin, missing badly. He doesn't bother to pick it up, even though—or maybe because—I'm standing right there. I pick it up and toss it in, feeling a tad humiliated. Is this how the school janitor, Mr. Hopkins, feels?

The boxers wrap their hands with long strips of cloth, and I try to observe inconspicuously. I note how they start the wrap at the wrist, then work up to the knuckles and slide the strip between each finger. They finish by wrapping the entire hand in an alternating cross pattern. It seems simple enough. Hopefully I'll be able to replicate it when the time comes.

When I emerge from the locker room, the gym is jumping. Fighters of all weight classes spar, work the bag, jump rope, and lift weights. All of this activity makes me want to box ten rounds—even if I don't know how to yet.

I pull a wide broom from Hank and sweep around the nearest ring so I can get a good view of the action. Two guys in headgear spar; both stand nearly six feet tall with ripped physiques and appear to be middleweights. One of them is damn gorgeous. He looks a bit like Zac Efron—if Zac were Latino and bulkier. Okay, this is so not why I'm here, but still—*bonus*.

Their punches are powerful but deceptively fast. Latino Efron takes a left to the eye. I nearly boo the other fighter. I've never seen live boxing in person, and an up-close view of these behemoths trading shots makes me wonder if I truly want to pursue this. My memory flashes to Rex and his crew working me over. I don't have much choice. I never want to be that helpless again.

In the far ring, two smaller boxers go at it. Their pace is faster; gloves fly in a blur of motion. One fighter has the other against the ropes, picking apart his defense. To my mild shock, the one pressing the advantage is a girl—redhead, my height, possibly the same age as me. Her ponytail whips about as she unleashes a savage swirl of punches.

I shake my head at the thought of myself, a queer teen who wants to learn how to fight, surprised by a girl boxer. I guess we all have prejudices lurking in our minds.

The girl's trainer calls time, and she heads to her corner. She sips water from a bottle, swishes it around, spits it into a bucket. She glistens with sweat, but also an aura of confidence. This girl is badass.

Her trainer, a grizzled Latino man, yells, "Full!" and sets the pail on the ring apron. Oh, is he talking to me? I trudge over, peek into the liquid, and shudder.

"Don't worry," the girl says, peering down at me. "Girl spit's the same as guy spit."

"You mean still disgusting?"

"Right, only more fragrant."

The trainer replaces her mouthpiece and clicks his stopwatch. She flies out of the corner and resumes her barrage. Girl can throw a punch. Her sparring partner remembers he can fight back and connects with a straight right that stuns her momentarily. She brushes off the blow. Girl can take a punch too.

I'm so mesmerized by her power, I forget I'm supposed to be working. Luke reminds me by yelling, "Hey, new blood! Stop ogling that fighter and get back to work!"

The girl grins at me, allowing her opponent to pop her with an overhand left. She snarls and unleashes a combination of jabs and a left hook that floors him. Damn, I could watch her fight all day. But I can't. Before Luke can yell at me again, I lug the bucket to the restroom, dump it down the sink, and replace it on the apron.

Later, while I change out the trash bag from the men's locker room, Luke comes in. With the thoroughness of a detective, he inspects the stalls and urinals.

His grimace slowly upturns into a smile. "Not bad, young blood. Floor hasn't looked this spotless since I mopped Mike Tyson's barf off it twenty years ago. You might just do."

"Thanks, Mr.—uh, Luke. Um, so I was wondering, can employees use the gym during off hours?"

Luke chews his chapped lip. "You keep the place this clean, you can live here for all I care. Hell, I do." He lumbers out of the locker room.

Looks like my gamble paid off. Now comes the hard part.

After I scrub and mop the women's locker room—which

takes a couple hours—Luke lets me off for the day. My arms and feet ache, but I can't go home now. I came here to learn how to box, and that's what I'm going to do.

My hoodie is covered with grime and cleaning solution, so I strip it off and shove it into an empty locker. Luckily I wore my Pacquiao T-shirt underneath.

At the counter, I ask Luke for a pair of gloves.

"What kind?"

"Er, the . . . boxing kind?"

Luke snickers. "I can see you're a seasoned vet at this, kid." From below the counter, he pulls a smaller pair of gloves with less padding than the sparring variety. "These are for working the bag. That's all you should be hitting for now. You can work up to sparring later." He looks me over. "Much later."

I want to protest, but he knows better than I do. With a nod, I turn on my heel.

Luke clears his throat. "Don't forget these." He holds up a pair of hand wraps. I grab them and scurry away.

The gym is near closing, so thankfully there are few witnesses to see my first time on the heavy bag. I take up a lefty fighting stance with my right shoulder leading and fire off a jab. *Ouch, that didn't feel right.* I try another, and the bag spins away like a wobbly top. "Ow."

Okay, this is not working. Ugh. With all the superhero comics I've read, you'd think I'd be able to throw a decent punch.

"You're hitting the bag with the top of your fist," Luke calls out. "Keep that up, and you'll sprain your wrist something nasty." He appears at my side. "Gotta hit it with the front of your fist. Don't bend your wrist. Try it again."

I follow his directions and strike with a straight wrist.

"Better," he says, "but try to hit the bag dead center so it don't spin." I snap off a straight left. "Good. Make sure you don't clench until right before impact."

For the next half hour, Luke guides me through striking technique, proper stance, and how to move with the bag. My strikes grow sharper, more confident. While I still have a way to go, Luke's teachings have already made a huge difference.

I work the bag, lose myself in the repetition. Sweat flies from my brow as I rip off combination after combination. A final left hook rattles the bag's chain.

"*Hoo-wee*, you got some pop in you, kid!"

I beam. Maybe Manny and I share more than just our Filipino heritage.

Luke squints at his watch. "Okay, time to knock off."

"Will you show me the speed bag first?"

The old guy sputters out a wheezy chuckle. "Kid, I may be an amazing coach, but I can't teach you how to box in one night. At least, not for free."

"Okay, how about instead of paying me to work, you teach me to box?"

Luke sizes me up. His stare is so intrusive, I want to turn away.

"How'd you get that shiner, son?" He points to his eye. "Not fooling anyone with that makeup."

I take my time answering. If Luke noticed the bruise, could Mom have seen it also? "I'm, uh, I just got into it with some punks is all. I don't go to the safest school."

Luke's eyes glaze over. "I know what it's like putting up with

bullshit from bigger kids. World's not built for our type, son."
Pretty sure he means short people, but there's another "type"
more relevant to my situation. For a moment he's silent. "Tomorrow. Speed bag."

He waddles up to me, hands me a small wad of bills, and
heads toward the locker room exit.

With a swallow, I count my pay for the day. Forty dollars. I
can't remember the last time I held so much money. Actually, I
can: never.

"Thanks, Luke," I call.

"Don't thank me yet, kid. You're gonna really earn it tomorrow." He snickers, which nearly makes me want to run and
never come back. "Get some rest."

Rest. Yeah, right after my five-mile run back to Mac-
Arthur Park.

On my return jog, my stride is sluggish. I slow my pace as I
enter the shadows beneath the belly of the 101 overpass and
once again approach the homeless shantytown. Whenever I
pass through here, I tell myself I'd give them money if I had
any. Now that I actually have a few dollars, I'm not so ready to
part with it. While not a huge sum, my Jab Gym pay could help
Mom with expenses. Would it be fair to her to give it away to
strangers? Granted, they're strangers in dire need, but strangers nonetheless. Still, what if this same excuse had stopped
Manny Pacquiao from helping Mom and me?

No, I can spare a small amount.

I stop in front of the veteran with the cardboard sign and

drop a five-spot in her basket. With a shaky hand, she picks up the money and whispers, "Gracias."

A warmth, a pure elation, fills me. I've never been able to help anyone like this. Is this how Manny felt on that day at the park? I'm not naive enough to think that five dollars is going to change the woman's situation, but helping her out even a little bit makes me smile.

It's a school night. I should head home for some well-earned z's, but the only thing waiting for me is an empty apartment. I get that Mom has to work late, but sometimes being home alone all the time can get, well, lonely. I make a detour down Beverly toward Rosie's place. With only a couple weeks until the contest, she and Brandon should be working on their zombie comic book well into the night.

Rosie's neighborhood is a slight upgrade from my own; instead of old, small apartment buildings, it's old, small single-story houses. The Sanchez family residence is a corner house that looks like all the others, with the exception of a bright orange front door. Back in sixth grade, Rosie decided she wanted to dye her hair orange like her mom's—a decision vetoed by her dad. To appease her, he agreed to paint their front door to distinguish their house from the cookie-cutter norm and, as Rosie put it, "Let the world know somebody awesome lives here." After her mom passed, he let Rosie dye her hair orange after all.

Before I can knock on said orange door, it swings wide, and Rosie pulls me into the foyer. Even by the front door, the tangy aroma of Mr. Sanchez's cooking entices me.

Their home is cozy and outfitted with worn yet comfortable furnishings. Vibrant sketches of landscapes and portraits grace the walls. One is of Rosie as a young girl with her tongue poking out of the corner of her mouth. She used to model for her mother, who was a gifted artist in her own right. Mrs. Sanchez, rest in peace, certainly captured her daughter's mischievous spark.

"Will you talk to your man, please?" Rosie gestures at Bran, who sits on the couch, hunched over the coffee table, head in hands.

I plod over to Brandon and peck him on the cheek, but he only grunts in acknowledgment.

On the coffee table, several pages of their zombie comic book are laid out in no obvious order. Most are rough layouts of pencil sketches, but a few pop with rich colors and finished speech balloons.

"What's the problem?" I ask, not sure if I want the answer. "Looks great so far."

"Yeah, it's amazing. Except for one thing. Zombies can't talk!" Bran points at a page with a pair of teenage girl zombies holding hands. One with long red hair is saying, *"I'm so glad we're facing the zombie apocalypse together!"*

Rosie groans. "Why not? Who says?"

"Only every zombie movie ever made."

"Dude, you said you wanted queer representation in our book."

"Not *undead* queer representation!"

"Bobby, back me up here. Zombies can talk, right?" She glares at me. "Right?"

Just what I want, to be caught in the middle between my guy and my best friend. My gaze jumps from one to the other, knowing that whatever answer I give will be wrong. "Well, um, I don't . . ."

"Bobby! Hola!" Mr. Sanchez pads in from the kitchen. He's a rotund man with a jovial disposition whose few remaining strands of hair are always combed neatly back. "These two at it again?" He chuckles warmly. "Earlier, they were arguing about whether vegetarians who become zombies would eat humans."

Bran shoots up from the couch. "Who cares?!"

"I'm a vegetarian. I care!" Rosie shouts.

"Nobody wants to see a zombie eat a salad!"

Mr. Sanchez steps in between them. "Okay, okay, bring it down, you two. It's not that dire." He points at a page. "Rosie, that zombie on page five is looking extra gruesome. I love it. Finish it up, sweetie."

"You think?" Rosie takes a seat on the couch, examining the page in question. "It is fairly horrific." She snatches up a pen and glides it over the paper in swift, confident strokes.

Mr. Sanchez puts his hand on my shoulder. "Hey, you kids hungry? Made a batch of my famous tamales—for both veggie- and meat-eaters alike."

"Grub truce?" Bran holds his fist out to Rosie.

"Grub truce," she replies, bumping his fist with her own.

Flattery and tamales. Good old Mr. Sanchez seems to always say the right thing.

We gather around the dining table and dig in—chicken and sweet corn tamales for Brandon and me, green chili pepper and cheese for Rosie. Whenever I eat with Rosie and her dad, I'm conscious of her mother's absence, which reminds me of the terrible bond Rosie and I share. A bond born of the pain from the loss of a parent. She gives me a lopsided smile and squeezes my hand, and I wonder if she knows what I'm thinking.

At first, the conversation is lacking, but Mr. Sanchez loosens us up with tales of his adventures as a mail carrier. One story in particular, involving a toddler, a Chihuahua, and a toy lightsaber, cracks us up.

For a moment, Mr. Sanchez reminds me of my dad. While Dad was slimmer and nowhere near as loquacious, he had a similar throaty laugh. The thought floods me with childhood memories: Dad and I watching *The Princess Bride* and laughing the whole way through, Dad teaching me to ride his bike and lifting me up when I'd fall, reading his old comics together at the park on a lazy Saturday. In all of these, I can't picture the details of his face. He's just a blur. An idea that refuses to take form.

I turn quiet. Bran notices and raises a brow at me. Before everyone finishes eating, I thank Mr. Sanchez for the food and say my goodbyes.

"Come on, you just got here," Bran says. "You can't hang out a little longer?"

"I gotta get going." I lean in for a hug, but he barely returns it.

At the apartment, Mom arrives as I'm brushing my teeth. I'm usually asleep by the time she gets home, so I smile when I see her, dripping toothpaste from the corner of my mouth. I tell her about my new job and hand her half of what remains of my pay. It's not a huge amount, but it should cover some groceries. It's about time I started contributing, and it feels good to do it.

"A boxing gym?" she asks. "Is that how you got that bruise?"

"Uh, yeah, just doing a little sparring after work. Barely stings."

Her brow crinkles. When did her once-flawless skin develop so many lines? She takes a long breath and says, "Okay, Pacquiao Jr., just keep up your grades. And be careful."

If she only knew the truth.

So I lied. Again. My motto of self-preservation extends to Mom as well. I was too young to realize it at the time, but after Dad died, she struggled with depression. There were whole days when she wouldn't speak or even acknowledge me. Nothing was more terrifying to nine-year-old me than starving while my mom refused to get out of bed.

Mom gradually pulled herself out of it, but that was the loneliest, scariest time of my life. Ever since, I've made the choice of shielding her from any and all crap that I have to deal with.

I am *not* losing her over this crap with Rex.

ROUND 9

Monday arrives, and Rosie and I march to first period, my hater radar set on high alert. Her royal bitchiness Charlotte Wilkes and her court of butt smoochers saunter up beside us. Great. Just the person I want to see to start the week on a high note.

"Hey, Agbayani," Charlotte says, "I heard T-Rex stomped all over your eyeball. Squished it like a grape." She gets in my face, examines it like it's a science experiment gone wrong. "Ew, nasty." She and her minions giggle.

"Oh, it's not so bad. My eyesight's totally fine, actually. I mean, I can still see your nose hairs sticking out like needles on a cactus." I turn to Rosie. "Hey, do Charlotte's nose hairs stick out like needles on a cactus?"

She squints at Charlotte's nostrils and grimaces. "Ew. They really do."

"See? Perfect twenty-twenty vision."

"Shut up!" is the only comeback she can manage before pinching her nostrils and stomping away. *Oh, Charlotte. You wordsmith, you.*

In the middle of Mrs. Jennings's lecture on absolute value, I get a call slip to report to the front office. On my way out, she gives me the side-eye for interrupting class again. As if it was my choice.

I'm directed into Principal Peterson's office, where Mrs. Cisneros, along with Rex, Eddie, and Jorge are waiting for me. Looks like Mrs. C chose not to forget about what happened after all. Wonderful.

Rex and his crew glower at me through slitted eyes. Can't say I blame them. I did beat them to a bloody pulp and steal their dad's cherished bicycle.

No, wait. That was them. I glare the hell right back.

Principal Peterson stands, his hands perched on his hips, belly resting on the edge of the desk. He's actually a fairly handsome man—or might be underneath all the wild facial hair. According to the rumor mill—also known as Charlotte Wilkes—Peterson's wife left him a few years ago for a semi-famous golf pro. He's been alone ever since. Unfortunately, his questionable choice of pluming muttonchops probably isn't helping to change his relationship status. They remind me of fangs on a horror movie alien, shooting out, ready to sink into the flesh of unsuspecting students.

"Have a seat." Peterson motions to an empty chair beside Rex. I would rather chomp off my own tongue and eat it for dinner, but it's not like I have much choice. I plop down next to the jerk. "Bobby, is it true that these boys assaulted you after school last Thursday?"

I gnaw my lip, stalling. How I answer will determine whether or not Rex and his crew take things further. "I-it was just a misunderstanding. Nothing big happened."

"See, just like I said." Rex smiles smugly. "We was just messin' around. Little dude here's my kaibigan. Right, pare?"

He holds up his fist for me to bump. I want to shove it down his mouth and keep pushing until it sprouts out his other end. Instead, I ignore it. His lips press together in a thin line.

Mrs. Cisneros groans and shakes her noggin like she's a bobblehead. "Come on, Bobby. They ganged up on you. When I ran up, they were kicking you around like a soccer ball."

"Wasn't us," Rex says. "We don't do that."

"Yeah, we don't do that," Eddie echoes his brother.

Mrs. C arches a brow and turns to the principal. "Look at his eye!"

Peterson leans forward, studies me, muttonchops ready to pounce.

I shrug. "I crashed my bike. Totaled it. Can't even ride it anymore." I glance at Rex. If he catches my meaning, he doesn't show it.

Mrs. Cisneros springs up from her chair. "Come on, Bobby. Why are you doing this?"

I squeeze the armrest and ignore her question, but what I really want to do is scream at her. Mrs. C means well, but she doesn't realize she's seriously messing with my future health.

As if we're the only two people in the room, she levels a hard glare at me, making me break eye contact. "Somebody needs to be brave enough to put these guys in their place. I thought that would be you, Bobby. Don't make me wrong."

Her words hit me harder than Rex's punches. But she has no idea what I'm going through, what's at stake. Does she really expect me to narc on a guy who supposedly put another kid in a coma for ratting him out for shoplifting? If Mrs. C could've just let it go like I asked, everything would be fine.

Maybe.

Rex clears his throat. "Y'know, we should get back to class. We're missing out on our quality education." He smirks as if he's the one in charge here.

The principal folds his arms. "You're right. I've heard enough. You boys can leave."

"Cool." Rex starts to rise.

"You three are suspended for two days. You can return to classes on Wednesday." Peterson picks up his phone, punches an extension. "Yes, security, we have a few students who need to be escorted off the grounds."

"What?" Jorge says, slamming his hand against the armrest of his chair. "I didn't even do nothing!"

His outburst jolts me. Jorge has been quiet throughout the meeting, so much so that I'd forgotten he was even there. I share his outrage, mostly because Peterson only suspended them for a couple of days. I guess that's the going punishment for beating me bloody.

"Hey, it's all good," Rex says. "Just an early vacation is all."

"One more thing," Peterson says. "The next time any of you three find yourselves in my office, you will be expelled. Now wait outside."

As Rex exits, he shoots me a steely-eyed stare. I sink a little lower in my chair, wishing I could crawl beneath the cushion and disappear.

"A couple days?" Mrs. C says. "That's all you're going to do?"

Peterson shoots her a look that silences her. "Will you give us a moment, please?"

Mrs. C gives me one more disappointed glance and leaves.

Peterson waddles around his desk, sits down beside me. "You have anything you want to tell me?"

I shake my head.

"I know what goes on out there. If they bother you again, let me know."

Yeah, I'll call you from the hospital. "Okay."

He exhales sharply. "All right. Get back to class."

When I exit Peterson's office, Rex and company are sitting in the lobby. I pass them, head down, eyes trained on the floor.

"Should keep your head up, bruh," Eddie says. "You gonna wanna see what's coming next."

Rex curls his lip into a snarl. "Oh, he ain't gonna see us coming. That's for damn sure."

My chest tightens at his words. On wobbly legs, I flee into the deserted halls. Great. My bruises haven't healed, and Rex is already making plans to add to them. And all the training sessions with Luke at the Jab Gym might not be enough to save me.

ROUND 10

In between classes, I meet up with Rosie at her locker and fill her in on Rex's suspension. Not surprisingly, she's already heard. And judging from all the stares I'm getting, the rest of the school has too.

"At least you'll be safe at school while they're out," she says, pulling a worn paperback of *The Handmaid's Tale* from her locker.

"Yeah, the operative words being 'at school.' What about every minute after?"

She squeezes my shoulder. "Then I guess you'd better start saving up for running shoes. After you buy me that burrito you owe me."

I shake my head, smiling. Only Rosie could say something so snarky yet comforting. She shuts her locker. Before we can leave, Jimmy Valdez, a freshman with excessively matching clothes, strolls up to us. His blue and white Dodgers hoodie matches his white sneakers with blue laces.

"Hey, Rosie," Jimmy says. "I, uh, like your hair. Orange is one of my favorite colors. And my favorite fruit. And juice. But not with pulp. My mom always buys it with pulp. I hate that. Gets stuck between my teeth."

Rosie blinks. "Lovely."

Jimmy winces. The conversation—if you can call it that—stalls. "Okay, bye." He hurries off, muttering to himself.

"That is one smooth-talking stalker you got there," I say. "He sure can match an outfit, though."

"Shut up. He's harmless. And kind of cute."

Biology class drags. The second hand inches around the clock like a dying caterpillar. I can't focus on the talking head up front, also known as Ms. Singletary, who's deep into an extended lecture on nucleotides and RNA. My mind is too crammed with everything that's been happening.

At lunch, Rosie and I sit at our usual table near the library stacks. While she sketches a new comic book panel, I pass the time reading issue #40 of *All-New X-Men*, which Bran loaned to me. It's another landmark in comic book queer representation, depicting the young mutant Iceman coming out to his teammate Jean Grey. Bran knows me so well—even the embarrassing little secrets I can't tell Rosie. When I was a kid, Iceman was my secret crush out of Marvel's merry band of mutants. He was funny and cute, not to mention he can turn his entire body into ice, which means he's literally the coolest hero ever. Now that he's out, it's nice to know my elementary school crush may have been reciprocated. I mean, if he were, well, *real*.

The comic is a fun read, but it does little to pull my thoughts away from the day's drama. I take my poetry notebook from my bag, and work on another tanaga. Writing poetry has always been my escape, even more so than reading comic books. Maybe because I'm taking action, channeling my anger or sadness into something creative. I write, cross out, and rewrite. As always, I quietly clap out the twenty-eight syllables.

Charlotte, please go far away!
Take a trip, maybe down south
The Grand Canyon's nice, they say
And also big as your mouth!

It's amazing how four short lines can lighten my mood so quickly. I show the poem to Rosie, and she snorts out a laugh.

The bell rings, and we exit the library and navigate the grounds toward her locker. While we walk, an idea hits me. It's a bit out there, but if I know Rosie, she'll be down to help.

"Hey, your boy Jimmy Valdez—he's an office aide during fifth period, right?"

"Yeah, but he's not 'my boy.'"

"You think you can ask him something for me?"

Her eyes narrow. "Like?"

I look off to the side. "Nothing big. Just, y'know . . . Rex's address."

"Seriously? Would you also like the number of a good chiropractor? Because you'll need one after Rex rearranges your spine."

We arrive at her locker, and she whirls the dial with her combination.

"It's not like I'm gonna knock on his front door. I'm just gonna, y'know, sneak into the backyard and take my bike back."

"That is completely insane," she says, stuffing a folder into her bag. "Which may be why I'm starting to like it." She tilts her head as if considering my request. "Do you at least have a plan?"

"Yeah, I'm gonna sneak into the backyard and take my bike back."

"I think your plan needs an actual plan. Work on it. I'll see about Rex's addy." She pulls out her phone and types out a text.

After school, Rosie and I take the Metro bus up to the Villain's Lair. She needs to go over some sketches with Bran, and I . . . well, I never need an excuse to see my guy and browse the racks. As soon as we enter, Bran comes out from behind the counter and greets me with a hug and a kiss on the cheek. The store's completely devoid of customers, so I let him. At Rosie, he merely nods. Looks like their working relationship is still a bit frosty.

"Hey, Larry," Bran says to his boss, who's at his computer, "okay if I take my fifteen?" Larry gives a thumbs-up, and Bran leads Rosie into the back room.

Larry shoots me a grin, and I know exactly what's coming. "Hey, Bobby. Want to help shelve some maquettes we just got in?"

"Sure," I say with a shrug. Usually I'm down to help out, but I need to get to the Jab Gym soon, and I'd much rather spend what little time I have with Bran instead of doing his job for him.

I spend the next ten minutes unpacking a box of Marvel Zombies maquettes: everything from zombie Hulk to zombie Wolverine. It's like Brandon's ultimate Christmas wish list. Too bad I could never afford to buy him one. I line the figures up in a glass display case, positioning them so they're attacking a J. Jonah Jameson maquette.

When I'm finished, I look over a display of graphic novels

on the counter. Amid the colorful covers of superheroes flying into action, a hardcover edition of *Runaways* catches my eye. I pick up the book with the respect it deserves and flip through it. The story centers on a diverse group of teens who run away after finding out that their parents are supervillains. It's one of my favorites, and not just because the story and art are first-rate.

"*Runaways*, volume one. Nice," Bran says from over my shoulder. "Do you remember when I first told you about this title?"

"The day we first kissed. You used the promise of back issues to lure me into the storage room so you could put the moves on me."

"Yep, it totally worked too."

I smirk, return the book to its perch, and let slip a sigh.

"Hey, let me get it for you," he says. He moves to retrieve the book.

"No, it's okay."

"Come on, I want to. It's not a big deal. Employee discount, remember?"

"Bran, you don't have to keep buying me stuff," I say, a bit harsher than I mean.

He blinks at me. "All right. Sorry."

Rosie joins us and says, "Well, hey, if you're treating, there's a cute She-Hulk tee that'd look super dope on me." Bran walks off toward the register without replying. "What? Green's my color."

I need to get to the Jab Gym for my shift and some much-needed training. Before I can say bye, Rosie grabs my arm.

"No frickin' way." She points toward the front of the store.

Outside the window, Jorge's unmistakable shaved head stands out among the pedestrian traffic. He appears to be alone. Strange seeing him without Rex and Eddie. His eyes meet mine, and he scurries away.

I dodge around displays, nearly trample over a small boy in a Batman shirt, and shove open the door. Three storefronts down, I spot Jorge weaving through the crowd. I sprint after him—only he's faster than he looks. He hops on a transit bus that speeds off before I can reach it.

Damn.

What the hell was he doing here? Did he follow us just now, or did he already know where I'd be?

Rosie and Bran catch up, and we walk back to the Lair. On the way, I tell Bran about Jorge.

"Looks like Rex is making his attack dog keep tabs on you," Rosie says. "Not good."

We reach the front of the shop, but Brandon doesn't go in. "What the hell do they want? Why can't they just leave you alone?"

The answer to his first question is fairly obvious, but replying *To beat me until I bleed freely* probably won't do much for Bran's peace of mind. To the latter question, I say, "I don't know. They're assholes."

Rosie grunts. "World is full of 'em."

I check the time on my cell. "I gotta get to work." I move past Bran, hoping to make my escape before the onslaught of questions, but he catches my arm.

"You got a job? Since when? Where?"

"It's nothing. Just sweeping and cleaning up . . . at the Jab Gym."

"What the hell's the Jab Gym?" Rosie asks.

"Just a gym where they do gym stuff and, you know . . . boxing."

They glance at each other. Rosie folds her arms, raises her brow. "B, what are you up to?"

"Is this because of that Pacquiao fight we watched?" Bran says.

"No. I don't know. Maybe. Is there something wrong with wanting to defend myself? I'm learning a lot there. Come on, you guys know my motto."

"Getting punched in the face on purpose doesn't sound much like self-preservation," Rosie says.

Bran frowns. "I don't know if I like this."

"Great. This is why I didn't tell you guys before." My voice rises with every sentence, earning stares from passing pedestrians. "Why can't you guys have my back?"

Bran shifts his jaw, as if weighing his answer. "I don't want you to be hurt again."

"Just use the pepper spray," Rosie says.

"Pepper spray is not gonna fix this! You guys didn't get your asses literally kicked in. That is not happening to me again."

"Okay, okay, breathe." Rosie rubs my arm. "I actually think it's a good idea."

"I guess," Bran says. "What, are you going to fight their whole crew? That's a good way to get yourself killed."

"They're coming for me either way. I need to be ready."

"Well, there is, you know, a certain philosophy that says violence just leads to more violence."

"Who are you now, Martin Luther Gandhi? You're writing a frickin' zombie comic book!"

"Yes, exactly! A comic book! As in fictional. If you try to fight those guys, the beatdown you'll get will be straight-up real."

"I am doing this, Bran. I need to do this."

He stays silent for a drawn-out moment. Finally, he replies, "Do what you have to do."

Not exactly the ringing endorsement I need, but he'll come around. Hopefully. I can't believe he came at me with that nonviolence noise. He just doesn't understand how things work beyond his safe, rich neighborhood.

"Well, I gotta go." I move to leave.

"Maybe I should drive you," Bran says, but I'm already breaking into a jog.

"I'm fine, Bran." I give a wave without looking back.

When Manny Pacquiao was a young boy, he stowed away on a boat and traveled five hundred miles to Manila to become a professional boxer. So running five miles to the Jab Gym to learn to throw a punch is no big deal. At least that's what I tell myself when I'm laboring at the halfway point.

The whole way over, I keep alert just in case.

ROUND 11

By the time I reach the Jab Gym, sweat coats every part of me, but instead of being spent, I'm refreshed. I stroll inside, and Luke lets me behind the counter.

"Here, try these on, kid. Should be about your size." He hands me a pair of red boxing boots. "If you're gonna train, gotta use the right gear. You ain't getting in my ring in those raggedy-ass sneakers."

I slip on the boots, which are much lighter than my high-tops, almost like thick socks. I do a couple jumping jacks, and immediately my movements feel faster.

"Well, how ya like 'em?"

I strike a fighting pose. "Nice. Just like Wonder Woman's. Do they come with a lasso and fancy tiara?"

"Yeah, this ain't professional wrestling, kid." He squeezes my shoulder. "Okay, today we're gonna get organized and tackle this problem head-on. What do you say?"

"Dope." My skin tingles. Luke is actually taking a real interest in my bullying problem. Hopefully we'll start on the speed bag first thing.

"Okay, let's get to work." He ushers me to his office in the bowels of the gym.

Up against the far wall, beneath the lone window, sits

possibly the most uncomfortable-looking cot in the world. The middle sags, nearly touching the floor. Luke sleeps on that thing? No wonder his posture is horrible. Scattered stacks of papers, a bunch of those old videocassette things, books, and piles of other random junk litter the office. Who knows how long he's been accumulating it all. Decades, probably.

Luke gestures at a rusty cabinet. "Okay, file the papers by member registration, equipment rental, receipts, and bills. Then you can get to everything else."

My shoulders slump. I guess the speed bag will have to wait. This had better be worth it.

I wade through the piles of papers, resisting the urge to trash them all. In between sweeping, mopping, and emptying out spit buckets, I spend the first couple of hours finding a home for every piece of scrap paper. A good third is old lottery tickets—played with the same lucky numbers that never came through. I file them away in the trash.

On the wall behind Luke's desk, lost amid a clutter of old flyers, hangs a frame covered in a thick layer of dust. I pull a rag from Hank and wipe it off, revealing a faded photo of a young boxer and his trainer. They pose in a ring, the trainer with his arm around the boxer's shoulder. The trainer appears to be Luke, decades younger, fifty pounds lighter—and actually handsome. Damn, Luke was a hottie back in the day. Good for him.

Suddenly, I feel creepy for ogling my boss's younger self. I replace the frame on the wall, pull a broom from Hank, and sweep the floor.

After my break, I dive into Luke's video collection. The

tapes consist of hundreds of fights—most are labeled. Some I recognize, a few I don't. There are Mayweather vs. Mosley, Margarito vs. Cotto, and Holyfield vs. Tyson II—also known as the "OW! HE BIT MY EAR OFF!" fight.

My breath catches when I come across tapes of Manny's key battles against Érik Morales and Juan Márquez, as well as his one-punch knockout of Ricky Hatton. Looks like I may be spending even more of my off-hours here than I thought.

"Awesome," I say as Luke pads by.

He pauses outside the doorway. "Good to see you enjoying your work, kid."

The voice in my head replies, *Oh, yeah, I'm ecstatic to clean up your decades-in-the-making landfill of a mess. Huzzah.* Out loud, I say, "Yeah, good times."

He disappears down the hallway, and I set about organizing the tapes alphabetically on a wooden shelf that stretches across the back wall.

Luke also owns dozens of books on boxing, both instructional and biographical. A few sport a library filing number on the spine, which makes me wonder about the small fortune he must owe in late fees. Books on Muhammad Ali, Rocky Marciano, both Sugar Rays, De La Hoya, and, yes, Manny Dapidran Pacquiao grace the office. A veritable pugilist hall of fame. I place the books on a lower shelf with the respect they deserve. Being surrounded by the all-time greats in boxing history makes me bounce on the balls of my feet with excitement. I can't wait to learn more.

For the remainder of my shift, I empty every trash can in

the gym, heft each bag over to Hank, and wheel the old cart out to the back dumpster.

At quitting time, Luke waddles into the office and claps slowly. "Damn, son. This place is cleaner than my ass after a waxing."

"Uh, thank you?" I can't help but snicker at his crassness. He and Rosie would definitely click. "So, Luke. Would it be okay if I checked out some of these old fight videos?" I gather up the cleaning supplies and load them onto Hank; Luke might grant my request if I keep busy.

He doesn't answer, his attention fixed on the formerly dusty photograph.

"Hey, Luke."

He blinks, then pivots toward me. "What's up?"

"Mind if I watch some fights?"

"Sure, kid. There's a good one of me and my ex-wife. She got a mean right hook." Is he joking? Damn, I hope so.

With all the nonchalance I can pull off, I hold up the Pacquiao book. "Oh, and you mind if I borrow this? I'm kind of a big Pacman fan."

Luke smirks as he glances at the MP emblazoned across my chest. "Really? Hadn't noticed." He shrugs. "Keep it."

"Seriously?"

"It's yours."

I nearly hug him but think better of it. The gift makes me pumped for my workout. Manny has become my goal. I skip to the locker room and store the biography in my pack.

First up, I jump on the heavy bag. With each throw, I focus

on Luke's pointers: hit the bag with the front of my fist, dead center, clench right before impact. I lose myself in the repetition. Before I know it, a half hour passes.

Next, I hit the free weights. Working out with milk cartons served its purpose, but curling actual dumbbells is a definite improvement.

In between sets, my attention focuses on the redhead from the other day while she works the speed bag. She strikes in a blur, like a woodpecker going to town.

Her eyes lock on to mine, and she finishes with a stinging right that rattles the bag. "I know the glare of my awesomeness is distracting, but would you mind not staring so hard?"

My cheeks warm, and I avert my gaze. "Sorry. You're pretty fast."

"Go ahead, finish."

"Finish what?"

"Most guys say, 'You're pretty fast . . . for a girl.'"

"Wow, that's, uh, fairly sexist. You'd be fast for a cheetah." She laughs, which encourages me to keep the conversation going. "How long have you been boxing?"

"Since I was in junior high, about, what . . . four years now? God, has it been that long?" Her eyes seem to lose focus for a moment. "How about you? How long you been strapping the gloves on?"

"Oh, uh. Not long." Just over twenty-four hours to be precise. "Um, I mean, not as long as you."

"Maybe we could spar sometime. Show me what you got."

That would take all of three seconds, but okay. I blink,

hoping to stall. "Oh, yeah. Let's throw some leather." *Throw some leather? Good God, shut up now, please.*

"Sweet." She unhooks her speed bag. "I'm Vicki, by the way. Vicki Connolly."

"Bobby Agbayani."

"Good to meet ya." She jabs her fist into mine, then disappears into the women's locker room.

"Don't even think about it." Luke materializes by my side with a small duffel bag under his arm. "That girl could deck you with her pinkie finger."

Nice to know he has so much faith in me. But I can't deny that the thought of trading blows with Vicki makes cleaning the head more appealing in comparison. "I could learn a lot from her, though."

"Yeah, she could learn you some math. As in how many teeth she'd subtract from your mouth. Now come with me."

Luke brings me over to the mat area, where a line of seven orange cones are laid out a few feet apart. "Let's get you on some footwork drills."

"Footwork? When am I gonna get to hit someone?"

"Boxing ain't just about punching, boy. If you got crap footwork, you got a crap fighter. Watch any bout—the guy who loses his footwork first is the guy who loses the fight. Now watch and learn."

With a nimble step that belies his weight and age, Luke sidesteps through the cones in an intricate pattern. He reaches the end of the line and comes back. "Okay, your turn. Take it slowly at first."

My first couple of times through, I falter with the steps and kick over a few cones. Luke has to show me the movements a second time before I commit them to memory. By my fourth try, I have the routine down and whip through the cones with ease. I'm sure there's a bad joke in there about queer guys being light on their feet, but if fitting the stereotype makes me a better fighter, I'm good with it.

"Excellent." He claps. "From now on, before you hit anything, you start every workout with footwork. Hear me?"

"I do."

"Good." From his pack, Luke pulls out a worn speed bag, the leather cracked along the seams. "Now, ready to hit something?"

"Oh, you know it." At last we're getting to it.

The metal hooks click as Luke hangs the bag. Before I can step up, he sticks out his arm and restrains me. "Easy there, antsy boy. You need to learn to watch and learn. Okay, first thing. Always keep your fists up by your peepers, like so." He puts his hands up and demonstrates. "You want to hit the bag twice with one hand. First, strike through the bag with the flat of your knuckles, then rotate your forearm and come down on the bag with a hammer fist."

He switches to his left and does it again, landing the second punch as the bag returns. "One, two. One, two. One, two. One, two." The bag and his fists blur into motion like a cyclist pumping down a straightaway. The old guy still has skills. He steps back, gestures with his chin. "Okay, give it a try. Don't get discouraged if it don't come at first. It'll take some time."

My first few punches are awkward, off-center. I can't seem

to get the right balance between speed and power. I lunge instead of striking.

Luke squeezes my shoulder. "It ain't about hitting it hard or fast. It's about hitting it right. Solid. Got it?"

Out of reflex, I nod, even though I'm not entirely sure what he's saying. I try again. I fail again. The bag morphs into Rex's head, wobbling back and forth, mocking me. I growl and unleash a ridiculously overpowered punch. Fighters nearby stare. Another new kid struggling at the bag. Big news.

"Whoa. Easy," Luke says. "You ain't gonna get this down in five minutes. It's gonna take a good while. Just slow it down and focus on form."

He's right. I need to trust in the process, be patient. Only I have no patience because I don't have time. Another beatdown is waiting for me, tomorrow or next week. And when Rex or any other homophobic douchebag comes to test me, I have to be ready.

For the next hour, I force myself to follow every one of Luke's teachings. I slow my pace. I strike the bag solidly. And eventually, it starts to come. I'm not a whirlwind of speed and technique like Vicki or Pacman yet, but I make some progress. And tomorrow I'll get better. Hopefully.

After I manage to keep the bag going for nearly half a minute, I ask Luke when I'll be able to get some sparring in. He coughs out a wheezy chuckle and retreats to the front counter.

By closing time my arms are as heavy as concrete, and I struggle to push the exit open. Not good.

Especially since Jorge is waiting for me outside.

ROUND 12

My first instinct is to check for a sneak attack on either side of me, but the sidewalk is clear. Apparently Jorge came alone. Is he here on Rex's orders or on his own?

I raise my fists to my chin like Luke taught me and crouch into a fighter's stance, but Jorge makes no forward move.

"You like boba?" he asks.

My hands dip slightly, and I blink. Why the hell is he asking me about an intergalactic bounty hunter? He points to a store sign across the street that reads BOBA TEA in red block letters.

Oh.

"Come on. My treat." Jorge dashes across the cracked road before an oncoming truck can pass. The driver brakes and blasts his horn.

His treat? Is he serious? Why would I ever do anything with this bald-headed delinquent? The time on my cell reads 9:12. I should head home, but curiosity gets the better of me, and I follow him across the street.

I enter the mom-and-pop shop, half expecting to get jumped. It's empty, save for a middle-aged Chinese lady sitting behind the counter, her shoulders slumped forward.

"What's your flavor?" Jorge asks me as he scans the lengthy drink menu.

"Taro."

"That's a good one."

"It's a wannabe ube flavor, but it'll do. What do you want?"

"Honeydew milk tea's chido."

"No, what do you *want*? As in why are you following me around like a creepy-ass stalker?"

He winces, but doesn't reply. He steps to the counter, gives our order, and—even after my less-than-friendly comment—pays for my drink. A few minutes later, we're enjoying our ultra-sweet beverages at a window table as if we're not mortal enemies.

As the sugar rush hits me, I recall the image of Jorge flipping his balisong right before they jumped me. He probably has the knife on him now. I glance around furtively for something to use as a weapon, but only see the napkin dispenser on our table. If Jorge even slips his hand inside his pocket, he's getting a face full of napkins.

The conversation is nonexistent, the only noise the slurp of tapioca balls through extra-wide straws. From what I've seen at school, Jorge has never been the talkative sort. But if he doesn't want to talk, why drag me over here?

"Well, this has been great. Thanks for the bubble tea." I rise, straighten the wrinkles in my hoodie. "Totally makes up for you kicking the shit out of me."

"Wasn't me, man."

"Whatever."

"It was all Rex and Eddie. You were too out of it to know, but I never touched you. Refused to, actually." Jorge holds up his left hand, plants his elbow on the table. "How you think I got this?" His pinkie finger hangs off from the others in a bent, grotesque shape, its color the shade of a rotting plum. "Rex's way of making sure I don't step out of line again."

This is the most I've ever heard Jorge speak, which, for some reason, makes me believe his story—but not quite forgive him. I sit back down and take another sip of the taro to wash down the bile coating my tongue.

"So basically, you stood back and watched while they worked me over. Thanks, I can see now that you're just bursting with moral character."

I keep my eyes on the doorway, half expecting Rex and Eddie to stride through it.

"We ain't angels, güey," Jorge says between sips. "Some fool ain't showing us respect, we're gonna teach respect. Some vatos just need a lesson in proper decorum 'n' shit, you know? But what they did to you? That ain't right." Jorge takes an extra-long swallow, as if his tongue isn't used to this much talking. "Mi tío, he funny like you. Into other vatos—since always. He stayed true to hisself no matter how much people beat him down. But he chido—he a good dude." He chews his straw then puts down his drink. "Was good, anyway."

I lean in closer. "Your uncle—he passed away?"

Jorge shakes his head. "Killed. Found in an alley two blocks from our house. Face kicked in beyond all recognition." He swallows hard, eyes glistening. "Look, I ain't got no problem with you—never have. Make sure you don't end up like my tío. He took care of me when I was little. More than my own papi ever did."

Maybe Jorge's a decent guy after all—but the mention of his dad erases any sympathy I may have felt.

"You know that bike you guys jacked from me?" I say, my words even and measured. "That was my dad's. It was the last thing he gave to me before he died. I want it back."

Jorge's eyelids flutter, and he looks out at the stream of headlights blurring by. "That's messed up. I feel you, I do, but you need to let that go. You got more pressing shit around the corner." After a final slurp of his drink, he rises. "Rex . . . he coming for you."

With a final nod, he exits the store and heads west without looking back.

Should I tail him? Maybe I'll get lucky and he'll lead me to Dad's bike. Or more likely he'll lead me to his crew and another beatdown.

No—it's late and I have homework. I make the smart move and sprint home, scanning the street for Rex the whole way.

After a protein-heavy dinner of hard-boiled eggs and chocolate milk, I zip through two hours' worth of English and algebra in half the time. Now I can finally dig into Manny's biography. My excitement almost makes me forget how exhausted I am.

ROUND 13

The next morning, I try to stay focused in algebra, but my mind is fixed on the Manny book. I take notes during Mrs. Jennings's lecture, but they're sloppy and not nearly as detailed as usual. After ten minutes, I lose all interest and cave. I pull the Pacquiao bio from my bag, hide it in my lap, and read.

Soon the classroom walls disappear, and I'm back in the motherland with the champ. Despite dropping out of school due to extreme poverty, Manny passed his high school equivalency exam. That doesn't sound like such a bad idea. Maybe I could do the same. It would be a lot safer than risking bodily harm here at Worst-Luck High every day.

"Bobby?" Mrs. Jennings calls.

I look up. It takes me a moment to realize she's talking to me. "Uh, yes? Can you repeat the question?"

Mrs. Jennings throws me a frown she usually reserves for hopeless students like Eric Ocampo. "I asked you to read problem sixteen aloud for the class."

"Problem sixteen. Right. Sure." I scan the pages, but see no such number. I flip the page, then the next one. And the next.

Eric leans over my shoulder, his breath on my ear. "Page one twenty-six. Dude, follow along."

Great, I'm being scolded by a drug addict who probably hears something entirely different whenever Jennings says "math." Not very scholarly, Agbayani. I wince, turn to the right page, and read the problem out loud.

Over my next three periods—US History, Art, and Spanish—I try to stay focused strictly on schoolwork. My notes are thorough. Maybe too thorough. Somehow I doubt we'll be tested on Mr. Olsen's extensive grunge-band vinyl collection, but if he mentions it, I'm writing it down.

I devote all of lunch to reading the Pacquiao bio while Rosie works on her secret art project. I try to sneak a peek, but she's being extra covert.

"Hey, did you know when Manny Pacquiao was a young boy living in poverty in Tango, he had to climb a mountain every day to search for food?"

"Really?" She pauses from her sketching and looks at my MP T-shirt. "Did he wear that same shirt? Because it sure smells like it."

I take a whiff of my collar. She's right. Time for an overdue laundry day.

"Hey, whatcha working on? That for the comic book?"

She shuts her portfolio. "Nothing. Side project."

When the final bell rings, Rosie and I plod through the halls and navigate the metal maze of cars in the parking lot. A horn blares. Brandon waves at us from his Bimmer across the street. One of the perks of Bran being homeschooled is he's usually finished with his school day much earlier than us public school peons, which often results in a ride home for Rosie and me. We dodge through the impatient traffic and stroll up.

Bran clicks the automatic locks open. "What's up, pogi

guy," he says, calling me the Tagalog word for handsome. "I hear you owe this lady a burrito."

I glance at Rosie.

She shrugs. "People will gossip. It's disgusting." She fake coughs. "Shotgun!" She dashes around the back bumper and gets into the passenger seat. "Come on! I didn't have lunch. My ass be hangry as hell."

"Okay, okay." I settle into the back seat. "I got the day off from the gym. Let's grub."

"And not no fake-ass Taco Bell, neither." Rosie slams the door.

"Come on, how can you not love their Mexican pizza? That sounds completely authentic."

"I will smack the light brown off you, Agbayani."

"Not before I lick it off," Bran says.

Rosie holds up a finger. "Hey, there will be no tongue action in my presence. Not while I'm not getting any!"

Brandon punches up "Perfect Getaway," a dope track by Echo Park native Emcee Klassy. We vibe to the laid-back groove as Klassy name-checks Historic Filipinotown and spits mad flow about getting away with her friends. Bran always picks the best track for the ride.

Bran heads over to El Charro, a cozy Mexican restaurant on Sixth Street and home of the most incredible shrimp tacos I've ever tasted. Since I'm in training, I forgo all things tortilla wrapped and order the all-protein machaca con huevos. Rosie gets her veggie burrito—with extra guacamole, of course.

After we order, Bran opens his wallet and pulls out one of his credit cards, but I step in front of him. "My treat," I say.

He arches a brow. "You sure?

"Yep." I hand the cashier a wad of cash—the remainder of my pay from the Jab Gym.

"Um, maybe you should be saving that. I can pay—it's no problem."

I wince. "I got it." Bran always pays when we go grub—which makes me feel bad enough—but the one time I have some extra cash, he can't let me treat. *Why can't he just let me have this?*

When our dishes arrive, I take a moment to breathe in the aroma of juicy beef and bell peppers. Rosie, however, immediately slices her burrito in half, and ample amounts of guac seep out.

"Now that's what we need in our comic," Bran says. "Zombie ooze oozing out of every zombie orifice."

Rosie grimaces. "Ugh. Can you not use the words 'ooze' and 'orifice' while we eat?"

"Hey, it's only a couple weeks till the contest. Just wanna keep us on point."

While we eat, I update Bran and Rosie on my impromptu boba meetup with Jorge. Rosie, of course, is her usual trusting self.

"Uh-uh." She shakes her head. "Do not listen to anything that juvie inmate has to say."

"I don't know, he seemed pretty sincere. Denied ever taking part in jumping me. And I vaguely recall Rex yelling at him to join in when he wouldn't."

She rips a bite from her burrito. Through a mouthful, she says, "I repeat: do not trust him."

"He sounds sincere," Bran says. "Maybe Jorge could help, tell you what Rex is planning."

"You mean like a spy?" Rosie shakes her head. "Yeah, *right.*"

"Sure, why not? Sounds like this Jorge is sick of being Rex's attack dog. Besides, people can change, you know."

"Sure they can." Rosie rolls her eyes. "Maybe that's how things work in comic books or up in Richie Rich Silver Lake, but down here that kind of thinking can get you killed."

Bran bristles at the dig. "Whatever. I think you should give him a chance, B."

I glance at them, each taking opposing sides like a gullible angel and a paranoid devil perched upon my shoulders.

"Well, Jorge also told me about his gay uncle who was, well . . . he was beaten to death. Jorge was pretty torn up about it. He's not a homophobe like the rest of their crew."

Rosie coughs. "Oh my God, Bobby. The queer relative who was killed by gay-bashers? That's the number-one way homophobes get you to lower your guard!"

I drop my fork, startling Bran. "What? What are you babbling about?"

"It's Gay Infiltration 101, B."

I manage to refrain from rolling my eyes. Could she be right, though? Was Jorge lying to me? If so, why? I don't want to be naive like Brandon sometimes can be, but I also can't become the poster child for paranoia like Rosie, always seeing conspiracies everywhere and trusting no one.

Bran's cell buzzes. Not hard to guess who it probably is. "Hey, Dad," he says into his phone. "Yeah, it's my day off." His brow crinkles into a frown. "Yes, I'm hanging out with Bobby. We are dating, remember?" With a groan, he shoots up from his chair and moves to the front door.

My head droops, and Rosie squeezes my forearm. Nothing to see here, folks. Just another nagging phone call from my boyfriend's dad, who despises me.

Another minute of back and forth, and Bran finally hangs up. We finish our food in silence; none of us acknowledge the phone call. It's as if it didn't happen. By the time we exit the restaurant, sunset has crept up on us. Beneath a brooding violet sky, we trudge down a side street to Brandon's car.

Rosie yanks my arm. "Shit."

Rex leans against Brandon's BMW. Eddie stands beside him, gripping a wheel wrench at his side. A purple bruise discolors the left side of Rex's scowling face. I can't imagine who'd be big enough to slap Rex around, but I must admit, I appreciate the results. Eddie also sports a nasty bruise by his eye.

I step in front of Brandon and Rosie. "You guys following me now?"

Rex brushes his fingertips against the Bimmer's red hood. "Not too hard when your boy picks you up in this dope ride. You just begging for trouble, rolling around in this thing."

Eddie raises the wrench and, with a double-handed swing, bashes in the back window. The car alarm blares like a banshee cry. He holds the tool up to the driver's side window.

"If I was you," Rex says to Brandon, "I'd kill the alarm before my bro here does more damage."

Brandon pulls out his keys and with a click of his thumb,

silences the wailing. "Okay, okay. It's off. Just don't do any—" His protest gets drowned out by Eddie smashing in the driver's side window.

"Assholes!" I rush Rex, but Brandon locks my arm up and blocks me.

"Don't," he says.

Rex sits down on the front of the hood and says, "Better listen to your girlfriend there."

Before I can stop her, Rosie steps to him and jerks his head back with a slap.

He blinks and rubs his cheek, which turns fire red. "Tanga bitch." He rises and drives his fist into Rosie's stomach. Coughing, she falls to the concrete.

"Rosie!" I brush by Bran and run over to her. Big mistake. Rex kicks me in the ribs, and I crumple to the ground. Rosie and I lie on the pavement, coughing. More kicks come, blasting pain through my gut. I try to stand and fight, but my muscles have other ideas. I fall back down. Rex drops on top of me and curls his fingers into a fist.

One chance.

I dig into my back pocket for the smooth cylinder as Rex cocks back his arm. I aim the nozzle, flick the safety, and unload the brown pepper spray into his face. He screams. I shift my aim to his open mouth, and his shrieks turn to gags. Rex falls to the concrete, clawing at his face.

"Get in the car," I say to Rosie, helping her up.

Bran lies sprawled out on the sidewalk while Eddie repeatedly slams his heel into his gut. His groans spur me on. The world whirls around me. I stagger toward them, wanting to drive a punch through Eddie's jaw, but I can barely lift my arms. I settle for giving him a taste of pepper spray. Eddie joins Rex in a chorus of howling and coughing.

I hook my arm under Bran's shoulder and manage to drag him over to the car and into the passenger seat. Rosie is in the back, laid out amid the shards of glass. Behind the wheel, I push the round starter button. Nothing happens.

"Bran!" I push the button repeatedly. "It's not starting!"

Rex stumbles toward us, gripping the wrench, the brown spray smeared across his cheekbones like a horror-movie mask. He screams something unintelligible. I have three seconds, maybe less, before he reaches me.

"Step on the brake!" Bran says.

"What?!"

"Keep your foot on the brake and push the button!"

A hollow *thud* rattles the car. Rex crouches over the front bumper, his acne-scarred cheeks flushed red, his pompadour a deflated mess. A newly formed crater decorates the hood.

I step on the brake, press the starter, and the engine roars to life.

"Your punk ass about to get bodied!" Rex lunges for me through the shattered window.

I yank the stick into reverse and peel out, clipping a parked minivan's headlight. With an expletive-filled scream, Rex hurls the wrench, and it connects with the windshield. Cracks sprout across the glass, but it holds.

A good half block passes before I whip the car around and

continue driving forward. A *thunk-thunk-thunk* pounds in my ears. *Did we blow a tire?* No—it's my pulse, blasting in my skull like a trip hammer.

"You guys okay?" I risk a glance at Bran.

"Yeah," Bran replies, despite being hunched over. I grab his hand, squeeze it. I find Rosie in the rearview mirror. She's too shell shocked to answer.

We ride in silence toward Rosie's house. The wind rushing through the shattered window makes me flinch at things that aren't there. I keep seeing Rex in random cars behind us. I take several extra turns just in case.

Bran leans back, lets out a string of rapid-fire coughs. "So, that was Rex?"

"That was Rex," I say.

"They were out for blood," Rosie says in between heavy breaths. "What the hell are we gonna do about that pinche dickwipe?"

"I don't know. Working on it." I check the rearview again and make a right onto Rosie's street.

"Well, do it faster. Because Rex is gonna be back terrorizing the school tomorrow, and he'll make a beeline straight for us."

"I know, Rosie. I was kind of in the room when Bruno Scars got suspended."

Bran snorts. "*Bruno Scars?* You stay up late thinking up this stuff, don't you?"

"Huh?" Rosie says. "Bruno what now?" Bran chuckles to Rosie's dismay.

When he quiets down, a thought hits me. "Hey, listen, you guys notice what happened back there?"

"Uh, yeah." Rosie says. "Extreme violence and terror?"

"Not what I meant." I pull up a few doors from Rosie's house—just in case—and kill the motor. "I'm saying Jorge wasn't with them."

After we drop off Rosie, I offer to come home with Bran to help explain to his parents what happened to the car. He furrows his brow and gives me the look—the one people make when they can't tell whether or not I'm joking. I rarely get the look from Bran; we usually connect on everything. The exception being his dad.

He squeezes my arm. "Better let me handle it." He guides the damaged Bimmer away from the curb and through the neighborhood.

"What are you going to tell him?"

"Nothing. If we're lucky he won't ever find out about any of this."

"Wait. How are you going—"

"Don't worry. I have some money saved up."

"Oh." Great, Bran has to use up his savings all because of me and my Rex drama.

"Hey, don't worry, it's only a couple of windows. Shouldn't cost too much."

Does he really mean it, or is he just trying to make me feel better? Ugh. He's probably right. If his dad knew I was the reason their luxury car got trashed, it would mean another entry on the Reasons to Not Date Bobby the Lowlife list. I get it. Doesn't make it any easier to accept.

When we get to my apartment, we sweep up the broken glass from the Bimmer's interior in silence. Something's up.

Bran usually only clams up when he wants to tell me something I won't like. Confrontation and Bran are not friends.

I dump the last of the glass into a trash can. "Go ahead, say it."

"What?"

"Whatever it is you think I need to hear."

"Look, I just—I'm not entirely sure this boxing thing is such a great idea."

I suppress a sigh. "The other day you said you were cool with it. Said you had my back."

"I don't know. You've been spending all your time at the gym. We barely see each other."

"What are you talking about? I just saw you yesterday."

"Yeah, for like, ten minutes." He looks toward the ground. "Why do you think I pick you guys up after school? Why do you think I'm working on this comic book with Rosie? I thought maybe then we'd see each other more."

"Bran, I can't spend every free moment I have with you!"

"You don't understand. You get to hang out with Rosie at school. You're surrounded by people all day. I don't have that."

I bite my lip. I never really considered how lonely it must be for Bran to be homeschooled, but right now I'm not in the mood to console him. "Yeah, I get to be around assholes who want to cave my skull in with a steel pipe. It's a party."

"So maybe fighting them isn't the smartest move."

"They're gonna come at me whether I learn to fight back or not. It's not like I have a choice here, Bran."

"You can run." He looks away. "You did it today."

"Because you and Rosie were there! I couldn't let you guys get hurt!"

"I don't want you getting hurt, either! We're not talking about a schoolyard brawl here, Bobby. That guy wants to permanently reshape your face with a tire iron. Why don't we just call the police?"

With a slow breath, I try to calm myself. My voice rises anyway. "The police? Are you kidding? They might end up shooting us all!"

"Come on, you're exaggerating."

If there was ever an indication that Bran doesn't understand how things work for people of color outside his posh neighborhood, this is it. "I don't need this. You're not helping." I stomp up the apartment path.

"Then what can I do to help?"

Without looking back, I shout, "Anything else!"

ROUND 14

Wednesday morning. The day Rex and crew return from suspension. I'll never understand how permission to miss school is considered an actual punishment. *Hey, kids! Commit a hate crime, get a two-day vacation!* That's what the PSA poster should read.

With my hood pulled down to my eyebrows, I navigate the jammed halls toward Rosie's locker. I dodge all eye contact but still catch the murmurs and wisecracks aimed my way. Today's an exciting day here at Worst-Luck High. The queer kid's going to get the epic beatdown coming to him.

And everyone gets to watch.

Before I reach her locker, Rosie pulls even with me. She draws in close, and her voice takes on a furtive tone. "Good move with the hoodie. Best to stay in stealth mode."

I bristle at her comment. "Yeah. I'm just cold."

"Oh. Sure. No sign of the hulking homophobe, by the way."

"Good," I say too quickly. "I mean, I didn't ask."

We make it to first period without a Rex sighting. When I slip through the doorway and into the safety of the classroom, I exhale and my cheeks burn hot with shame. I yank off my hood and fall into my seat. *Damn coward.*

Eric Ocampo leans forward, close enough for his rancid druggy breath to assault my nostrils.

"Today's the day, pare. T-Rex is back. You gonna kick his ass for saying all that shit about you?"

Despite my better judgment, I engage him. "What shit is that, exactly?"

"You know, bruh, like how you supposed to be into dudes and shit."

Oh, Eric. Word's been all over school for the past week and he's still in denial. Might as well set him straight about me not being straight.

"I am into dudes."

"Shut up." He sinks back into his seat. "For real? You bakla 'n' shit?"

"That ain't a cool word, but yeah, I'm queer."

"But we had sleepovers when we were kids. You slept in my bed."

I face him. "Yep, and you looked so adorable in your Pikachu jammies." I pucker my lips in an air-kiss.

Eric's stunned expression nearly makes me crack up. He says nothing for a few seconds, and it feels like an eternity of peace. "Aw, you messing with me, right? Yeah, you got me." He leans closer. "Hey, bruh. You got that homework?"

I want to shout various expletives at him, but Mrs. Jennings begins her lesson. I exhale and try to focus.

Thirty minutes later, I have no idea what Jennings is lecturing on. Something about polynomials with coefficients. I can't concentrate, and I couldn't care less. My thoughts jump from the drugged-out gago sitting behind me to the gay-bashing a-hole waiting for me somewhere beyond the classroom door. I'm done with it all. The constant shade thrown my way, the gossip, and most of all, the waiting. Funny how the more I try to avoid trouble, the more it finds me. Let's see what happens if I step right into it.

The bell rings. I burst from my seat and wade into the hallway traffic.

"Bobby! Wait up!" Rosie pulls even with me. "Uh, where are you going? History's the other way."

"To find you-know-who."

"Okay, that's one plan. Another would be to turn around and get your ass to class."

"I'm sick of hiding."

"Okay, sure. Maybe you should put your hood back on, though."

I give her the side-eye.

"What? It's a good look on you."

Ahead, Principal Peterson stands in the middle of the hall, telling students to go to class. I'm so glad he's here to help, or else I might accidentally go to the cafeteria for US History.

"Agbayani. Staying clear of trouble today, I hope."

"Of course, sir," I reply. "You know me."

Peterson nods and continues down the hallway toward his office.

We round the corner. Halfway down the hallway, Rex and a few of his crew fling crushed soda cans at a trash bin. Eddie's there, but not Jorge again. Is he not at school, or was he kicked out of their crew? Or did he ditch them?

They whoop it up, acting like a kennel of dogs that hasn't been fed. Not wanting to be their next meal, I nearly do an about-face. Too late. Rex spots us. His bruises from the other day have faded but are still noticeable.

"Hey, Agbayani," Rex calls. "And Agbayani's beard."

"Oh no." Rosie steps in front of me. "What'd you just call me?"

Rex curls his upper lip into a sneer. "My bad. I meant his bodyguard."

I place my hand on her shoulder. "Easy."

Traffic stalls around us as students take notice of what's about to go down. "Kick his ass, T-Rex!" Charlotte yells.

"Hey, how's your boyfriend's car?" Rex says. "Heard it got rear-ended. You know, 'rear-ended'?" Rex cracks up, and his boys join in as if they're on salary.

Their cackles make my molars gnash. My motto runs through my head. *Self-preservation, self-preservation, self-preservation . . .*

Screw it.

"Whew." I wave a hand in front of my nose. "Your breath, Rex, it's . . . what's the word I'm looking for? Oh yeah. *Peppery!*"

Rosie nods. "Oh, it is damn peppery."

I grin at him, even though it probably means my prolonged, painful death. "Get it? 'Peppery'?"

Smirking, Rosie holds up her pepper spray and waggles it back and forth.

Rex's face flushes. Eddie shouts, "Ay, let's end this punk ass now!"

Rex's fingers clench, and the cords in his neck contract. My breath catches and my muscles freeze. But only for a second. I remember what he did to me, what he did to Brandon and Rosie. I make a fist of my own.

I turn sideways and drop into fighting stance, hoping I can catch him with a quick left. But Rex stays rooted. He closes his eyes and breathes. His hand unclenches. *Wait, is he trying to calm himself?*

"Nah. This bitch ain't worth bruising my fists over."

The crowd gapes as Rex actually walks away from a fight. A couple students make their disappointment known with a chorus of boos, and the gathering breaks up. The booming in my chest quiets, and I exhale.

Like a gnat, Eddie buzzes after him. "Ay, where you going? Let's stomp that little bitch."

Rex socks him in the arm. "Shut the hell up, ya damn gago. Get to class."

"And I am not a beard!" Rosie shouts at their backs. "I'm a fag hag!" She turns to me, eyes popping out like hard-boiled eggs. "Okay, what just happened?"

I shrug. "I scared him away?"

"B, you are completely delusional. *We* scared him away."

The warning bell sounds, and we make our way to second-period history.

"Fag hag? Really? Not a cool word, Rosie."

"Okay. How 'bout queer peer?"

"Better."

"Gay bae?"

"Please stop now," I say. "Hey, you notice who wasn't kicking it with Rex again?"

"God, not your 'Jorge is a double agent' theory again." She shakes her head. "You read too many comic books, Bobby."

I nearly reply but manage to rein in the snark. She's not wrong.

Even though Rosie's probably just being her usual paranoid self, I don't try to dissuade her. I'm not going to convince her Jorge's on the level during the short trip to class, so I let it drop.

Before fourth-period Spanish lets out, I text Rosie that I want to kick it at our old table during lunch. I am so done with spending every lunch period cooped up inside the library, hiding my food in my bag and sneaking bites when the librarian isn't looking. Not to mention that moldy old book smell. Ugh.

Okay, so maybe I don't hate the library. Maybe I hate myself for hiding there.

Rosie replies: FINALLY! MUST. HAVE. PIZZA!

We meet at her locker and slog our way through the river of bodies toward the quad. She gets a Rice Krispies Treat craving, so we make a detour toward the vending machines. She's a fiend for anything marshmallow.

When we exit the double doors, I glimpse a familiar shaved head near the vending machines. Jorge sips a soda, his back against the building. He looks like someone used his face as a treadmill. Even yards away, I can see the purple circling his right eye. He winces as soda dribbles over his bloated lip.

He sees us approach, tosses the soda into a trash can, and hobbles around the corner.

"Jorge!" I yell. "Wait up!" He's limping, so we catch up easily.

He scans the area and leans his arm against the building for support. "Can't be seen talking to you, güey," he says, his words slurred.

I point at Jorge's bruises. "Rex's handiwork?"

"Him and Eddie. Both them fools."

Rosie grimaces. "Lovely friends you got there. What do they do for your birthday? Kick you in the nuts for every candle on your cake?"

I shoot her a look that says, *Shut up, please, before you scare away our only source of intel.* I turn to Jorge. "You really need to get away from those assholes."

"What you think I been doing, güey? Why you think they kicked my face in?" His voice cracks, and he steadies himself. "Dude wasn't too happy I didn't show up to jump you."

"Why don't you fight back? You got that balisong."

"That's just for flipping. For show. I ain't never used it for real."

Should've known. Balisong flipping is like doing yo-yo tricks, only with the added fun of possibly slicing your hand open. Actually fighting with one is something else entirely.

"We saw Rex in the halls," I say. "For some reason, he wasn't his usual punch-happy self. Thought we were gonna throw hands, but he backed off. Any idea why?"

"Oh, he's still coming for you, just not at school. He don't wanna get kicked out."

Rosie furrows her brow. "Hold up. Why would Rex even care about getting expelled?"

"Let's just say it wouldn't be good for his health. Rex is still out for payback. And he ain't gonna stop till he puts a serious beatdown on you." Jorge puts his hand on my shoulder, like he's paying his final respects before I depart the mortal coil. "You might wanna move somewhere safe. Like maybe back to the Philippines."

ROUND 15

As I stroll up to my locker, Mr. Hopkins is rummaging through his cleaning cart. He thumbs through a rainbow of brightly colored cleaning bottles and chooses a red one. He sprays the graffiti and wipes it clear in three strokes. At last, my locker is hate-message free. That's some extra-strength cleaner. All my scrubbing barely made a dent.

"Thanks for cleaning that up, Mr. Hopkins," I say.

Sure, he took his sweet time getting to it, but I'm still grateful. Maybe it's the first step in changing my luck for the better. Besides, we custodial workers need to stick together. I know what it's like to clean up after people who couldn't care less about your work.

Hopkins drops the cleaner into his cart. "No problem, uh . . ."

"Bobby."

"Glad to help, Bobby."

"Hey, you mind me asking what cleaner you used? I've, uh, got a lot of dirty toilets to clean." He gives me a blank stare. "Job related."

A grin splits his lips, and his eyes widen. "Well, I'll tell ya, it's a secret recipe of my own creation. Just mix equal parts

Ajax and vinegar. Guaranteed to eat through rust, graffiti, and, if you're not careful, maybe your hands."

"Cool. Thanks."

He tips his scruffy Lakers cap and pushes the cart down the corridor at a leisurely pace. How anyone can have enthusiasm for such a tedious job I will never know, but I could stand to learn a lesson or two from him.

I'd never paid attention to Hopkins's supply cart before, but I give it a good once-over. It's more modern than Hank, more streamlined, and it doesn't have its junk heap character. It looks a little plain, like a Harry or maybe a Stanley.

Good God. I'm naming custodial carts now. *Thank you so much for that, Luke.*

Toward the end of sixth-period English, Mrs. Cisneros springs a pop quiz on *Animal Farm*—the entire novel. Usually, a pop quiz wouldn't be cause for alarm—they're a standard part of her curriculum—but I haven't read the last few chapters. I scan the test, which consists of fifteen short answers and fill-in-the blank questions. Great. If it were multiple choice, I might be able to guess my way to a B-minus.

The first ten or so questions are fairly easy, and I run through them in no time, but the final five are a mystery to me. I read over number eleven.

11. No animal shall kill any other animal without _____.

My shoulders tense, my stomach twitches. I have no idea what the answer is. *No animal shall kill any other animal without . . . claws? Barbecue sauce? An unregistered handgun?* This is what I get for neglecting my studies and reading the Manny biography nonstop.

I run through the novel's story and themes, mentally cross my fingers, and write down "reason" in the blank. Not a bad answer, but it's still a guess. And I never guess.

The clock reads three minutes until class ends. Have to hurry. I fly through the final questions, writing down my best educated guesses and a couple I know are completely wrong. The bell sounds, and students race to the front to turn in their papers. I'm in no such hurry.

On my way up to Cisneros's desk, I'm tempted to ball up my quiz and trash it, but her eyes find me before I reach the wastebasket. No way to avoid it. I hand her the test, my head down.

Nausea grips me as I trudge toward my locker. Hopefully I didn't screw up my class grade too badly, but I need to do better.

I *will* do better.

After school, I change into my Pacquiao shirt inside the restroom and head to work. Instead of jogging down Sunset, I take Temple—just in case Rex is waiting for me on my usual route. When we throw hands, I want it to be on my terms. I want to be ready.

Temple Street is usually calmer than Alvarado—less traffic and fewer pedestrians—but now every little sound is amplified. I flinch at the growl of a motorcycle and give a homeless man pushing a grocery cart a wide berth. Every other block or so, I glance over my shoulder. Everything is a potential threat.

If only I had my bike, I wouldn't be so vulnerable out here.

At the gym—after ten minutes of ransacking the custodial closet—I find the Ajax to make Hopkins's special cleaning solution. Luckily, Luke keeps an old bottle of vinegar at the back of his fridge. Wearing extra-thick cleaning gloves, I mix the concoction together. The solution bubbles and stings my eyes.

I set to work, hoping Luke will finally let me spar if I finish his list of chores early. The super cleaner cuts through the lingering rust on the faucets and toilets, helping me finish the job in half the time. Along with my usual tasks of changing spit buckets and mopping up, I dust the trophies on display and clean the front window—which takes forever. It's a huge frickin' window.

The middle of the week must be slow—only a few of the regulars show during my shift. Unfortunately, Vicki isn't one of them.

On my break, I pop in the video of Pacquiao vs. Ricky "the Hitman" Hatton, one of Manny's signature bouts. I only get a fifteen-minute break, but that's plenty. It's a short fight.

During the promotional tour, Pacquiao and the Englishman Hatton dispensed with the usual over-the-top antagonism used to hype a match. They kept their rivalry on mostly friendly terms. In England, they played a game of darts—which Hatton won—and Hatton presented Manny with a Manchester City Football Club jersey.

Their friendly relationship didn't stop Hatton from a bit of prefight gamesmanship. In an episode of HBO's 24/7, Hatton blasted Manny's offense as predictable and one-dimensional. "Same move every time," Hatton said, relaxed and confident. "Right hook, roll under. Right hook, roll under."

In the opening moments of round one, no sign of the fighters' friendly bond remains. The action is fast paced. Manny allows Hatton to be the aggressor; he lets Hatton charge in, then welcomes him with a right hook. The maneuver works repeatedly. Hatton may know the right is coming, but Manny is too fast for him to counter it.

When Hatton backs Manny into the ropes, Pacman circles away while landing a right hook at an odd angle. This is what makes Manny so dangerous. He can land a punch from anywhere at any time.

Pacquiao connects with a brutal flurry of punches: straight left, right hook, left. Hatton has no defense and little answer. With fifty-six seconds left in the round, Manny whips a right hand into Hatton's jaw and slips beneath a Hatton left. Ricky goes down. Right hook, roll under. Right hook, roll under. Just as Hatton had said.

Hatton follows the ref's count on one knee, his confidence gone, replaced by cold realization. But Ricky is a warrior, a proud one. He rises at the count of eight.

Pacquiao moves in for the knockout, unleashing a storm of lefts and rights that overwhelms Hatton. I crouch into a fighter's stance and copy Manny's assault blow for blow. Rex takes shape in my mind's eye. As my fists slice the air, I feel as if Manny's spirit moves through me.

With six seconds remaining, Manny batters Hatton with a blaze of combinations and sends him to the canvas once more. Dazed but still game, Hatton rises again. Before Manny can end the fight, the bell ends the round.

Hatton fares better at the start of the second. His counter for Manny's right hook is to tie him up and get in some hard shots up close. The strategy works for a spell. But when the fighters untangle, Manny circles Hatton and resumes his onslaught.

The clapping signal warns the fighters that ten seconds remain in the round. Manny strikes, but not from where Hatton expects. Hatton focuses on Pacquiao's right, which leaves him completely open for the left hook. The punch smashes into Hatton's jaw like a jackhammer through concrete. It is arguably the most devastating blow of Manny's career, leaving Hatton sprawled out in the middle of the ring. The fight is over. The ref doesn't even bother to finish his count.

I rewind the punch multiple times, study it, mimic it. Every muscle in Manny's body moves in perfect sync to power the blow. His technique is flawless, and it is both inspiring and discouraging. I am nowhere near as fast or powerful, but Manny makes me want to train even harder, to get better.

I eject the tape and get back to work.

For the rest of my shift, I clean and organize the gear behind the counter, sweep and mop the restroom floors, and empty the trash. The latter is particularly fun since somebody left me a lovely present in the trash can, which appears to be barfed-up spaghetti—extra garlic. The stench gives me a much-needed jolt that keeps me from nodding off.

While I work, my phone vibrates and I get a text from Rosie: got rex's addy. when you wanna do this?

Wow. She was finally able to get the address from Jimmy. Never underestimate the persuasive powers of an orange-haired hottie.

I text back: Tonight. Borrow your dad's car? Pick me up at 9:30?

I type in Jab Gym's address. Before I tap send, I add: Do NOT tell Brandon.

Bran has been worried about me enough. He doesn't need to know we're planning a virtual suicide mission to get my bike back.

A minute later, she replies back: um, bran's here now. working on the comic. sorry?

Wonderful. I'm going to hear it from him now. And ten seconds later, I do: Thanks for keeping me in loop. WE will pick you up.

Ugh. I should've known they'd be together. They've been working on their comic book nonstop for weeks.

The last few minutes of work drag, but finally seven o'clock comes. Quitting time. I emerge from the locker room, fists wrapped, ready to train.

Like I promised Luke, I get in some footwork drills to warm up.

"Nice." Luke motions me over. "Okay, ready to do some boxing?"

I throw a straight left, right hook combo, à la Manny. "Hell, yes. Lead on, Freddie."

Luke blinks. "Who the hell's Freddie?"

"You know—Freddie Roach, Pacquiao's trainer. You're kind of like my own Coach Roach."

"Youngblood, do I look like a roach to you?"

"What? No. What?"

"Roaches are a pain in the ass. They never die even when you try to stomp their guts out." Luke blinks twice. "Actually that kind of fits. Come on."

He leads me toward the back ring, where a pair of teen

120

fighters spar in headgear, their punches snapping back and forth like whips. The hair on my arm tingles. Finally I get to step in the squared circle against actual human competition—but Luke shuffles past the ring and continues to the far mirror wall.

"All right now, take up a fighting stance."

"What's going on? You said we were gonna get down to some boxing."

"Yeah, shadowboxing, son. Best kind of training."

I fold my arms and try to restrain the snark monster within. Nope, can't do it. "Please tell me I did not stick my nose into vomit marinara just so you can show me how to beat up my reflection."

"Son, all the greats shadowboxed. Tyson did it, Frazier did it. Hell, Ali did it in a pool full of water. You telling me you better than them?

I should trust him, but the next time Rex comes at me, I'll need to be able to hit more than just air. I have to get some rounds in. Like now. "I just want to get in the ring, Luke. Get in some real action."

"I'm in here trying to teach you, boy. You don't wanna get taught? Fine, I got better things to do."

"No, no, you're right. Sorry. You're the master. I'm the Padawan."

"The Padawhat?"

"Nothing. Please. Impart."

Luke's eyes narrow, and he sighs like he's ready to give up on me altogether. "All right, no more questioning, no more complaining. Just listen and obey."

"Listening and obeying."

"Okay, the best thing I can teach you about shadowboxing is to box like it's a real fight. Visualize your opponent in front of you."

"Visualize my opponent. Got it." I wait for him to continue.

"Well, what you waiting for? Get in a fighting stance—show me something."

I drop into my lefty stance, fists up, and throw some rapid-fire combinations.

"Hold on, hold on!" Luke pulls my arms down. "What the hell you fighting, a housefly? Snap your punches forward and back, forward and back. Full extension. And slow down. No way you keeping up that pace a full round. Throw like you would in a real fight." He pulls out a stopwatch and clicks it. "Again."

I try to be mindful of his every word. My jab snaps like a slingshot, and I bring it back sharp and clean. My punches slow to a more realistic pace.

"Good. Widen your stance a bit. And show me some foot-work. You wouldn't stand still in a real fight, would you? Dodge your opponent's blows. Step with your jab."

I'm no longer myself. I'm Manny driving a straight left into Oscar De La Hoya's chin over and over. I circle, slip under a Ricky Hatton left and sting him with a right hook.

"Better."

I dip and dodge against a roll call of Pacquiao's fierc-est opponents: Morales, Mosley, Márquez. None of them can touch me.

"Time," Luke says, clicking his timer.

Through blurred vision, I glance at him and realize my brow is dripping with sweat.

"That was two minutes. Standard round. Rest for a minute, and we'll go again."

My breaths are short, but I manage to form words. "Oh. *We* will?"

The minute feels like a few seconds. I'm still breathing hard when Luke starts the timer again. My arms are like weights, dragging my fists down, making my punches sloppy.

"Hands up. Always. Drop your guard and you will get popped. Repeatedly."

I ignore the fire in my limbs and make the correction.

Luke gets distracted. In between combos, I follow his stare to a man in a wrinkled suit at the counter. New customer, apparently. Too old to be a fighter, though. Trainer maybe? No, the bags and worry lines etched in his face give him away. Most likely a parent who caved to his kid's ambition to be the next Floyd Mayweather.

"Keep at it," Luke says and pads over to the counter, taking the stopwatch with him. He welcomes the man with an obligatory handshake. Luke's palm brushes the countertop with the membership prices. He's giving him the Jab Gym spiel. This may take a while.

Great. When's the round supposed to be up? I punch air and dodge pretend opponents until my breaths turn to gasps. I bend over, try to slow my breathing.

"Nice moves," someone says. I crane my neck to see Vicki Connolly grinning at me from inside the ring, her gloved hands resting on the top rope. She rocks full sparring attire, including headgear. "Wanna try them on me?"

At the counter, Luke leads the customer into the locker room, probably taking him on a tour. My first thought is to decline Vicki's offer and continue shadowboxing, but a sudden flash of Rex and his brother beating on me makes me reconsider.

"Never again," I mutter.

"Excuse me?"

"Nothing," I tell her. "Yeah, I could use some ring time. Be right back." I dash over to the front. Since I reorganized the equipment earlier, I know where to find what I need without looking. I reach behind the counter, grab some headgear and a set of sparring gloves that fit me, and rush back.

Vicki's trainer says, "Go easy on 'im."

She snickers and accepts her mouthpiece from him. *Mouthpiece?* Crap. Now would be a good time to put my own in, except for the fact I don't own one.

Before I can call time-out, she's on me with a pair of opening jabs, which I manage to barely dodge. I sidestep right and counter with a couple jabs of my own. I miss badly but follow up with a straight left that would make Manny proud. And to my surprise, I tag her. Big mistake.

She shrugs it off and connects with a right hook that makes my jaw rattle. Another blow stings my nose. I can only assume it was her left, because I didn't see it coming. Tears drown my eyes. I cover up and backpedal out of range.

Blood coats my tongue. One of my teeth is loose. And this is why boxers wear mouthguards.

Right as Vicki steps to me, I raise my glove. "Wait, wait. Hold up."

Vicki frowns. "Hey, where's your mouthpiece? Did I knock it out?" She scans the mat.

"Stupid-ass fool!" Luke stomps toward the ring. "What the hell are you doin' in there?" I open my mouth, but he cuts me off. "I'll tell you what you're doin' in there. Making a stupid-ass fool of yourself!" He stomps back to the counter.

"Luke, wait." My foot catches the bottom rope, and I stumble out of the ring.

"Well, that was quick," Vicki calls after me. "Come again."

I wince, but I can't worry about her right now. I dash after Luke. He squeezes through the counter opening and disappears into his office. I brace for the door slam, but it doesn't come. He leaves the door wide open, so I enter.

Luke sits in the old swivel chair behind his desk, digging through a drawer. He pulls out a nail clipper and sets to work on his fingernails. I never noticed how long and dirty his nails were. They look like grotesque claws. Good thing I'm dieting, because I just lost my appetite for good.

"All right, okay," I say. "That was messed up. Sorry."

In reply, he clips a nail.

"Um, I just wanted to get some ring time in. You know, against a real opponent."

Clip, clip.

"Look, these guys at school. They're about to put a serious beatdown on me. I need to learn how to defend myself. Like now."

Clip, clip.

"Would you mind stopping that, please? This is important."

Luke continues cutting and cleaning his nails, devoting ample time to his thumb. "Do you believe personal hygiene is important?"

"What?"

"I said, do you believe personal hygiene is important?"

I sigh but play along. "Yeah, yeah. Yes, I do."

"Excellent. Glad we finally agree on something. I actually believe personal hygiene is the most important part of maintaining a positive self-image. If you look like a raggedy-ass bum, people gonna treat you like one. And nobody listens to a raggedy-ass bum. Since you don't listen to me, I gotta assume you think—"

"I don't. No, that's totally not it."

"No? Then I guess you got a personality defect that makes you do the opposite of whatever I tell you. Either way, we are done here."

My eyes lock on to his. "As in, done for the day?"

"As in, I ain't wasting another damn minute on your stubborn ass."

"Come on, Luke! It was just one time! I'm sorry, okay? Gimme another chance!"

"Uh-uh. I've trained too many fighters not to know how this is gonna play out. I am too gray and too grown for this shit."

No, this is not happening. Gotta stay calm, reason with him. I exhale slowly. "Look, I . . . I screwed up, but—"

"You can keep using the gym, long as you keep the toilets

clean, but you can get yourself another so-called coach to ignore."

He severs another nail, and the hollowness of the sound seems to bring the conversation to an end.

First I start screwing up in school, now this. *What the hell am I going to do now?* I had an amazing teacher, and I screwed it up. Utterly and completely. With Luke's help, I could have learned to defend myself, maybe even survive the rest of the school year. Now the chances of that happening are about the same as Rex quoting Mahatma Gandhi.

I drag myself from the office. Vicki has moved on to working the heavy bag. With each punch she throws, my cut lip seems to throb more. Even if she still wanted to go a round or two, no way am I up for it, so I return the headgear and gloves.

I have some time before I have to meet Bran and Rosie, so I watch a sparring match between Latino Efron—I really need to learn his name—and another boxer. The two fighters move with grace and precision, which only underlines how much I have to learn. Suddenly it occurs to me that I've most likely cleaned their urine off the bathroom floor. Where was their grace and precision then?

Yep, I'm in a mood.

I retrieve my bag from the locker room, pull on my hoodie, and slip into the night air. So far, my day has been par-for-the-course crappy, but if things don't go right at Rex's, it could get even worse.

ROUND 16

I only have to wait a few minutes before Bran's BMW slows to a stop in front of the gym. No evidence of Rex and Eddie's handiwork remains. The car's shattered windows have been replaced, its dents fixed as if they were never there, and its red finish glistens beneath the streetlamp. Even after months of dating, I'm still amazed how easily things come for Brandon's family. Money may not fix all of life's problems, but it sure fixes your broken stuff real fast. I dash across the street and slide into the back seat.

Rosie has come prepared, sporting stealth gear: black pants and a matching black sweatshirt. Bran, on the other hand, sticks out in a red-and-white sweater.

"Thanks for coming to get me," I say.

Bran pulls into traffic. "You sure about that? Because your 'don't tell Bran' text kind of makes me think you didn't want me to know."

"Look, I just didn't want you to worry."

He shakes his head. "Seems to be your excuse for everything lately."

Rosie clears her throat loudly. "I didn't come all the way out here to listen to you two hash out your drama. I do not want to hear it."

"What's up with you?" I ask.

"What's up with me? The only way I could get Rex's addy is if I promised Jimmy Valdez I'd go to the Valentine's dance with him!"

"Damn, seriously?" A chuckle escapes my lips, earning me the evil eye from Rosie. "You didn't have to go and do that."

"You think I want to go to the dance with him? Mr. Always Matching wants to wear an orange cummerbund and bow tie to match my hair!"

This bit of news sends Bran and me into a laughing fit.

Rosie holds up her phone. "You two better shut it, or I delete Rex's address right now."

"You're right, you're right. We gotta get serious." I stretch my neck until it cracks and put on my game face.

"All right." Rosie flicks her cell to a map screen. "Head toward Lake Street Park. Take Temple."

Silence dominates the rest of the drive as the reality of what we're about to attempt starts to hit us. In the middle cup holder, Bran's cell buzzes, shattering the quiet. The caller ID shows it to be Bran's dad. The phone vibrates a few more times before he flicks the screen, rejecting the call. Great. His dad calling is just the omen I need right now.

Rosie directs Bran into a low-lit residential area with narrow streets. The houses are small, single story, and surrounded by low fences. He kills the lights and pulls into a space a couple of houses down from Rex's place. Lights illuminate the closed window blinds as silhouetted figures move about inside.

"Maybe we should come back when nobody's home," Bran says.

I shake my head. "It's been nearly a week. He might sell it. Hell, he might've already." I lean forward between the front seats. "Okay, I'll check out the backyard—you guys wait here. Keep the motor running." I move to the door.

Rosie grabs my arm. "You'll need backup. One of us should go with you."

"I'll go," Bran says.

I point at his red-and-white sweater. "Not in that thing you're not."

He turns to Rosie. "Switch shirts with me."

"What?"

"You heard me." He pulls off his sweater, and I can't help admiring his toned abs.

"Wait, so I get to be the wheelman?" she asks, brow raised. "You're gonna let me drive?"

"Don't make me regret it." Bran tosses her his sweater. "Now change."

"Fine, but both of you look away. I don't care if you're queer. You're not peeping my goodies."

We avert our eyes as she pulls off her sweatshirt. She tosses it to Bran, who slips it on. It's a tight fit, but now he'll blend in with the shadows. Bran and I exit the car, and Rosie scooches over behind the wheel.

Keeping low, I lead Bran over to Rex's house. We hop the front wall and dash to the side chain-link gate, which stands about six feet tall. I pull on it, but it's secured with a padlock. Muffled yelling comes from inside the house, and Bran motions with his thumb that we should leave. I frown, shake my head. This is perfect; Rex's family will be too distracted with their drama to hear us. I point up, telling Bran I'm going to climb over.

I jam my shoe into a link and pull myself up. The gate rattles loudly. I wince and steady myself. As I swing my legs over the top, my pant leg gets caught. I lose my balance and fall but grab the gate before I hit the ground. Bran springs up, unable to help me from the other side. My arm hair tingles while I listen for any sign that we've been detected. The yelling continues.

I lower myself to the ground and tiptoe alongside the house in pitch-black darkness. A few yards down, I step on something round and roll my ankle. *Shit.* Pain throbs through the joint, and I grit my teeth to keep from crying out. I pick up the object—a baseball—and fling it over the fence.

Grimacing, I limp to the end of the house and peek around the corner. In the scant patches of moonlight, I make out a patio and a weed-ridden yard with foot-high grass. A rusted grill rests in the corner beside a deflated basketball.

My breath catches. Draped in shadow, a bike leans against a patio post. I scramble over to it, but it's not mine, just an old beach cruiser with flat tires.

Through an open window, the commotion grows louder, the words more distinct. Keeping my head low, I peek inside. Rex, Eddie, and an older Filipino man argue in the kitchen. Dirty pots and dishes are piled up in the sink, and beer cans litter the counter. The man—a few inches taller than Rex and even more muscular—dominates the room, making it seem smaller than it already is. He downs a can of San Miguel beer, crushes it, and cracks open another.

"Place's always a damn mess," the man says, slurring his words. "Clean this shit up."

Rex leans against the counter, his eyes darting from the man to Eddie. "Okay, Dad, I-I'll wash the dishes. Why don't you just get to bed?"

Eddie sits at the table, slurping from a bowl of soup. "Maybe we wouldn't be living in such a shithole if you'd throw your beer cans out once in a while," he mutters.

"*What?* What did you say to me? I am so sick of your fucking mouth!" Mr. Banta rushes Eddie, rears back, and smacks him across the cheek. The soup bowl goes flying. With a cry, Eddie topples from his chair and slams headfirst into the floor. "You little punk!" Mr. Banta kicks his son in the side repeatedly. I wince. Eddie had done the same to me.

"Eddie!" Rex rushes over and grabs his dad's shoulder from behind. "Dad, stop! Stop it! Please!"

Mr. Banta swings his arm back and smashes his elbow into Rex's eye. Rex stumbles back into the stove. Their dad whirls and rams his fists into his son's stomach repeatedly. Rex coughs and cries out.

Oh my God. What did I wander into here? A part of me wants to help Rex and Eddie, but after what they did to me, why should I? Maybe they deserve this.

No. Nobody deserves this.

But I'm not here for them. They'd probably turn on me if I helped, anyway.

Mr. Banta rains more blows down on Eddie, and the brutality makes my stomach swirl. I don't want to see any more. I turn away and see another bike leaning against the house. *My bike!*

Dad's bike.

I can't believe it's within my grasp. All I have to do is grab it. The only problem is it's right by the screen door, mere feet from the extreme violence going down inside. I try to steel myself, but my breath quickens and my body trembles.

Rex screams and tackles his father into a chair. "Eddie, get out of here! Go!"

Eddie stumbles toward the screen door. I dash over to the bike and wheel it toward the side pathway as fast as I can. Before I can round the corner, Eddie flings open the door and staggers outside, clutching his stomach. His eyes bulge when he sees me.

"What the fuck?" Eddie shouts. "He's got the bike!"

I hurry down the side of the house, but my ankle slows me down. "Bran! Help me!" I lift the bike and try to hoist it over the gate to his waiting hands, but the wheel bounces against the top. I lose my grip, and it clatters to the dirt.

"You're dead, bitch." Eddie storms toward me.

Bran rattles the gate. "Just leave it!"

I try lifting the bike over again, but Eddie reaches me first. With a two-handed grip, I hurl the bike and nail him in the kneecap. He howls and falls over. I glance at the bike a final time and launch myself over the gate. Bran braces my landing, and we rush back to the car and climb in.

Rex bursts out the front door and barrels straight for us.

Rosie freezes.

"Go go go!" I yell, shaking her shoulder.

Rex slams his fist against my window, blood seeping from the edge of his mouth. Rosie shrieks. She shifts into drive and peels away, clipping the side mirror off a parked truck. She speeds through the neighborhood, taking turns without slowing, and emerges onto Temple. Bran and I keep our eyes behind us, but nobody gives chase.

My breathing finally slows. I slam my fist against the door. "Damn it. I had my bike. I *had* it!"

"I knew this was a bad idea!" Bran shouts.

"You didn't have to come, you know. I had to try." I tried and I failed. Now Dad's last gift is probably lost to me forever.

"Whatever. We're just lucky nobody got hurt."

I become quiet, knowing the truth. Maybe none of us were hurt, but Rex and Eddie sure were. Their dad saw to that. Given the brothers' violent tendencies, I can't say I'm surprised that their dad's a monster. Despite being overly strict at times, my dad was kind and never raised a hand to me. What would I have become if I'd had a dad like Rex's? Still, lots of people have messed-up parents and don't try to make the world their own personal MMA match.

As the glow of red taillights stream by, I recall Bran's words from earlier in the week: *Violence leads to more violence.* If he's right, how will fighting Rex and Eddie solve anything?

ROUND 17

Thursday crawls by. I don't mind, since—according to Jorge—I'm safe at school. In my last period, I get a text from Brandon, the seventh he's sent today. Only this time he's sent me a tanaga.

> *I know I worry too much*
> *Sorry for all the hubbub*
> *Just promise you'll be careful*
> *And I'll give you a back rub*

It sends a tingle through my stomach, like the first taste of halo-halo on a hot day, or when a new Marvel trailer premieres. I should reply, but I'm still irked at his coddling me. Plus, this is beyond petty, but he's totally stealing my shtick. Tanagas are *my* thing. Like Rosie's things are art, paranoia, and an irrational hatred of all things Taco Bell. You don't see me badmouthing their Burrito Supreme. I slide my phone back into my pocket.

The second I enter the hallway after the final bell, Rosie appears at my side. "Let's go," she says, pulling on my arm.

"What? Where?"

"Just keep up." She bolts into the throng of students. I have to race through the crowd just to keep her bobbing ponytail within sight.

Two minutes in, I realize where she's headed. I pull up even with her as we pass through the double door exit. "Teacher's parking lot?"

"Last place Rex would try anything."

I say nothing. Rosie's only looking out for me, but I'm not thrilled with the idea of running from Rex, despite Jorge's warning. Still, I can't fault her logic. The parking lot is already swarming with the first wave of teachers trying to make a quick getaway from the school grounds. Too many faculty witnesses for a proper beatdown.

It's hard to reconcile the Rex who's out for my blood with the one last night who saved his brother from a vicious beating. I'd never seen that side of him before. He was nothing short of heroic. I guess even Rex has his moments.

A honk from a car horn pulls me from my thoughts. Parked at the curb with the motor running, Brandon waits in his BMW.

I grimace at Rosie.

She mock gasps. "Hey, lookee who's here. And with us needing a getaway car. How lucky."

I love that Bran came, but I keep my expression blank. Can't make it that easy for him.

He looks at me. "Hey."

"Hey," I reply, avoiding eye contact.

Rosie shakes her head. "Aw, you two with your constant flirting. It's disgusting."

Before she gets in, I claim the back seat; no way am I sitting next to Bran. We give each other the silent treatment during the drive. He sneaks a glance at me in the rearview mirror, and I quickly look away.

"Coming over tonight?" Rosie asks Bran.

"Yep. I want to go over the splash page again."

"Yes, yes, more blood, longer entrails."

I shift in my seat. It's cool they're spending time together, but I can't help feeling like Hawkeye in the Avengers—not needed. Comics have always been our thing—mine and Bran's; it's what brought us together, despite our different backgrounds. Now our thing has become their thing.

Bruno Mars's "When I Was Your Man" comes on the radio, quite possibly the most depressing song about relationship regret ever. The lyrics make me squirm. It could totally be our breakup song. I cringe even more when I picture Rex karaoke performing the song with his wannabe Bruno hair.

Then the chorus hits, and Rosie belts out the words in her own unique Rosie way. Her singing sounds like the last gasps of an alley cat dying of throat cancer. I grit my teeth to stifle a laugh but fail big time. Brandon and I sing along. Nothing cures your worries like an over-the-top group sing with your best buds.

When the song ends, Rosie shouts, "Bruno Scars! Ha! I get it now! 'Cause of Rex's acne! Brilliant!"

Today is Bran's day off, so after we drop off Rosie, he invites me over to check out the latest comics he snatched up with his employee discount. I have a couple hours before I need to be at the gym—plus, we do need to talk. We haven't had any alone time in weeks. I can't even remember the last time we kissed. Was it that night at the Lair?

Plus, his dad is usually still at work after school, so bonus. I have to take advantage of the times I can visit without having to deal with Mr. Elpusan's judgmental crap.

At his house, Bran offers me an individually wrapped ube mamón, and one look at the purple sponge cake weakens my resolve. The boy seriously knows my kryptonite. Normally I'd scarf it down and ask for seconds, but I'm deep in training. I eye the dessert warily. "No, thanks."

"Fine."

Bran seems to take my refusal as a personal rejection and shoves the sponge cake back in the pantry. Oh, boy. He can be so pouty. Fortunately, conversation isn't required for a good comic book marathon.

We hang out on the floor in his room with a few purple Villain's Lair shopping bags spread out between us, each filled with Bran's latest picks. He dives into a stack of *Captain America* issues while I flip through Marvel's latest limited series event, *Secret Wars*. The story and art are high quality, and the stakes are nothing less than the fate of reality itself, but after a couple of issues my eyes wander. Maybe dealing with all my real-life drama has soured me on escapism. Or maybe it's something else entirely? I set the comics aside and pull the Pacquiao bio from my bag.

I read about the lead-up to Pacman's bout with welterweight champion Miguel Cotto, another larger, taller fighter Manny bested in twelve rounds. During Manny's training camp, Tropical Storm Ondoy hit the Philippines, devastating Manila and taking nearly eight hundred souls. Despite the fight looming, Manny took a leave from training to aid the relief effort. He helped raise money, donated funds, even packed supply kits and passed them out to survivors. And then he went and won the fight. The more I learn about him, the more impressed—no, the more in awe—I become.

"What is it with you and Manny Pacquiao?

I peek out from behind my book. "What?"

With a creased brow, Brandon leans against his dresser and studies me. "You're sitting in a room full of the dopest comic books, but you can't get your head out of that Pacquiao book. What's up with that? Why are you so obsessed with the man?"

I shrug. "I dunno. I can relate to Manny. His struggle, his story."

"*His* story? He's a megarich, famous boxer. You're a dirt-poor kid from MacArthur Park. How can you even begin to relate?"

His questions stir something in me. Something I didn't even realize I'd been feeling. The answer floods through my being and pours out in a burst.

"No. See, Manny's me. He is *me*. Look, Bran." I wave my hand at the piles of comic books. "Look at all these superheroes we pretty much worship. None of them look like you and me. None of them are Pinoy. Zero. Manny's real. He's our super-hero. And he's us. He is *us*."

Bran's head dips low. "Okay, I get it. He is fairly awesome, not to mention incredibly cut. It's just . . . I don't know. I just wish you were that into *me*."

"What? No, no, no. Please tell me you're not jealous. It's not even like that."

"I guess."

I move closer. "Oh my God, you're so cute."

Bran pushes me away. "Shut up."

"Come on now, B, you know you're my only guy."

I peck him on the cheek a couple of times. At first, he plays like he's ignoring me, but then kisses me back full on the lips. Damn, his lips. They're soft and sweet like marshmallows, and it's been way too long since I've tasted them. His tongue slides into my mouth and caresses my own, sending shivers through my chest and down my core. We sink into each other's arms, and my hands find their way to his perfectly round, perfectly firm butt. I breathe in his scent, and my head swirls, and nothing matters in the entire world but us.

And then we roll over a pile of comics.

"My *New Mutants* 98!" Bran shouts. It's the first appearance of Deadpool, worth several hundred dollars.

"Shit! Sorry!"

"Kidding." He tosses the comic. "Reprint."

"Punk." I tackle him and kiss him harder.

Seven minutes into our makeup make-out session, Mrs. Elpusan calls Bran from downstairs. "Brandon! Take out the trash!"

"Trash day is Monday, Mom!" Bran yells.

"Now, please."

He groans, gives me one more all-too-brief kiss, and dashes from the room.

She has both good and bad timing: I don't want to stop, but I also kind of do. Bran and I have yet to do the full-on deed. Maybe all the sex-ed indoctrination at school and teen pregnancy PSAs have gotten to me, but I'm just not ready. Which is mildly hilarious because there isn't actually any danger of either of us getting pregnant. More to the point, I don't want our first time to be while his mom is within earshot. I swear, the woman can hear through ceilings.

Through the window, I watch Brandon drag the trash cans through the backyard, his reflection glistening in the pool's still water. A minute later, he tramples back into the room. "Sorry about that."

"No big. Hey, you got an extra pair of swim trunks?"

A few minutes later, sporting a pair of red Hawaiian-print trunks, I cannonball into the deep end of the pool, my arms wrapped around my knees. I plunge to the bottom, kick off with the balls of my feet, and break through the surface with a shout of "Excelsior, true believers!"

At the shallow end, Bran descends the steps into the water with a tad less fanfare. "You're such a dork," he says, shaking his head. His cut arms and abs glisten in the pristine water. Who says geeks can't be in shape? Yum.

Okay, I didn't come out here to ogle my boyfriend, however pleasing the view may be. Have to stay focused. I breaststroke over to him until I can stand straight up so the waterline covers my shoulders.

Bran stares at me with an ever-widening grin.

"What are you looking at?" I say, rubbing my arms.

"You, Mr. Ripped Guy. Suddenly I'm starting to like all this training."

My cheeks warm, and I splash him. "Whatever. Can you stop ogling me so we can do this?"

"Okay, okay. You sure this is going to help?"

"Hey, it was good enough for 'The Greatest,' aka Muhammad Ali." I take up my lefty fighting stance with my arms underwater. "Okay, time me. Two minutes."

He holds up an old stopwatch he found in his dad's toolbox. "And . . . go."

I start with a couple of jabs, and it's like I'm moving through mud. I knew the water would slow me down, but I'm surprised at how much. I fight through it and fire off some straight lefts and even throw in a couple of uppercuts. A few punches break the surface, making me lunge and throw off my timing.

Bran holds up a finger at the minute mark, and my arms sag.

"Keep it up!" he says. "You got this."

His encouragement helps me dig in with multiple combinations. My arms and lungs burn, but I power through.

"Time." Bran clicks the watch.

With a wheezy breath, I choke on a gulp of water and cough it up. I wade over to Bran and prop my arms up over the ledge.

He squeezes my shoulder. "You okay?"

I nod, too spent to speak.

"Brandon!" his mom calls from the open kitchen window. "I need your help. A spoon fell down the disposal."

"Maybe you should follow it in, Mother," he mutters, then glances at me. "I know, I know. That was mean." He places the stopwatch on the ledge, springs from the pool, and snatches his towel off a patio chair. "Be right back." One exasperated slam of the sliding door later, I'm alone.

After a minute of slow, even breaths, I'm ready to go again. I wade out to deeper water, hold in a full breath, and completely submerge. Hopefully, this will keep my movements in sync from my head down.

This time, I focus on hand speed, alternating left and right punches like I'm working the bag. With each throw, my moves turn more fluid, more powerful. My fists become torpedoes knifing through the water. My lungs expand, begging for release. How long has it been? Thirty seconds? Forty?

I sneak in one more combo, burst through the surface, and swallow air like a wino downing his last sip.

"Hello, Robert." In a patio chair, looking like a mafioso in a pin-striped business suit, sits Brandon's father. "So you're taking up boxing? Interesting." He purses his lips. "Are those my swim trunks?"

"Oh. Brandon let me borrow them." *And thank you so much for that, Bran.* I'd rather be wearing nothing than his dad's trunks, which would be fitting because I feel incredibly naked right now.

I climb the ladder and collect my towel on the table beside Mr. Elpusan. The man makes my arm hair stand at attention. It's like my Spidey-sense warning me of danger. How can his dental patients stand him hovering over them with lethal instruments in his claws? To put some distance between us, I scurry over to the patio counter and pour myself a glass of water.

"So, Brandon's car. Did you have something to do with wrecking it?" Judging by his pronounced smirk, I do a horrible job of hiding my surprise. "Brandon thinks I don't know about it, but he can't hide something that costly from me. My mechanic is very loyal."

"No, sir, I didn't do anything. It was some punk kids who attacked us."

"Kids from your neighborhood, you mean." I stay quiet, avert my eyes. "I thought so. You know, despite this anniversary thing Brandon's been going on about, it's all just a silly phase he's going through. It won't last out the year."

I nearly laugh in his face. I want to. But this is Brandon's dad, and it wouldn't be smart to insult him at his own house, wearing his swimming trunks.

"No, it's really not," I say. "This is who Brandon is. It's not a phase, and he's not experimenting or whatever you want to call it. He's just being who he is. And the sooner you accept that, the better off you'll both be."

The edges of his lips curl into a hint of a smile. "Oh, no, no. You misunderstand me. I'm no homophobe. I know my son is gay. I have no issue with that; I embrace it. It's you, Robert, who is the phase. *You* will not last."

I flinch. My shoulders sag. Could what he said be true? Am I only a phase? A temporary distraction? Just some dirt-poor kid Bran's messing around with because I'm different? Forbidden? I search for a biting remark, but for once, when I need it most, my powers of snark fail me.

Then Brandon steps out onto the patio, and it's too late. He notices the tension and raises his brow at me. "Hey, Dad," he says slowly, then turns to me. "Ready for another round?"

"I . . . I need to get to work." My eyes cling to the floor, and I dash inside to change.

I'm all set to get my usual jog in, but Bran insists on driving me to the Jab Gym. He doesn't like the idea of me being alone on the streets with Rex in berserker mode and out for my blood. Not wanting to spoil our freshly minted truce, I reluctantly agree. I'm late, anyway.

The drive over is short and uneventful. My thoughts jump from Mr. Elpusan's crushing words to making things right with Luke, but settle on the impending threat of Rex. Lately, everything always comes back to Rex. Whenever we stop at a light, I can't help checking behind us.

"So, hey, what did my dad say to you?" Bran asks, his eyes focused on a slow-moving Mercedes in front of us.

"Nothing. Just asked about school. The usual boring parental chitchat."

"Really? Because it looked like you were about ready to sock more than just the water."

"What? Not even." I swallow hard. "Look, we just had a disagreement about, y'know, um, the Dodgers."

"The Dodgers? Since when do you watch baseball?"

"I watch baseball."

"Name one Dodgers player."

"Um, Jackie Robinson."

"I meant from this century."

I clam up. Of course I don't watch baseball. It's like watching a bunch of guys loitering in matching pajamas.

"Okay, whatever. Don't tell me."

He pulls up in front of the gym with the care of someone who just got his car out of the shop. Before exiting, I hug him and say, "By the way, thanks for the poem. It was sweet."

"Oh, *now* you say thank you. Thought you were going to pretend it didn't happen."

"Well, you can't just write me a poem and think everything would be cool. 'Cause I would *never* do that."

"Ha ha."

"I promise I'll be careful, okay?" I shut the door behind me. "And you owe me a back rub."

I linger in the lobby, watching Bran drive off until his Bimmer is just a red blip in the afternoon traffic.

ROUND 18

Luke ignores me my whole shift. He still shouts at me to empty spit buckets, sweep up, and do all the other miscellaneous duties that come with this oh-so-fun job. He just doesn't talk to me about anything else. Not boxing, not Manny, not even an inappropriate crack about his ex-wife—which I'm ashamed to admit, I kind of miss. Apparently now we're merely manager and employee. Guess I can't blame him. I've definitely earned the cold shoulder.

On my break, instead of snacking on the protein bar in my bag or taking in a Manny fight, I write Luke a tanaga.

Sorry I didn't listen
I'll obey now without fail
If you please train me again
I'll even cut your toenails

Reading it over, I groan. Not every mistake can be smoothed over by tearing off a quick poem. It's a cheap move that I've relied on way too much. Luke would probably either laugh at me or fire me—quite possibly both. Besides, the poem's not exactly honest. No way would I cut Luke's toenails. Yuck.

I delete the poem from existence.

No, the best course is to keep working hard and hopefully, eventually, he'll train me again. But so far the best course has been a total failure. In between my usual duties, I tidy up Luke's office, sweep and mop his floor, and even leave him an ube mamón cake that Bran gave me on his desk. None of it works. Later on, I find the sponge cake wrapper in his wastebasket. He didn't even say thank you. Rude, dude.

Guess I don't have much choice but to continue training on my own. I can do this. Luke already taught me how to work both bags and shadowbox, and maybe Vicki will spar a few rounds with me. This time I'll make sure to remember my mouthguard.

Note to self: buy mouthguard.

At the end of my shift, I load up every trash bag in the gym onto Hank and wheel the rickety cart out to the back-alley dumpster.

So there's a 'roid rager out to spill large quantities of my blood, and the one person who could've truly helped me will barely speak to me now. Plus let's not forget that my boyfriend's father loathes me, and there's a good chance said boyfriend will be booting me to the curb any day now. I'd ask what else could go wrong, but the universe might actually answer.

To cheer myself up, I make a game of seeing how far I can toss each bag into the open receptacle. My first try is from a spot even with the back door, about fifteen feet away—a perfect free throw. I shoot. Nothing but dumpster.

I back up to an imaginary three-point line near the end of the alleyway and line up my final shot. *Three, two, one . . .*

Right before I let the trash bag fly, something hard smashes against the side of my head. Pain surges through my skull. The alley tilts and whirls, and I drop to the concrete, fighting to steady myself.

Rex stands over me. "Little bitch! You come to my house?" He kicks me in the side, and it's like a grenade goes off in my belly. I cry out. I try to crawl away, but he stomps my back with the heel of his shoe. My next howl makes the first sound like a whisper.

I roll over and stick my hand up at him. "Rex, you don't have to do this. I . . . I know about your dad. I saw what he does to you and Eddie. You don't have to be like him."

His face twists into a mask of rage. "What'd you say?" he yells. "What the hell you say to me, bitch? You trying to analyze my ass? Like you know me?" He points to his bruised face. "You're the reason this shit happened!"

If I didn't realize it before, I do now. Rex cannot be reasoned with, and whatever this thing is between us, it will end in violence.

With a two-handed grip, he pushes Hank over, and the cart topples toward my face. I roll out of the way, and it crashes onto the ground, scattering brooms, trash bags, and cleaning supplies.

Rex kicks me in the side twice, hard, and I cough. My body trembles like I might heave.

"Bruh, you sick? Sounds like you need some meds stat." He produces his own can of pepper spray. "Better down the whole bottle."

As Rex presses the button, a long stick slams across his shoulders, cracking in half. He drops to the ground along with the canister, revealing Luke behind him, a half-broken broom in his hands.

Luke shoves the splintered tip against Rex's throat. "Boy, you better get the hell out my alley before I crack open your skull." He slams the broom against the pavement, inches from Rex's head.

Rex clambers to his feet and shoots me a glare. "We ain't finished, bakla bitch." He stumbles toward the alleyway exit.

"Go on! Get!" Luke chucks the pepper spray in Rex's direction, missing badly. He grabs my hand and helps me sit up. "You okay, youngblood?"

"Think so. That was totally badass. Thanks, Luke."

"Yeah, well, nobody messes with my friend."

"I . . . I don't know what to say. That means a lot."

He rights Hank back on its wheels and pats it fondly.

I shake my head. "You were talking about Hank, weren't you?"

"Of course." He gathers up the supplies and wheels his "friend" toward the door. "Come on, kid. Let's see if we can figure this shit out."

I follow him inside. "Wait. So you'll train me again?"

"Depends. Got any more of them purple cake things?"

"Uh, sure. I mean, I can get more."

"Then I guess you got a trainer again."

Luke sits me down in his office and tells me to lay it all out for him. So I do. I spill on my graffitied locker, Rex and his violent obsession with me—even him jacking Dad's bike. Everything. I manage to get through it all without curling up into a ball of emotional goo. Guess I needed to vent to some type of an authority figure who wasn't interrogating me like I'm the one who did something wrong.

To Luke's credit, he listens without interrupting once and doesn't even flinch about Brandon and me, which makes me totally love the guy. I never had the chance to come out to my dad, but I like to think he would've been fine with it—just like Luke. Wishful thinking maybe, but wishful thinking is all I have.

When I'm finished, he paces the room, stroking his stubble. "Okay, here's what we do."

With the conviction of a Baptist preacher and the persuasiveness of an infomercial, Luke schools me on how to put an end to Rex's special brand of queer-bashing. His hands thrust into the air. Then his palm slams his desk as if to smite all purveyors of bigotry everywhere.

My first reaction is maybe the old dude has taken one too many punches to the head. There's no way his scheme will work. Am I even capable of what he has planned? I don't know. So many things could go wrong. But what other choice do I have that doesn't involve me getting beaten to death in an alley?

"So, whatcha think?" Luke asks.

I exhale slowly. "Yeah. Yes. Let's do it."

"All right, then. Go home, catch some z's. You're gonna need 'em."

I text Brandon. Twenty minutes later, his BMW pulls up to the curb.

While Bran drives, I tell him every detail of Luke's plan. He listens without interrupting. Even if he doesn't like what he's hearing, he usually lets me finish before saying so.

"So what do you think?" I ask as he brakes outside my complex.

"I think your boss is about to make you jump off a cliff, and there's no coming back." He turns to me. "Can I come too?"

"Always."

Bran grins, dimples in full effect. He leans over to kiss me, but I flinch and pull away.

"Oh. Sorry," I say. "Just a little too public out here for me. Um, you wanna come inside for a little?"

He sighs and looks away. "Maybe another time." He flicks a switch, unlocking the doors. The moment is ruined, and it's entirely my fault.

Ugh. Brilliant.

I fumble with the door handle and get out. Bran pulls away without saying goodbye. His father's words echo in my head: *You're just a phase.*

Whether Mr. Elpusan is right or not, what just happened couldn't have helped. Should I tell Bran about what his father said? What would that accomplish? It's not like he's going to say, *Yep, my dad's right. You are just a phase.* He isn't cruel. I could just as well be a phase without him knowing it. Better to keep quiet about it.

Once I'm inside, I text Rosie all the details of the plan. My palms turn moist, waiting for her reply. I need her on board.

She replies back: About time!

ROUND 19

When I arrive at school on Friday, I avoid my usual routes. I steer clear of the west entrance and enter campus through the teacher's parking lot. I need to avoid Rex. Not for the whole day, just until I have a big enough audience.

The entire school should do.

On the way to first period, I take a shortcut past the drinking fountains to find Rex and his crew terrorizing an underclassman. Like the living clichés they are, they dump the kid in an oversize trash can and crack up like it hasn't been done a million times by a million bullies before them. On the plus side, Jorge's nowhere to be seen. Looks like he's ditched them for good.

I slip into the bathroom and wait it out in a stall. A minute before the bell rings, I crack the door to find the hallway clear of all homophobes and delinquents. I sprint to math class and slide into my seat as the bell sounds.

During morning classes, my mind wanders to the plan. I find myself jotting it down over and over until I've memorized each point.

Finally, lunch comes.

Rosie meets me at our old table. I could use a little banter as a distraction, but we're uncharacteristically tight lipped. She chews her lip incessantly while my gaze flits about the lunch tables.

She pulls out her sketchbook and draws, holding the book at an angle so I can't see. Her hand flies over the pad, and in a minute, she's finished. She flips the book around and shows me a detailed drawing of me in a superhero costume, complete with a cape. Across my chest are the letters B.A.

"Sweet," I say. "B.A., of course, stands for Bare Ass. I have the power to moon people in a single pantsing."

"No, it's for Bad Armpit. You subdue foes with a headlock and bad body odor." She adds more shading and definition to my abs, which I definitely appreciate.

"Well, you're the real superhero if you can whip up a sketch like that so fast."

As the quad fills up, a few kids throw us surprised looks—probably since we've finally come out of hiding—but for the most part, we're left alone. And then Rex and company make their appearance, strutting over to their own table across the way.

I glance at Rosie. She nods, her jaw set. We leave our bags at our table, and I lead her over into enemy territory.

"H-hey, Rex," I mumble. "Give me . . . I—I want my bike back." The table chatter drowns me out, and nobody looks my way. I chew my lip, and my eyes find Rosie.

She squeezes my arm. "You can do this," she whispers.

"I want my bike back, Rex," I say louder. "And I'll fight you for it."

Heads turn, and a cloak of silence envelops the crowd. Rex's eyes bug out, and he's overcome with a fit of laughter. Eddie joins in, followed by everyone else. Only Rosie and I aren't in on the joke.

Rex steps out from the crowd and stands barely a yard from me. "Cool, I'm always down to fuck you up. After school then, bitch."

"So you and your brother can jump me again? Uh-uh. I'm fighting just *you*. Three rounds in the ring at the Jab Gym one month from now. Winner's decided by knockout or whoever gets the loudest cheer from the crowd when it's all over. If I win, you give up the bike and leave me and my friends alone for good."

"What? Why would I go through all that when I can just kick your ass when you walk home?"

"'Cause you're not gonna say no to kicking my ass in the ring while the whole school watches. You love an audience. Besides, you're not gonna punk out in front of everyone right here, right now. Are you?"

"Ay, let me end this little bitch now," Eddie says.

Rex glares at his brother. "Shut it, Eddie." He takes in the crowd before turning back to me. "Okay, I'll be happy to destroy your bitch ass in the ring. But not in no month. Next Friday night."

Great. Wasn't expecting that, although I probably should have been. I can't fight Rex in a week. I need that month to train—not to mention learn how to actually fight. "No, it's . . . that's not the deal. We fight in a month so—"

"I don't give a goddamn what you got to say. Next Friday, I'mma beat the faggot out you—in the ring or not. Your choice."

The crowd jeers and my face burns. I want to sock Rex in his bigoted, pockmarked face, even though it would probably result in a very public beatdown. How can so many cheer for such irrational hatred? I'll never understand it.

Not everyone supports Rex, though. A few glare at him or shake their heads. Someone even yells out, "Homophobic dickwad!" I nearly crack up because the heckler is Rosie.

Like she's done for me so many times before, Rosie's comment brings me back from the edge. My fingers unfold, and a slow breath settles me.

"Friday night, then. Bring the bike." I retreat through the crowd, Rosie at my side.

"One week?" she says. "One week? What the hell?"

"Not like he gave me any choice." I avert my eyes. "It'll be okay."

She makes a noise that's half sigh, half grumble. "Are you going to be ready in time?"

"It'll be okay," I repeat, knowing I didn't actually answer her question.

"A week?" Luke scratches his white stubble like he's trying to uproot a tick. He paces behind his desk as I sit in a rickety chair made of splinters. "One week. I don't know. Gimme a month and you'll be ready to take on the ghost of Joe Louis. But a week? Nah, can't do it."

"What are you talking about, Luke?"

"You strapped on gloves for the first time two days ago. And you been in the ring, what, all of ten seconds? One week ain't enough."

I shoot up from the chair. "Come on! I challenged Rex in front of the whole school like you told me to! I can't back down now!"

"Look, I'm just . . . I'm trying to protect you. The ring's a dangerous place, kid. If you step into it unprepared, you will get hurt."

"Then prepare me! Show me how to kick this guy's ass! 'Cause if I don't meet Rex in the ring, he might kill me outside of it."

His gaze catches the framed photo of himself and the young fighter. He stares at it for a moment as if forgetting I'm in the room. *What is with this guy? Why does he keep flip-flopping on me?*

"Luke," I say. No answer. "Hey, you there?"

My voice seems to send a shiver through him, yanking him from his thoughts.

He lets out a sigh that sounds like defeat. "Okay, kid. I won't leave you hanging. Friday night it is."

"Thanks, Luke." I restrain myself from leaping over the desk and hugging him.

"But you'll have to work hard every day. Till your body hurts like it's never hurt before. You ready to do that?"

"Hell yes."

"You gonna argue and not listen to me again?"

I raise my chin, fold my arms. "Hell no." Luke's taking a chance on me, and I will not let him down again.

"All right, then. Let's start with some shadowboxing." He squints, almost daring me to disagree.

I pop up out of my seat. "Shadowboxing it is."

Stopwatch in hand, Luke leads me down to the full-length mirror. For a two-minute round, I throw jabs, hooks, and uppercuts at my reflection. He reminds me to keep my gloves up and my feet moving side to side.

"Time." Luke clicks his watch. "You're fast, kid. That's your biggest advantage."

I appreciate Luke's praise, but I can't get too excited. Being faster is not only my biggest advantage, it's my only one. Rex has me on size, strength, and experience.

"Okay, round two." He punches the timer again.

By the end of the third round, I'm barely breathing hard. The jogs to and from work have helped my conditioning. Which means—because he swiped my bike—Rex is responsible for my increased endurance. I'll make sure to thank him come Friday.

When Luke calls time, my skin glistens with a thick layer of sweat. I feel like I've been dunked in a tub of mucus. I plop down on a bench for a breather, but Luke allows me only a few minutes' rest before he has me do it all over again.

Somewhere in the middle of what could be round six, my arms sag to my sides. Luke claps twice, making me flinch. "Come on! Power through! Keep them fists up! Always, always protect yourself, or you will get hurt!"

When we wrap up an hour later, the gym is deserted. My lungs are burning like I've been inhaling needles, and my gloves feel like fifty-pound weights. I'd have a better chance of lifting Thor's hammer than going another round. Luke wasn't kidding about aching like hell, but it's a good ache. One I've earned.

After showering and changing into sweats and a hoodie, I stick my head into Luke's office to say bye. He's slouching in his swivel chair, staring at the old picture frame, now propped up on his desk. Sensing his serious mood, I try to duck out quietly.

"He's my son."

"Oh." I stay rooted in the doorway. Somehow, entering would feel like intruding on his moment of reflection. "What's his name?"

"Ray. Named him after the great Sugar Ray Robinson. He's quick like him too." Luke grimaces. "Well, he was."

I wince. *Was?* "You trained him?"

"Yeah. Kid was a thoroughbred, could lift twice his weight, and lightning fast. Great fighter, better than I ever was." A hint of a smile slips through his melancholy, but it quickly fades. "Had a habit of dropping his left when he was gearing up to throw the right. Back in '95, fighter named Javier 'the Matador' Perez made him pay for it. Lit up his left eye for nine rounds, detached his retina. Ray's sight was never the same. Neither was his fight skills. He blamed me. Can't exactly say he was wrong. My job was to protect him."

"I'm sorry." The words sound hollow.

With weathered hands, Luke gingerly replaces the frame on the wall. "Nothing to be sorry about, kid. My boy's doing just fine. Started a family, moved back east. Atlanta. Guess he didn't want his kids to get hoodwinked into the ring by their gramps." He bats away a tear. "Fathers and sons, y'know?"

I do know—totally. "I'm sure you did everything you could for him, Luke." Quiet seconds pass. Should I stay or leave?

Luke decides for me by flopping down on his cot and muttering, "Night, kid. Hit the lights for me." He rolls over to face the brick wall.

He'd mentioned he lives here, but actually seeing him curled up for the night in a lonely corner makes my shoulders droop—especially after his confession about his son. I'd invite him back to the apartment if we had any room.

As I'm leaving, Luke peeks over his shoulder. "Hey, kid. Tomorrow you step in the ring."

"Okay, cool. Night, Luke." I flick off the light.

I stride through the main gym and click off lights as I go. No wonder he'd been so strict with my training. He doesn't want a repeat of what happened to his son. Which means more than just my own life is on the line—so is Luke's psyche and already fragile emotional state. More pressure. Woo-hoo.

My arms throb when I inch the front door open. Like Luke said, I'm feeling the ache big time—physical and otherwise. I push on and jog into the night.

Five minutes in, my cell vibrates, and I slow to a halt right in front of a doughnut shop. Not good. The chocolate éclairs on display nearly make me forget I'm in training. I shuffle away from the shop's window and check my phone. A text from Rosie reads: get your geek butt over here. ur boyfriend is compromising my artistic vision!

Uh-oh. Looks like Bran and Rosie are having another one of their writer/artist standoffs, and they want me to play referee.

On my list of Agonizing Things Not to Do, being caught between my best bud and my guy is up there with bending back a toenail and dousing it with hot sauce. Still, they only have a week before the contest; somebody has to get them to communicate.

Mr. Sanchez opens the door, greeting me with a shake of his head. The house is surprisingly quiet—I thought I'd be walking into a war zone—but the grimace on his face tells me all is not joyful in zombie-comic town. "See what you can do with them," he says, and disappears into the kitchen.

On opposite ends of the couch, Bran and Rosie sit, ignoring each other. Rosie fiddles with a marker; her portfolio containing their comic sits on the coffee table, unopened.

"What's up?" I say. "How goes the comic brain trust? You know? As in, *braiiiins!*"

And . . . nothing.

Bran fake snickers. "Didn't you know, B? Zombies don't eat brains—they feast on a bloodbath of tofu and carrot sticks."

Rosie slams her marker on the coffee table and rises. "Oh, you wanna see some zombie shit? I will rip your earlobes off, rich boy!"

Bran's eyes bulge, and he pulls his knees up in self-defense.

I grab Rosie's arm before she can reach him. "Stop it, Rosie!"

"All right!" She flings my hand away, seething. "All right."

"I can't do this," Bran says softly. "Maybe we should just forget the whole thing."

"Whatever." Rosie storms from the room and disappears down the hallway. A second later, a door slams.

Bran turns away from me. "Don't start."

I'm about to head for Rosie's room when Mr. Sanchez pops his head out of the kitchen.

"You boys hungry? We have enchiladas. Just have to heat them up. Come on, help me out in here."

"Okay, sure." I head toward the kitchen, but Brandon stays planted in his seat. "Bran?"

He gnashes his teeth for a beat, then follows after me.

The kitchen's overflowing with culinary equipment and doodads. Pots and pans hang from a rack directly above the island; bags of bell peppers, onions, and garlic occupy counter space; dozens of spices line multiple shelves. Mr. Sanchez may be a mailman by trade, but he could probably moonlight as a master chef.

Mr. S peeks inside the refrigerator, emerges with a glass baking dish, and pulls off the foil covering. "Could use a bit more cheese." He retrieves a block of cheddar and a metal grater and hands them to me. "Do the honors?"

After washing my hands, I take a seat at the table and set to the task. Even cold, the aroma of sharp cheddar and tangy tomato sauce makes my stomach grumble. At the counter, Mr. S prepares a salad with avocados, red beans, and feta cheese while Bran slices lemons for lemonade.

I grate the cheese, and a dull pain pulses through my arm. With each thrust, I imagine myself back in the gym, shadow-boxing. The work is slow, and five minutes in, I've barely covered half the dish. I take a break and notice a framed pastel drawing on the wall of a Latina woman with shoulder-length orange hair. I'm fairly sure it's Rosie's work, just as I'm certain who the subject is.

Or was.

"Rosie's mother," Mr. Sanchez says. "Rosie drew her from memory. Didn't even use a photo as a guide."

"She's beautiful. Wish I'd known her."

He brings the salad over to the table and sits down across from me. "You know, when her mom passed, Rosie had a tough time of it. It was only the two of us, and honestly, I wasn't as available for her as I should've been. I'm just glad you were there to help her through it, Bobby."

I nod, not knowing what to say. Mrs. Sanchez died from breast cancer when Rosie and I were in seventh grade, which was a huge part of the reason we'd bonded. There weren't many other kids who could understand the ache of losing a parent to illness at a young age. The pain is always present, even on the good days.

"Your wife was very beautiful," Bran says. "Rosie has her eyes—and hair."

"Oh, that's not all she got from her. Leticia was a wonderful artist—loved to draw. She taught Rosie so much." Mr. Sanchez gazes at the portrait, apparently lost in thought. "You know, she was a vegetarian too. It was hard for me at times, especially when I was craving me some pork ribs. But Rosie wanted to be like her mother so much, she stopped eating meat when she was still in grade school." He turns to Bran. "I know some of Rosie's story ideas are a bit out there, but maybe it's her way of remembering her mother—of honoring her."

Bran takes this all in with softening eyes. "I didn't realize."

"Well, it really just occurred to me."

The meal is delicious, but I stick to my training diet and only sample half a chicken enchilada. Bran eats even less. Sounds from the TV filter in from the living room—apparently Rosie's back from her self-imposed exile.

Bran excuses himself and exits the kitchen. While he and Rosie talk, I help Mr. Sanchez with the cleanup. He washes, I dry. Before long, laughter spills in from the living room. As I wipe down a plate, I wander to the edge of the doorway and listen in.

"Are you sure about this? I mean I love it, but that's a hell of a lot of changes," Rosie says. "And we've only got a week till the contest."

"Plenty of time. We can knock out the script tonight. Pull an all-nighter. Unless you need your beauty sleep."

"Psssh, boy, I'm pretty enough already."

Bran chuckles. "All right. Let's do it."

"Hear that, Bobby?" Rosie calls. "We're good now. You can stop your sad-ass attempt at eavesdropping and get your behind in here."

I put the plate on the counter, wave to Mr. Sanchez, and join my friends. "Good to know. 'Cause I was about to ghost the both of you till you came to your senses."

"Ooh, then our plan was working." Rosie shoots me a grin.

"Hilarious. I've gotta get going." I peck Bran on the lips and give Rosie a hug. "Please don't hurt him," I say to her. "I like his earlobes where they are."

Outside, I fill my lungs with the night air and exhale fully.

Hopefully their truce lasts beyond tonight. I have enough chaos in my life without my best buds adding to it.

As soon as I attempt to break into a run, my body quickly tells me it's not happening. My muscles feel like they're about to burst through my skin in protest. Looks like I'm walking home.

ROUND 20

Six Days before the Fight

The ache in my arms wakes me long before the alarm clock sounds. I stand up and stretch, and my joints crack. I throw a combination and wince. I throw more and block out the pain. It's Saturday, and today I finally spar in the ring with Luke coaching me. No amount of sore muscles will keep me from stepping through those ropes.

When I trudge into the kitchen, Mom's already fixed my breakfast: three hard-boiled eggs. All protein. She's paid attention.

"Good morning, anak," she says, eating oatmeal at the table in her waitress uniform.

I return the greeting but stay quiet while we eat. So much has happened that I've kept secret from her, and the guilt makes my stomach acids churn. With the fight coming up next weekend, I should probably tell her about it soon. Somehow, telling her seems even scarier than challenging Rex.

"Mom, I-I need to talk to you about . . . well, about my job at the gym."

"Are you being overworked?"

"No, not really."

"Sexually harassed by your boss?"

"What? Ew, no."

She gulps downs the last of her coffee and rises. "Okay, then it'll have to wait until tonight. I'm running late."

"Uh, okay."

Mom pecks me on top of my head and rushes out the front door, and I release a sigh. I can always tell her later. At least I tried.

After clearing the table, I slip into my jogging sweats and head out. The run over to the Jab Gym is relatively easy for me now. Routine. My breathing is steady when I arrive.

Silence greets me when I enter the gym. I soak in the stillness, grateful for a moment of peace before the place becomes filled with the cacophony of the sweet science. With a skip replacing his usual waddle, Luke appears from the back. He looks rested and seems to have recovered from last night's moment of gloom.

"So, youngblood, ready to step in the ring for real this time?"

"You know it."

"All right, then." Luke rubs his hands together. "After you clean the head."

"Totally knew that was coming."

"Good on you. Major rule of boxing: always anticipate your opponent's attack."

Two scrubbed toilets and an hour later, I slip on headgear and sparring gloves and practically leap through the ropes. Vicki waits for me inside, sporting a grin that gives me a clear view of her mouthguard—which I forgot. Again. Fortunately, Luke appears on the apron with a mouthguard in hand. I barely open my mouth in time as he shoves it in.

"Now, don't get wild in there," he says. "Focus on defense, protect yourself. She likes to set up with the jab, fake right, and come with the left hook. Let her throw, then counter. Okay?"

"Got it."

I prop my gloves up and meet Vicki in the middle. We touch mitts, and she immediately comes with a quick double jab, stinging my right eye. The hook follows, smashing my chin. The sharp pain and tears welling up in my eyes remind me that I'm not shadowboxing anymore. I backpedal fast and wince as something bites me in the back. It's the ropes. I bounce off them right into Vicki's jab.

"Counter, baby," Luke says. "Counter!"

My jab keeps her off me but glances off her headgear and does little damage, if any. Vicki keeps coming. I slip in a straight left that stops her advance and follow with a right hook.

"There ya go!" Luke shouts.

Vicki shrugs it off and comes with a barrage of jabs and hooks, making me retreat into the corner. A haymaker of a right lands. *Ow. Big-time OW.* Girl has speed *and* power. I fight my way out of the corner with some desperation throws, one of which catches her on the chin. She ties me up, and we clench. This is the first time I've been this close to a girl—a sweaty one at that. The moment reassures me that I'm definitely not straight.

We exchange a few more skirmishes, which Vicki clearly gets the better of, before Luke calls time with a blow of his whistle. I stumble to the corner, hoping to plop down on a stool. Only Luke doesn't offer me one. Guess I'm standing.

"You doing fine, kid. Way to keep her off you."

"What are you talking about? She pretty much kicked my ass."

"Well, yeah, what'd you expect? She's been logging ring time for years. You can barely step through the ropes without bumping your noggin. I'm just impressed you kept her from laying you out. That's a win, kid."

I side-eye him. There's a compliment in there somewhere, I guess.

"All right, keep that guard up. You're dropping it before you throw the left, telegraphing it. And you can punch first every now and then, you know."

At the sound of Luke's whistle, Vicki pounces across the squared circle before I can take a step and lands an uppercut that jiggles my incisors. I ignore the instinct to turn to Luke and ask for a time-out. Sidestepping to my left, I avoid another haymaker and tag her with a straight left. She flinches, but only for a second. Then she's on me once more.

Whooping and clapping shake my focus. I catch in my periphery Brandon and Rosie watching from the edge of the apron, right next to Luke. *When the hell did they get here? Didn't they just pull an all-nighter on their comic book?*

"Woo-hoo! Go B!" Rosie shouts.

I risk a glance over at them. Bad move. When I turn back, Vicki's gloved fist smashes into my eyeball. Pain blasts through my face. Another punch sends me into the ropes, and I cover up and deflect most of her attack.

"Get out of there!" Luke yells. "Circle her!"

I bounce off the ropes, swerve right, and sneak in an off-balance jab-slash-straight-left combo that would make Manny proud. Bran and Rosie cheer even louder.

Vicki snarls. She seems to sprout another pair of arms like some kind of ancient idol as she hurls a series of combinations that stagger me. Luke shouts at me to raise my guard. I manage, but Vicki's onslaught picks apart my ineffective defense. The light blurs. The room tilts.

The soft mass hovering over me sharpens into focus and becomes Luke's face. "You okay, youngblood?"

Luke, Vicki, Brandon, and Rosie stare down at me. The fluorescent lights on the ceiling behind them clue me into the fact that I'm laid out on the canvas.

"I told you to go easy on him," Luke says.

Vicki shrugs. "I did." She kneels to my level, smirking. "You got heart, kid. Not to mention a sledgehammer of a left. Keep your guard up, though, or someone's going to mess up that pretty face o' yours." She rises and exits the ring with the swagger of the victorious.

Rosie bites her lip. "Oh, man. You don't look so good."

Arching an eyebrow, Luke says, "Yeah, well, that's what happens when you distract him and he gets clobbered by a nationally ranked bantamweight. Who are you two, now?"

Brandon sits down beside me and takes my hand. "I don't like this, B. At all."

"I'm fine, Bran." I try to stand, but a wave of nausea hits me.

Shaking, Brandon squeezes my arm. "That wasn't encouraging, Bobby. Rex is not a hundred-pound girl. He's going to kill you!"

"She lit your face up like a Roman candle, B." Rosie beams. "I like her."

"Ah," Luke says. "These must be those supportive friends you told me about."

I half sigh, half chuckle. "Luke, meet Brandon and Rosie. Rosie, Bran, this is Luke, owner of the Jab Gym, friend to custodial carts everywhere."

Luke bows slightly. "Good to meet you both. Now kindly keep quiet and let us work. And if I hear any more negative comments, you'll be booted off the premises. Nod now if you understand."

Bran nods. "Yeah. Yes. Sorry."

Rosie nearly says what I'm sure would be a characteristically snide comment, but I shoot her a warning glare and shake my head. She seals her lips and nods.

"Great. Now help your boy up, and let's go make popcorn." Luke leads our group to the back office.

Ahead of me, Rosie whispers to Bran, "She really kicked his ass."

"Right?" he replies.

I glare at their backs. "Nice to finally see you two agreeing on things."

"See how Pacquiao uses his speed to keep Margarito off him?" Luke asks through popcorn-stuffed cheeks. "He constantly beats him to the punch and circles away." He coughs, and a kernel flies from his lips.

We've gathered around his ancient TV/VCR setup to watch

Pacman's twelve-round domination of welterweight Antonio Margarito. My head's still foggy from fighting Vicki, and I have to squint at the screen's glare, but I do my best to focus.

At five feet, eleven inches and 150 pounds, Margarito dwarves Manny, who stands five feet, five inches, 145 pounds at weigh-in. Plus, Margarito boasts a six-inch-longer reach. Their height and reach differences are similar to mine and Rex's. Rex, however, has way more than five pounds on me. Try thirty.

In round three, Margarito backs Manny against the ropes, but Pacman sidesteps left while unleashing a right-left combo at an odd angle. Then Manny whirls away from Margarito's attack and stuns him with another flurry.

Luke nudges me with a meaty elbow. "Just like Pacquiao, your advantage is your speed, kid. See how he throws when he's on the move? That is exactly what you need to do against this—this . . . What's this kid's name?"

"Rex." I nearly grab a handful of popcorn from the bowl in Rosie's lap, but I catch myself, remembering my training.

"Rex, huh? Well, come Friday night you're gonna *Rex* that punk's face up good."

Tilting her head toward Luke, Rosie says, "I like this guy. He's like an angry hobbit. With puns."

In round four, the play-by-play announcer relates how Margarito told his corner team in between rounds that Manny has no power and his punches can't hurt him. The big red welt under Margarito's right eye tells a different story. Maybe Manny won't knock Margarito out, but he's definitely damaging him.

Round after round, Pacquiao adds more cuts and bruises to Margarito's face, like an artist painting a portrait of agony. Manny is far ahead on points, and unlike Margarito, he appears nearly unmarked.

Bran flinches and looks away when Manny lands a crushing right hook. Is he picturing *my* face getting pummeled? Is he worried that come Friday I'll end up like a bruised and bloodied Margarito? I guess I can't blame him, but his worrying is making *me* worry. I reach for his hand and squeeze it.

Rosie, however, loves the action, cheering and mimicking Pacman's jabs and hooks. "Yeah! Take that, ya punk-ass bitch! You just got punked, ya punk-ass bitch!"

Rosie and her antics. If only for a moment, she helps me breathe easy.

Pacquiao—along with his trainer, Freddie Roach—have good reason to want to punish Margarito. Leading up to the fight, Margarito was caught on video mocking Roach, who suffers from Parkinson's disease. The footage showed Margarito imitating Roach's shaky mannerisms and slurred speech. Not smart, Antonio. As if Manny needed any more motivation.

By the eleventh round, however, Pacquiao glances at the referee as if pleading with him to stop the fight for Margarito's sake. But the ref allows the bout to go the distance. Manny, to his credit, does not pursue the knockout. He eases up on Margarito and allows him to finish the fight standing, with dignity. This sense of honor and decency is why Manny is beloved the world over. Why *I* love him.

If I were in the same position against Rex, would I be as

compassionate? Would I let up and show him mercy? Maybe. But without question, Rex would not return the favor.

Maybe Bran's right to worry.

After the fight, Rosie stands up and hands me the empty popcorn bowl—wow, she downed the whole thing. "Well, all this blood and violence has been fun, but now I'm off to do something much more gruesome."

I stand and stretch. "Gonna work on the zombie comic?"

"Nuh-uh. Valentine's dance with Jimmy Valdez." Her posture slumps, and she pumps her fist in mock celebration. "Woo-hoo."

"Right. You really don't have to do this, y'know."

"I'm kidding—mostly. I'm actually kind of looking forward to it? He's growing on me. He's a good guy." She nods as if trying to convince herself.

After I change into civvies, Bran and I drop Rosie off at home. As he pulls away from the curb, he asks, "Do you want to hang out at my place tonight?"

Oh, boy. While I'm totally down to spend time with Bran, I can do without seeing his dad, aka Mr. You're Just a Phase, for, oh, the next century. "Let's kick it at my apartment instead."

"No offense, B, but there isn't much to do at your place."

"But we'll be alone."

Bran's grin is so wide, I can see it in my periphery. Without a word, he turns out of Rosie's neighborhood and heads toward my place.

When we get to my apartment, we spend the next couple of hours watching *X-Men: First Class*, the origin story of Marvel's team of mighty mutants. As usual, Bran gives his original take on the gay subtext.

"See, young Professor X and young Magneto are really a gay couple trying to make it work in a homophobic world that hates and fears them."

I nod. "They do make a fairly hot couple."

"Right? So the prof and Maggie travel the world together, looking for young mutants. Not just so they can teach them to use their powers, but because they want to start a family together. The whole movie is about same-sex adoption!"

I laugh, not because his theory doesn't make sense—it totally does—but because he's so ecstatic and firm in his belief. It's fairly adorable. I'm overcome with the urge to kiss him—so I do.

The credits roll, and Bran aims the remote and mutes the TV. "Y'know, it's not too late. We could go to the dance. Together. I mean, if you want."

Ugh. Should've known this was coming. "I don't think so, B."

"Come on. I can loan you a shirt and tie."

"I have a shirt and tie."

"Great! Get dressed, and we'll head to my place so I can change."

With a groan, I rise from the couch. "Bran, I told you I'm not ready for this. You keep saying you don't want me to have to fight, but then you wanna put me in a position where I might have to."

"Okay, I get it. Sorry." He exhales, and it's as if his whole body deflates. "I just wanted to . . . I don't know, forget it."

"What?"

"Dance with you." He chews the corner of his bottom lip. "I want to dance with you."

"Um . . . yeah. I don't do that. At least not with witnesses present."

"Oh, that will not stand. Nope."

He pulls out his phone, flicks the screen a few times, and a breezy dance track leaks from the speaker: Hailee Steinfeld's ode to self-empowerment, "Love Myself." Bran leaps to his feet and starts shimmying wildly while perfectly lip-synching the lyrics. I stare and giggle. He's sexy, adorable, and a complete dork all at once. "Come on. Shake that ube-loving boo-*tay*."

"I'm really sore, Bran."

He breaks into the robot and shifts into his Guilt-a-Tron voice. "Guilt-a-Tron is. A dancing. Machine. You will dance. Or feel guilt."

"Nope. No guilt here."

But he's undeterred. He grabs my hand and sways it to the beat. Before I know it, I'm moving my feet, bobbing my head, and actually dancing—if you can really call it that.

"There ya go!"

I know I suck at this, but Bran's giddy energy makes me not care. Our cheers nearly drown out the music as we try to outdo each other in a mock dance battle: Bran busts some dope popping moves, and I counter with some boxing footwork that hopefully passes for a B-boy uprock.

His eyes go wide. "Oh! Go Bobby! Go Bobby! Shake your brown thang!"

How have we never done this before? Dancing. It's what

couples do! Hailee gives a final lyrical shout, ending the track, and we plop onto the couch in each other's arms, kissing as we go down.

"Ow!" I pull away, my lips still tender from Vicki's smack-down. "Think we're gonna have to hold off on the make-out sessions for a little while."

"It's okay. I can work around it." He leans in and kisses my neck softly. I close my eyes and quiver as he makes his way up to my earlobe one soft peck at a time. *Damn, that is the spot.*

And then both our phones buzz.

We get a text from Rosie: please pick me up n get me away from this creep.

"Damn, that went south fast," Bran says. "The dance started like what, an hour ago?" He slips his phone back into his pocket. "Looks like we're going after all."

The only reason Rosie went to the dance with Jimmy was to help me. If she's not having a good time, we can't either.

We roll into the basketball-gym parking lot, pull up to the curb, and Rosie dashes over to us, four-inch heels in hand. I open my window. My girl's slaying in a black mini dress with her orange hair done up in a bun. She's gorgeous, despite the scowl marring her face. Jimmy trails behind her in a tux, and sure enough, his bowtie and cummerbund match Rosie's hair.

"Come on, Rosie! What'd I do?" Jimmy says, grabbing her wrist. "You can't just leave me here alone!"

She yanks her arm away and rounds on him, brandishing a pointy heel. "I dropped three weeks' allowance on these new shoes. Don't make me ruin them by gouging out your eyeball."

Before Jimmy can reply, she hops in the car and we peel out.

"You okay?" I say, turning around to Rosie.

"Just spectacular." She slams her fist into the seat and folds her arms together.

Bran glances at her in the mirror. "What happened?"

"He turned out to be a raging, infectious dickhole is what happened." She goes quiet for a moment, as if debating whether she wants to get into it. "So we were talking about Charlotte and how she's always up in people's business, and how someone should put that chica in her place, and how that someone should totally be me. It was a nice talk, y'know? He was sweet and kissing my ass at an acceptable first-date level. But then he had to go and call Charlotte a shitty word. That word that starts with a *d* and is not nice to lesbians?"

"Wow." I shake my head. "Seriously?"

"Yeah! I mean, Charlotte may be nosy, but don't be calling her that trashy d-word, especially around me. I called him on it, and the little punk doubled down and said I was over-reacting."

"What a jerk," Bran says.

"Right? That fool made me defend Charlotte Wilkes! I will never forgive his annoying matchy ass!"

I reach for her hand and squeeze it. "Sorry he ruined the dance for you."

"Yeah, well, not everyone's as lucky as you two."

I glance at Brandon. She's spot-on; I am pretty damn lucky. We fall quiet as Bran enters Rosie's neighborhood.

A chuckle from Bran breaks the silence. "Gouge his eyeball

out with your heel? Now that is some badass zombie-slayer action."

Rosie snorts. "I've been spending too much time with you."

Badass Rosie is right. A lot of people talk about being down for queer folks, but that's all they do—talk. Rosie's the definition of ride or die. Utter a gay slur around her, and it's a definite deal breaker.

ROUND 21

Five Days before the Fight

I'm clinging to the edge of sleep when a weight plops onto the bed, making it shudder. At first I shrug it off as just another Southland quake, but then a hand nudges my side. The nudge turns into a full-blown shake.

"Bobby," Mom says much too loudly. "You want to go to church?"

The morning is too new for me to form words. I let a groan be my answer.

"Good. Get dressed." She springs up from the bed.

She means it, but I hit my mental snooze button for some extra shut-eye. A shout of "Bobby!" jolts me awake for good.

I didn't lie to Bran; I do have a dress shirt and tie. But we haven't attended Mass in months—maybe even half a year—so I have to search for a few minutes before I find them.

Mom was raised Catholic, and she passed down the prayers, beliefs, and general dos and don'ts to me, but I wouldn't say she's devout. Well, not anymore. If she insists on going to church, there's a reason.

She misses Dad.

The melancholy can wreck her at any time: during the holi-days, Dad's birthday, even on the Fourth of July beneath a cascade of shimmering fireworks. About five years ago, we were celebrating the Fourth at Lake Street Park. Right in the middle of sharing a bag of pastillas, her eyes welled up, and it quickly turned to full-on sobbing. All I could think to do was sit still beside her, stare blankly at the exploding sky, and pretend nothing extremely uncomfortable was happening. At first I had no clue what was wrong, but then I remembered. Pastillas were Dad's favorite candy.

I guess returning every now and then to the familiar rituals of Mass helps her deal. When Dad was alive, we'd amble down to Beverly Boulevard to Our Lady of Refuge every Sunday. During the blessing, Mom would whisper to me to pray for Dad's recovery. I did so with brow tightly furrowed, believing that the harder I prayed, the more likely God would listen.

Apparently, he didn't.

After Dad died, I gave up praying for good, and Mom couldn't bring herself to attend church regularly again. Maybe she couldn't stomach celebrating a god who took her husband from her. Maybe she stopped believing.

Either way, I can't say I miss it, given the church's stance on my so-called sinful lifestyle. Still, whenever the pain of Dad's absence overwhelms her, we inevitably return.

On the walk over, I lug my backpack stuffed with my gym clothes so I can jog straight to the Jab Gym after Mass. Mom's not her usual chatty self, which is fine, because neither am I. All I want to do is get to the gym. I'm losing valuable training time by going with her. Plus I'm not really looking forward to entering a closed space packed with overly judgmental people.

But she's Mom. I have her back.

According to the church bulletin, Our Lady of Refuge was built back in the late 1980s. They've obviously done little remodeling since. The marble floor is cracked in places, most of the pews are warped and chipped at the corners, and the air holds a vaguely musty odor. As we enter, I take a whiff, and I'm six again, Dad holding my hand, guiding me to our pew.

Heads turn. Their eyes say what their lips never would in a place of worship. *Hey, here comes the gay sinner! Maybe he's come to repent of his evil ways!* Nice to know that the Westlake rumor mill includes churchgoing parents. They look like they could be Bran's titas and titos. Maybe even my own—if I knew them. My thoughts cling fast to Dad, and I remember his strength. His courage. I straighten my back, raise my chin, and glare right the hell back.

Mom flinches at the attention we've drawn. She probably thinks the stares are for her. Nodding, she motions me to a row near the back. I bet she wants to avoid being seen by any of her old circle of friends, because that would lead to small talk and the inevitable nosy-ass questions. *How are you? Where have you been? Are you seeing anyone? Aw, that's too bad.*

As soon as we sit, Mom buries her face in a hymn book. I do the same.

Within minutes, the church is packed, Mass being the one occasion most folks aren't on Filipino time. The pews are stuffed with neighborhood families and teens who attend Westlake. Latecomers line the side aisles against the walls. The crowd is mixed, mostly Mexican and Filipino. I wish Rosie were here—I could use the support—but she and her dad usually go to the

Spanish Mass later in the day. Thankfully, one of the modern allowances the staff has made is air-conditioning, so the church isn't too stuffy.

Mom throws herself into the proceedings. She recites each prayer perfectly, follows along with the readings, and replies to the responsorial psalm on cue. I'm barely there. I go through the ritual motions, but in my head I'm running through my sparring session with Vicki, figuring out what I can improve on and what I can use against Rex. Despite my slacked faith, I feel conflicted about contemplating violent acts in the middle of Mass. Kind of.

We come to the part I've been dreading, and I doubt Mom has been looking forward to it, either. The part that means actual physical interaction with your fellow churchgoers. Father spreads his arms and says, "Let us offer each other a sign of peace." On cue, the whole congregation turns to the person beside or behind themselves, offers a handshake, and says, "Peace be with you."

Mom and I hug and exchange the greeting. I let go, but she grabs on to me for a moment longer, shivering. Her breath tickles my earlobe. Finally, she releases me. Did she just blink away a tear?

An older man turns around and thrusts his callused palm into mine. I catch a familiar figure a few rows up, across the aisle. With a warm demeanor I've never witnessed from him before, Rex shakes hands with various folks. He looks like your average, nonviolent churchgoer.

Then his eyes meet mine, and he mouths, *Peace be with you . . . faggot.*

From cheeks to earlobes, my face burns. For a final insult, he gives a crisp wave, then whirls to face the altar. I want to run over and sock him in the back of his thick neck, but that might be seen as un-Christian.

Beside Rex stands Eddie and their father. Mr. Banta's muscled back and shoulders stretch the fabric of his dress shirt. I shudder at the memory of his powerful limbs working over the brothers. Sure, they're homophobic douchebags, but how could any man beat his children? Plus, homophobic douchebaggery is learned, which means he's probably the OG homophobe who taught it to them.

With a shake of my head, I cast away the train of thought. The last thing I should be doing is feeling sorry for Rex, because he won't feel an ounce of pity for me when we meet in the ring.

For the remainder of the service, my sights are locked on Rex. He waits in the Communion line, fingers clasped and head bowed, the picture of Christian supplication. Back at his pew, he kneels and chews the sacramental bread with eyes clamped shut, apparently in deep prayer. For a second, I wonder if the ritual will miraculously transform him into a kinder, more tolerant, and less violent person. Yeah, and maybe I'll sprout wings and become the first Filipino to fly to the moon.

Aside from the occasional stank eye from representatives of the holier-than-thou delegation, Mass ends without further drama. The procession files out slower than I'd like. We emerge into the smoggy morning, the kind that reminds Angelenos the air we breathe is most likely killing us.

"You okay to get home on your own?" I ask Mom.

"Yeah, I'm fine. Her lips curl into a half smile. "Well, better than an hour ago. Think I'll treat myself to some halo-halo— with ube ice cream on top."

The image of the purple ice cream melting over crushed ice and fruit makes me exhale. "That sounds delicious. Good for you."

I kiss her on the cheek and bolt to the restroom to change clothes. I don't want to leave her, but I've lost too much training time already.

And my time is running out.

ROUND 22

When I arrive at the red brick exterior of the Jab Gym, I'm breathing and sweating harder than usual. *Thanks so much, smog.* I stagger into the restroom to find Brandon mopping the floor in a cool Defenders T-shirt and high-end sweatpants. Even his bummy clothes are nicer than my church ones. Hank is parked against the wall, a dent in its side courtesy of Rex.

"Uh, Bran, what are you doing?"

"Well, someone has to keep this place clean while you're training. And that would be me."

"Wait, what? How?"

"Larry gave me the week off at the Lair. He said anything to help you win on Friday. And Luke—well, he said, uh . . ."

"What?"

"I don't really want to—"

A toilet flushes, and Luke emerges from the stall, morning paper under his arm. "I said I want the seat so spotless I can see my cheeks reflecting in it when I do my business." He gives Bran a thumbs-up. "Mission accomplished, kid." He shuffles from the room.

"Lovely." I turn to Bran. "What about the contest? Don't you and Rosie have to finish up your comic?"

"The writing's pretty much done. She just has to finish the

artwork. Plus, there's only so many times I can tell her to add more entrails to a panel."

"You don't have to do this."

"No, I do. You were right, B. You need to be able to defend yourself. Besides, cleaning toilets is a small price to pay if I get to see you. And maybe while I'm here you can teach me how to punch."

"Definitely." My cheeks warm. What did I do to deserve such a thoughtful—not to mention incredibly hot—guy? Maybe it's the universe's way of balancing out all the crap I've had to endure. If so, thank you, universe.

"Oh, and I got you a little something." He retrieves a gift bag from one of Hank's shelves. "Happy Valentine's Day, B."

I wince and break eye contact. "Aw, no. I didn't do anything for you. Sorry." *God, I am the worst boyfriend ever.*

His head slightly dips. "It's okay. You've had a lot going on."

"You're not gonna bust out the Guilt-a-Tron, are you?"

"I think I'll spare us the indignity this time."

From the gift bag, I pull out a brand-new T-shirt and unfurl it, revealing the MP Pacquiao logo in the red, blue, and yellow of the Philippine flag. "This is . . . wow. You're kind of incredible, y'know?"

"Well, no offense, but your old tee is looking fairly ragged."

"Yeah, it is." I take his hand and squeeze. "Thank you for this."

"You want to hug me now, don't you?"

"Uh, I would, but you smell like vomit and number two."

He sniffs his arm and grimaces. "I really do."

"Hey, I've been there." We hug, and I allow myself a moment

to sink into his arms, to take refuge in them. Then I get to work. The noncleaning kind.

Luke insists I start the session with footwork drills. I take it slow the first time through, making sure to dodge the cones and hit each step in the pattern. Then I do it again.

While I take a breather, Bran sweeps up near the ring where two fighters spar. His eyes seem to be more on the boxers than his work. Great, it's only his first day and he's already slacking off. Luke will not be pleased.

My third time through the cones, I pick up the pace. From the corner of my eye, I notice that Bran's attention seems to be on one fighter in particular: Latino Zac Efron.

Is he checking him out? Damn, and on Valentine's Day too? Is this because I didn't get him a present?

Stepping on a cone, I lose my balance and topple to the wood-paneled floor. *Shit.*

Luke appears over me, shaking his head. "Youngblood, did you really just get taken out by a plastic cone?" He offers his hand and helps me up. "Say it with me. If you got crap footwork..."

"You got a crap fighter." I groan. "Yeah, I hear you."

I replace the cone and turn back to the ring, but Bran has moved on.

So maybe he was checking out a hot guy. Or maybe he wasn't. I did the same thing on my first day—with the same hot guy. Doesn't mean anything. I try to forget about it and focus on training, but four words keep popping into my brain.

You're just a phase.

Back in the ring with Vicki.

Luke's whistle blares, and my sparring session—the sequel—begins. One mistake I made the first time was letting Vicki take the fight to me; I was much too passive. This time, I dash over to her before she takes a step. A trio of jabs sets up my left. The punch is solid and stuns her. I press my advantage with a right hook, and she ties me up with both arms.

"Break it up there!" Luke calls.

We push off and circle each other. Vicki nods, acknowledging the punch; the gesture is a sign of respect, and it gives me a jolt of adrenaline. Then she gives me an entirely different type of jolt. She fakes right and sneaks in a left hook, rattling my jaw.

I don't know what happened next, but when I open my eyes, I'm staring up at the ceiling, my back flat against the canvas. Pain throbs in my right eye as I roll over onto my knees.

"You okay, kid?" Luke calls from the side. "Kid?"

I fill my lungs slowly with air and try to block out the pain and steady myself. Finally, I nod and rise to my feet.

Damn, she knocked me down again. I had it coming. My guard dropped as I was about to throw the right, just like Luke warned me about doing. My teeth grind into my mouthpiece. I vow to correct the mistake and bring my gloves up to my chin.

Luke smacks the apron. "Remember now, protect yourself. And keep moving!"

My feet obey the command. I circle Vicki and pop her with a straight right while keeping my left up. A blur of a combination follows. I snap off each punch at a Pacquiao-like clip. She backpedals, clearly stunned.

"Woo-hoo, Bobby!" Rosie yells. *When did she get here?* She's always teleporting in like Nightcrawler from the X-Men.

Put her out of your mind. Remember what happened last time.

As if to remind me, Vicki connects with a left hook to my eye, but I roll with it and escape its full force. Her next punch—a right uppercut—lands solidly, and she follows it up with more combinations. I grunt through the pain and cover up.

"Move!" Luke shouts.

I do. Sidestepping left, I pepper Vicki's eye with jabs, then sweep my left in for a wide hook. She stumbles backward into the ropes. My fists work like pistons, pumping blow after blow through her defenses.

Luke's whistle erupts with quick, short bursts. "All right, all right. That's enough for now."

"Not bad, newbie," Vicki says. "Way to finish strong." We bump gloves and retreat to our corners.

"Better," Luke says. "Much better."

Rosie throws an awkward combo. "You were like a whirlwind in there. Bobby 'the Tsunami' Agbayani!"

"Huh. I kind of like that," Brandon says, sweeping up nearby. "It rhymes."

"Yeah, a little too much." I take a sip of water and spit it into the pail on the apron.

"Dibs on the merchandising," Rosie says.

"What? You actually fighting a girl, Agbayani? Why am I not surprised?" Rex strolls over, still sporting his Sunday finest, backpack hung over one shoulder. His gaze lingers on Vicki. "Yep, a ripped one, but still a girl. 'Sup, thickness?"

Vicki sneers, baring her teeth like a starved guard dog. "Step in the ring. Find out."

"God, I would so love to see that." Rosie clasps her hands together as if in prayer. "Please do that," she says to Rex. "Here, let me hold your bag."

Unbelievable. Jerk actually has the nerve to show up here before Friday. "What do you want?"

"Thought you supposed to be some kind of genius, man. Why else would I be here? I'm looking to train, get the feel of the ring."

Brandon, Rosie, and I exchange glances. *Oh, hell no. This is not happening.*

"That's hilarious." I jump to the floor. "Wow, who knew under all that toxic machismo lurked a shitty sense of humor?" I spit into the bucket with more force than usual.

"How about you keep your bullshit comments to yourself, Agbayani? Or I'll have to pummel your ass before fight night."

I turn to Brandon. "Wait, wait, wait. Did he really just say he's going to pummel my ass?"

"He really did. That has to be the gayest thing I've heard all week."

"Oh, damn." My jaw drops. "Are you one of us now, Rex? Are—are you joining the gays?"

Brandon, Rosie, and I crack up, our laughter turning heads.

"Ay, shut your damn mouth," Rex says, his cheeks a deep red.

"Hey, it's okay. It's great to see you embracing our lifestyle with such an open mind. Good for you."

"Ay, I ain't no bakla, so you all best shut the hell up."

"Okay, relax. Yeesh. Just don't pummel my ass, okay? It's taken."

Bran raises his hand. "Dibs."

Rex fumes, but he can't do anything about it. He's alone and outnumbered in enemy territory.

"Yo, you run this dump?" Rex asks Luke. "Where do I sign up?"

I shake my head. "There's no way you're training here, so you might as well—"

Luke clears his throat rather unsubtly and motions me over to the far end of the ring. He wraps his arm around my shoulder, bringing me into a two-man huddle. "I say we let him stay."

"What? Come on, Luke, business can't be that bad. We can—"

"Listen, you need to be smart about this now. We need to see what he's got if I'm gonna get you ready to fight him."

"What, so we let him train here so we can spy on him?"

"Exactly."

"You realize he's just gonna spy on us, right?"

"Of course. But when he's in the room, we lull him to sleep."

"I guess so." Before I can argue more, Luke plods past Rex.

"Come on, then." Luke waves at him. "Let's get you settled in. We got a membership package you're gonna love. Includes a towel and everything."

Rex mock salutes me and follows Luke to the counter.

Wonderful. My archenemy gets to prep for our big grudge match at my home base. He's going to punch the bags I punch, lift the weights I lift, and piss all over the toilet I clean. Unbelievable. Does Apocalypse get to train in the X-Men's Danger

Room? Does Iron Man have to worry about Thanos taking a big purple dump in Avengers Tower?

Brandon rushes over. "This is not a good idea."

"It really isn't," Rosie says.

If Bran and Rosie agree, I must really be in trouble.

ROUND 23

Four Days before the Fight

Across the neutral zone of the lunch area, Rex and his goon squad actually refrain from harassing or maiming anyone. I'm like an anthropologist observing predators in their natural habitat, anticipating a surprise attack on weaker prey. It's fairly chilling to watch. But nope, they eat their lunch like normal, nonsadistic people.

Of course, random acts of douchebaggery still show through. Eddie sets free an empty Doritos bag on the wind, making yet another contribution to the semi-landfill look of the school grounds. I swear, instead of the Wolverines, our school mascot should be the Raccoons.

How long will they be able to keep their base instincts under wraps? Will they make it to Friday? More likely the pressure will be too much, and they'll explode at some underclassman who can't defend himself. Funny how, less than a couple weeks ago, I used to qualify.

Afternoon classes crawl by. I don't even attempt to make a show of taking notes. Instead, I replay Manny highlights in my brain, only with Rex's head superimposed on De La Hoya's and Margarito's bodies. The Hatton knockout plays on a loop like a GIF. I'd give up my entire X-titles collection to put Rex on the canvas in a similar way.

The final bell rings, and on my way out, Mrs. Cisneros calls me over. She greets me with a frown I'm now accustomed to and hands me my *Animal Farm* pop quiz. My grade flares out from the top corner in angry red marker: 60 percent, D-minus. Damn it. I haven't received a D since—actually, I don't think I've *ever* gotten one.

"Your work has taken a huge downturn lately, Bobby. Everything okay?"

I shrug. "Yeah, sure. I'm good."

Her head bobs slightly as she regards me. "Is Rex still giving you trouble?"

Of course. Thanks to you, Rex and the Bigot Bunch won't leave me alone. "No, everything's okay. I'll get my grade up."

She waits for me to elaborate, but that's all I'm going to give her. Mrs. Cisneros says all the right teacherly things and probably does mean well, but everything has to be done on her terms, regardless of how it might come back to kick me in the gonads. My silence is more out of self-preservation than spite, although there is plenty of the latter.

For nearly ten seconds, she studies me like I'm some literary passage that needs puzzling out. Finally, she says, "Okay," excusing me. Wading into the jam-packed hallway, I vow to make good on my promise to pull my grade up. Not because of Cisneros and her disapproving grimace, but for Mom. For myself.

* * *

My focus during training isn't much better. I run through my footwork drills and again kick over a couple cones. When Luke holds up the mitts for me to strike, my punches glance off with barely half my usual power.

Rex snickers and pounds away at the heavy bag mere feet from the ring. Well, Luke's plan was to lull him into overconfidence with a pretend lackluster workout. Only I'm not faking. And apparently Luke doesn't realize. We're four days from fight night, and we're wasting time playing mind chess with a guy who probably doesn't care whether or not I can throw a decent punch. Either way, he will try to put a permanent hurt on me. Rex throws a final hook, then pads toward the locker room, smirking all the way.

"You're doing great, kid," Luke whispers in between throws. "He thinks you got nothing. Keep it up."

Over in the far ring, Latino Efron spars with another middleweight. He sneaks in an uppercut that stuns his opponent, but before he can follow it up, his trainer blows the whistle, ending the session. At his corner, he sips from a water bottle and spits in the apron bucket.

His trainer yells, "Full!"

When Bran comes over to retrieve the pail, Latino Zac smiles and says something to him. Bran laughs—a bit too hard. He lingers by the apron and carries on a conversation with the fighter.

You're just a phase.

With a snarl, I tear off a right hook, making Luke wince.

"Easy!" He pulls off the mitts and flexes his fingers. "Take five. I gotta hit the head." He moves behind the equipment counter and disappears down the hallway.

My pulse throbs in my neck like Morse code as I march over to Bran and his new "friend." "Hey, who's this?"

"Oh! Bobby, this is Javier."

Up close, he looks even more pogi—and more ripped. He nods at me. "What's up, amigo?"

He seems friendly enough, which only makes my blood burn more. I scowl at him. "Wanna go a round?"

The fighter stares at me from above and blinks. "You serious, güey?"

"B, that doesn't sound like such a good idea."

I side-eye Bran. "Don't you have a bucket to empty?"

He jerks his head back. "Excuse me?"

Javier takes out his mouthpiece. "Yeah, I don't spar with amateurs." He moves toward the ropes, but before he can exit, I climb into the ring.

"Come on, dude. Let's see what you got." I slip in my mouthpiece and smack my gloves together. He has me on height, weight, experience, and probably every other category worth noting, but I don't care. I'm sick of bigger dudes thinking they can take whatever they want.

Javier mumbles something in Spanish to his trainer, who just shrugs. He hands the trainer his mouthpiece, not bothering to put it on. "Okay, cabrón." He motions with his glove. "I got time to give you a free lesson."

"Bobby," Bran says, "don't do this."

In a single stride, I bound over to Javier. I throw a wild

double jab, straight left combo. He easily slips away, untouched. Before I can reset, his glove smashes into my jaw. Not sure if it was his left or right. My shoulder slams into the canvas, and I roll over as white-hot pain blasts from my gums to my temple. Seconds pass, maybe minutes. It's all a haze of fogginess and lights.

"Bobby!" Bran says, beside me. "You okay?"

I want to scream at him to keep away from me, but my mouth is too busy throbbing to cooperate. I crawl out of the ring and stagger past a blurry image that I assume to be Luke.

"What the hell happened?" the blur says.

The next thing I know, I'm stumbling into the locker room, even though I don't quite remember the walk over.

Bran follows me in. "What the hell was that?"

I flop onto the bench and fumble with my glove straps. "Nothing. Forget it."

"Bobby, talk to me."

"Why don't you go talk to your new friend Javier?"

"What?"

"I saw you flirting with him."

"Seriously? I said like two words to him. I wasn't flirting, I was being polite!"

"Yeah, right!"

Bran folds his arms over his chest. "What's this really about? What are you not telling me?"

"Oh, you don't know? It's about you and me and where the hell are we going with this thing? It's about your dad keeping you on a short leash, always blowing up your celly when we're together! It's about me being some ghetto kid curiosity that you're just gonna toss aside when you get bored!"

"What are you . . . ? Where is all this coming from?"

"Your dad told me. That day at the pool. He said I was 'just a phase' to you."

Bran's eyes bulge. "And what, you actually believed him?"

"No. I . . . I don't know."

"Oh my God, Bobby! Of course he's going to say that! My dad can't see past his damn bank account!" Bran's eyes start to flood with tears. "And . . . and who cares what he says! He doesn't know how I feel about you." He wipes his tears with the back of his hand. "And I guess neither do you."

"Maybe I don't know. I mean, you can be really sweet, but sometimes you don't seem to care about what I need. For six months, you kept pressuring me to come out when I wasn't ready, and you weren't exactly supportive when you found out I was learning how to box. Not to mention, you keep wanting to buy me stuff when you know I'm not comfortable with it. Maybe your dad is right. Maybe we're just too different."

Bran opens his mouth, but no words come. His gaze finds the floor as he exhales sharply, and he storms out the back exit.

What did I just do? As if I don't have enough drama complicating my life, I have to create more between Bran and me. So fucking stupid.

On the trek back to MacArthur Park, I try calling Bran multiple times, but his phone goes straight to voicemail. I settle for sending him a half dozen texts of the "I'm a jerk and I'm sorry" variety. When I arrive home, I have no energy to shower or change out of my sweat-soaked clothes, so I stagger down the hallway and belly flop into bed.

I sleep, but far from peacefully. In my dreams, a faceless mob chases me through the moonlit streets of Los Angeles, and I flee toward Unidad Park—where I felt safe ages ago. But the barred fence is locked. No matter how hard I shake it, the gate refuses to open for me. The stark faces of the mural look on with indifference as shadowy figures collapse over me. I cry out, but my screams die in my throat, muted.

Three Days before the Fight

Tuesday morning. The chirp of the alarm drags me back to a reality that's even colder than my dreams. My clock reads 11:32 a.m. I've overslept again and missed my first three classes. I yawn, and a sharp pain shoots through my bruised jaw and snaps me fully awake. Note to self: *Never challenge Javier to a fight while in a fit of jealousy. Better yet, never challenge Javier to a fight.*

I fumble for my cell on my night table. Bran hasn't replied. The only messages are from Rosie, who's been wondering where I am.

With a groan, I stumble out of bed. I take an extra-long shower and change into my new Pacquiao T-shirt. Its crisp fabric scrapes over my skin like sandpaper.

My arm joints crack as I hop the fence onto school grounds, thankfully, during the middle of lunch. With all the students mingling outside, I blend in easily. I enter the quad, and Rosie shoots up from our table, phone in hand, and bolts over.

"You don't want to be out here right now," she says, her face a stone mask.

"What? Relax. Rex isn't gonna try anything—"

"Trust me on this." She hooks my arm with hers and drags me away. "We have to talk. Without any Charlotte Wilkeses around to poke their nosy snouts in our business."

We march through the grounds, all the way to our table in the library. Seeing our former hangout makes my eyelid twitch. If Rosie dragged me back here, whatever she has to tell me must be serious.

"What's going on? Why are we—"

"You need to see something. It's bad."

"How bad?"

She hands me her phone without another word.

A headline in bold font leaps off the screen like a panther and rips out my heart.

MANNY PACQUIAO PROVOKES STORM BY CALLING GAY PEOPLE WORSE THAN ANIMALS

I scan it again, then twice more. After the fifth time, I still don't believe it. I flop onto a chair and read the article. It says Manny made the comments during an interview to promote his candidacy for the Philippines senate.

"This is some bullshit, Rosie." I slide the phone across the table like it's infested. "Fake-ass news hating on Manny 'cause he's running for office. Whatever."

Swallowing, she snatches up the phone and swipes to a new screen. "There's video."

Rosie sets the device on the table in front of me. Offscreen, an interviewer asks Manny if he's for or against same-sex marriage. Manny chuckles and answers in Tagalog while subtitles translate. He explains that same-sex marriage is prohibited by the church, and women were created for men and vice versa. Not exactly a slogan for GLAAD, but Manny's a devout Christian, which is hardly breaking news.

The next part, however, sends me reeling harder than any body shot from Rex:

"It's common sense. Do you see animals mating with the same sex? Animals are better because they can distinguish male from female. If men mate with men and women mate with women, they are worse than animals."

With each word, my spirit wilts under the glare of Manny's bigotry. I can't believe it. I refuse to believe it. Manny would never say such hateful words. Not the champion I know. Not the man who saved Mom and me with his generosity when we were at our lowest. Except the proof in high-definition video says otherwise.

I replay the clip once more, and Manny seems to be speaking to me directly. Mocking me, shaming me. Not only me, but Brandon as well.

Rosie pats my shoulder and squeezes it. "You okay, B?"

"Yeah, considering I just found out my hero likes to spread homophobic propaganda in his free time, I'm good." I wince at the flippant remark. Rosie's only being my friend. I grab her hand. "I'll be okay."

"Rex knows. Him and his crew were having a good cackle about it."

Of course Rex knows. Because why would the universe make it any other way? And as always, I'm the last to know about anything going on in the world, which happens when you're too poor to afford a smartphone.

"I'll deal with it. Like always."

My eyes become moist, my breathing short and labored. Before any tears can make an appearance, I pull myself up and flee from the library.

As I walk down the path, I pull out my phone and type a text to Bran, then quickly delete it. He hasn't answered my last six texts, so why bother? Guess I can't blame him.

I tear up and sniffle as a group of sophomore girls strolls by, staring. Great, just what I need. As soon as I'm out of view, they'll text all their friends about the gay kid crying and being all hysterical. Head down, I dash into the restroom and release a drawn-out, throat-shredding scream. I barge into a stall and slam the door shut—twice.

So, my idol, Emmanuel Dapidran Pacquiao—winner of multiple world boxing titles and donator of free Thanksgiving turkeys—shares the same backward beliefs as my worst enemy. His words were so filled with contempt, Rex may as well have been the one in the clip. How is this the same man who's shown the world so much kindness? The same man who went out of his way to be merciful to opponents in the ring?

I can't fathom this.

From my sitting position, all of the graffiti on the stall door is laid out before me. Dirty jokes and gang tags occupy space alongside racial slurs about every group on campus. My gaze drops. My shoulders follow. I can't find an escape anywhere. Sometimes it seems like the whole world is fueled by hatred.

I bolt from the stall and spend the remainder of lunch hiding in the shadows behind the gymnasium. School can't end soon enough. I need to get to the Jab Gym and hit something. Hard.

ROUND 24

With a fury I've never unleashed before, my fists smash into the heavy bag like a pair of pile drivers. The chain rattles in protest. And then it happens. In my mind's eye, Manny Pacquiao's visage materializes. Before, I'd only see Rex as my opponent—not only as a physical obstacle to defeat, but the homophobic mindset he represents. Now Manny is the face of that mentality. My punches turn harder, fiercer.

"Easy!" Luke calls from his foldout chair against the wall. He takes a bite from an ube mamón cake. "Don't hit it hard, hit it right."

His coaching is sound, reasonable, but I'm not in the mood for reason or a lesson in proper punching technique.

I pause in between punches as Bran walks by, wielding a glass cleaner and a rag. Wow. He still came to help out, even after my cringey behavior with Javier. Bran really is the best.

I wave to him.

Surprisingly, he nods back. Well, it's a start.

"Okay, let's hit the ring." Luke rises slowly from his perch and finishes off the sponge cake. "Get your headgear on."

Vicki and I spar again in the squared circle, but this time I set the pace. I'm all over her, attacking from multiple angles, fueled by Manny's betrayal even as I mimic his trademark tactics. Vicki's glove shoots by my ear. I barely duck under it. I spring up with a left uppercut that staggers her.

Luke pipes in with his whistle, signaling the break. Vicki pounds my glove with her own. As I pad back to my corner, Brandon gives me a thumbs-up from outside the ring. I give him a tentative smile in return. Baby steps.

"Easy," Luke says, offering me water. "Got yourself an audience." He jerks his head at Rex over at the heavy bag station.

From a slouched stance, Rex barely grazes the bag. When we make eye contact, he flinches and turns away. Could be he's come to the realization that this fight won't be the usual easy ass-kicking. Good. Maybe it's not sound strategy, but I'm done hiding who I am.

In more ways than one.

At closing time, I find Rex in the locker room, sitting on the bench in his street clothes, stuffing gear into his pack. My stride stalls, but I force myself to enter.

"You got some skills, Agbayani. And a mean left. I'm almost impressed." He jams his gloves into the bag as if they're responsible for his lackluster workout. "'Course I ain't no girl, and we ain't gonna be sparring come Friday."

"You wish you could box like Vicki. She'd take you apart inside two rounds."

"Uh-uh. Maybe if we were in a bullshit girl-power movie. And who said I was gonna box you, fool? I'm just gonna pound your face into a whole new shape."

The threat makes me quiver, try as I might to hide it. "You

don't know what you're talking about." My words sound weak, hollow, and only fuel Rex's verbal attack.

"Nah, kid. You're the one got it twisted." Rex rises and steps to within two feet of me, hovering like a drill sergeant. I try to meet his gaze, but I swallow and take a step back. "I heard what your hero Pacman said. Manny ain't down for your faggoty bullshit either. He says queers are worse than animals, and I'm right there with him. You and your boyfriend be living in mortal sin, and Manny and me gonna teach you some straight gospel. The hard way. So what I'm wondering is, why you rockin' that Pacquiao tee when he clearly ain't on your team? Think on that, pare."

I eye the crucifix hanging from his neck. I want to yank it off him and shout in his face that he's a hypocrite and a bully who hides behind his religion.

But I don't.

All my training, all my preparation is forgotten, and I'm reduced to the helpless kid that Rex beat bloody in a grassy field. He sniggers and struts from the locker room, leaving me shaking. I stumble backward onto the bench.

The squeak of rusty wheels announces Brandon's presence as he rolls Hank into the room.

"You hear all that?" I ask.

"Just the tail end." He sits beside me and takes my hand. "Forget about it, B. That asshole doesn't know what he's foaming at the mouth about. Girl-power movies are awesome."

I try to think of a witty reply, but my shoulders start to tremble. "I . . . I don't think I can do this, Bran. I don't think I can beat him."

"Hey, look at me," he says. I turn my head toward him. "You stood up to him. That means you already have."

He means well. His words are sweet, but words will not stop Rex in the ring or keep me from getting hurt—maybe permanently.

"He's right about one thing." I tug on the Pacquiao shirt. "Why am I still wearing this thing?"

"Well, maybe you don't want to believe that someone you looked up to—someone you saw as a good, decent person— could be so intolerant." He squeezes my hand, offering a half smile. "Or maybe you just don't want to get rid of such a thoughtful present from an amazing guy."

I return the smile, but it quickly fades. "Maybe I'm overreacting here. It's not like Manny goes around beating up queer people to a pulp. He's just following what he read in the Bible. What he believes to be true. At least he's not as bad as Rex."

"No, he's not." Bran shakes his head. "Manny is worse. Way worse."

"What? Come on, for real?"

"Manny isn't just some punk-bully nobody. He's probably the greatest boxer of his generation, yeah? The most famous Pinoy on planet Earth with influence over millions of fans. How many Rexes did he create with that interview? How many little kids are going to think we're no better than animals? That we can be *treated* worse than animals?"

I don't answer at first. Maybe because Brandon is right and I don't want to admit it. "I guess. I don't know," is all I manage.

Bran touches my chin and tilts my head toward him. "Well, this is what I know, Bobby Agbayani. I love you. I love *you*. I can feel it under my skin whenever I see you after we've been apart too long. I feel it in my chest when you step in the ring and get punched one too many times. And I know it in my heart that you make me a better, braver person when we're together. And anyone who thinks the love I have for you is evil . . . well, they don't have the heart to understand what love is really about. Also, they can kiss my queer brown ass."

Laughter bursts from us. It's cathartic. God, Bran is so cute when he acts tough.

When our laughs peter out, I take his hand in mine. "Thanks for still helping out today even after I was a jealous ass. And I'm sorry. I mean, about your dad. You're right. It doesn't matter what he says."

"Yeah, it really doesn't." He nudges me with his shoulder. "I still yelled at him, though. Then my mom joined in when she heard about what he'd said to you. My dad was a cowering mess—he looked like one of his dental patients. It was kind of fun."

"Wish I could've seen that."

"And hey, I'm sorry about everything too. I'll try to be more sensitive about your needs and what you're going through. I'll even let you pay most of the time."

I laugh. "Well, we don't have to go that far."

Bran leans over and sinks his lips into mine. For a long while we sit together, the only sound the rumble of rusty pipes. Maybe we won't last forever like in some fairy tale, but I know that what we have right now is real. And nobody can take that from us. Not his dad, not Rex, not Manny. Nobody.

When we rise to leave, I fling off the Pacman tee in one motion. I pull my hoodie from my bag and slip it on. On our way out, I toss the crisp new Pacquiao shirt into Hank's trash bin.

ROUND 25
Two Days before the Fight

"What?" I ask Rosie as my fists work the speed bag.

From a foldout chair against the wall, she waves her phone at me. "I said, more news on the Manny front. Do you want to hear?"

"I dunno. Do I?" Ever since the news of Manny's comments hit the internet, she's been updating me on new developments. Last night she woke me with a text at two in the morning to tell me that Manny had apologized on Instagram. Well, it wasn't much of an apology, actually. He did say he was wrong for comparing gays to animals, but he also doubled down on his beliefs by quoting Corinthians:

> *"Or do you not know that wrongdoers will not inherit the kingdom of God? Do not be deceived: Neither the sexually immoral nor idolaters nor adulterers nor men who have sex with men."*

Basically Manny's saying he's sorry for upsetting queer folk, but we're all still going to hell. Nice.

"Pacman lost his Nike endorsement," Rosie shouts. "Yep, dumped his butt quick style."

A part of me is heartbroken by the news. Manny worked

hard to gain such a major sponsorship, and to lose it in the span of a day has to be a crushing blow for him. But another part knows he had this coming. Millions of Nike consumers support LGBTQ+ rights, so there's no surprise the sports giant does not want to be associated with an athlete who spreads antigay bullshit.

Still, I can't help feeling sorry for Manny, and I'm pissed at myself because of it.

Before Luke calls time, I end the speed-bag session with a lackluster follow-through.

Luke clicks his stopwatch. "You okay, kid? We still got a few more sets."

I wave him off and head to the locker room, only Bran—sweeping up around the ring—cuts off my path with a push broom.

"Hey," he says, "don't lose focus, okay? Not now. Not so close to the fight."

"Come on, Bran. You saw that so-called apology Manny posted."

"Yeah, I did. All the more reason to get your butt back in there and train. Do the X-Men cancel a Danger Room session when some mutant-hating big bad attacks them in the press? No. Now get back in there and hit that bag like it's Rex's fat head."

A chuckle breaks through my dour mood. Bran always knows how to make me laugh when I need it most. "Okay, but you need to take your turn at the bag too."

"What? Uh, I don't know about that."

"Come on. You said you wanted to learn to fight. And I'm not gonna be around to always protect your pogi butt."

He gives me a lopsided smile. "Whatever." But his eyes zero in on a pair of fighters sparring, and he nods. "All right. Yeah. Let's do it."

Bran ditches the broom, and I find him some gloves behind the counter. While I get back to work on the speed bag, Luke goes over basic striking technique with Bran on the heavy one. After Bran's first few attempts, he grimaces, pulling his hand back in pain. Funny how, not two weeks ago, I was where he is, barely able to throw a punch without hurting myself.

When I finish my workout, the place is nearly empty. Despite being on the floor for most of the night, I haven't seen Rex since our confrontation in the locker room. He probably thinks he's ready and has had enough training.

Wish I were that confident.

One Day before the Fight

Rosie's Manny Watch continues Thursday at lunch. While I sort through the mini landfill of my locker, she materializes beside me. Without bothering to ask if I want to know the latest, she reads aloud from another article.

"*Hours after losing his Nike endorsement, boxer Manny Pacquiao published an Instagram post that quoted verses from the Bible with more antigay sentiment.*"

"Rosie, I happen to have this thing tomorrow. No big, just, y'know, the fight of my life. Trying to focus here. I get it, okay? Manny won't ever be grand marshal at the Pride parade."

"Oh, no, you need to hear this." She swipes her phone screen. "Dude quoted the Bible again. '*Leviticus: If a man has sexual relations with a man as one does with a woman, both of them have done what is detestable. They are to be put to death; their blood will be on their own heads.'"* She lowers the phone. "Seriously? *'Put to death'*? Can you believe this bullshit?"

No, I can't. I can't believe it. I don't want to believe it. I snatch Rosie's phone and see the proof for myself. The post includes a photo of Manny and his wife, Jinkee, along with the quote. Any religious nutjob could read it and feel justified in going on a killing spree. But, hey, as long as it's from the Bible it's okay, right?

Too much has happened in too short a time. I want to punch the lockers, but injuring my hand right before the fight wouldn't be the smartest.

"Why'd you have to show me this, Rosie? Damn!"

"Hey, I get why you're pissed, but don't be yelling at me. You're the one who worships the damn homophobe."

Before I can retort, a voice cuts in. "Is there a problem here, Mr. Agbayani? Ms. Sanchez?" Principal Peterson says, alternating his glare between us.

"No, not at all, sir," I say, even though I want to tell him the problem is him sticking his hairy mug into our business.

"Good to know." He steps closer to us. His muttonchops hover too close, a pair of hairy pincers about to snatch my nose. "Have either of you heard rumors of students participating in some sort of rumble tomorrow night?"

Rosie and I steal a glance at each other. Did he really just say *rumble*? As in switchblades and hair grease? *How old is this dude?*

"Uh, no, sir, we haven't," I say. "But, um, I have heard there's a completely safe boxing match of no more than three rounds happening at a fully sanctioned boxing gym."

"Really now? So this boxing match is in no way happening on school grounds?"

"Nope," Rosie says. "I mean, not that we know of."

"Good to know." Peterson passes us but stops and looks back over his shoulder. "Oh, and Agbayani? Good luck tomorrow night." He smirks and strides down the hallway.

"Wow," Rosie says. "Even Peterson wants you to win."

"He's probably just sick of seeing Rex in his office."

Aside from the typical haters and hecklers ready with prefight predictions of my doom, the rest of the day passes uneventfully. Bran meets me in the parking lot after school to give me a ride so I don't have to jog to the gym. Good thing too. I'll need all the energy I can muster. I'm sure Luke is going to put me through the wringer for our last training session before fight night.

"I said take the night off."

Decked out in full ring attire, I follow Luke out of his office and onto the main floor. The gym is packed with not only the regulars, but a good number of new members. Apparently my grudge match with Rex has had an impact on membership.

"Come on, just work the mitts with me a few rounds."

"You're ready, okay? Get out of here. Rest up. Save it for tomorrow." He gestures at Brandon, sweeping up by the ring. "And take your guy with you."

"Sweet," Bran says, placing the broom on Hank. "Thanks, boss man."

"You're welcome. And don't ever call me that again or you're fired."

"You know you don't actually pay me."

"And yet you drive a BMW."

"Yeah, I do!" Bran salutes him and practically sprints to the locker room.

"Vicki, couple rounds?" I ask.

She takes a break from slugging away at the wrecking ball bag. "You heard the man. Get on out of here. You were ready a few days ago when you rocked me with that sick uppercut. Just promise me you'll inflict ten times worse on that Neanderthal."

"Done." I bump gloves with her. "And thanks, you warrior badass." She gives me a sweat-drenched hug.

On my way to the locker room, I do a double take as I approach a heavy bag station. Flat footed in front of the bag stands a familiar teen with spiky blond hair: the underclassman that was beat up in the school quad, way back on Bran's and my anniversary. Wow, did he join the gym because of me?

The kid throws an off-balance punch and winces on impact. His technique—or lack of it—sorely needs work.

He waves at me shyly. "Hey, Bobby, right? Um, good luck tomorrow night. I'm rooting for you."

"Thanks, um?"

"Jason."

I nod and continue on. Before I take three steps, I make a U-turn back to the bag and drop into fighting stance.

"You're hitting it with the top of your fist," I say. "Gonna hurt your wrists. Hit it with the front. Watch." I fire off a jab and a straight left. "Try it. And hit the bag dead center."

He attempts to follow my directions, but his first few tries are sloppy, weak. The bag spins off to the side.

"Again," I say.

He throws another combo, which lacks power. "Ow," he says, grimacing. "Not sure if that helped."

"You trying to steal my job, youngblood?" Luke pads over, shaking his head. "Leave the coaching to the ones who know."

"Okay, okay," I say, lifting my hands, laughing. "Listen to this guy, Jason." I head toward the locker room. Kid has a long way to go, but so did I. Hell, I *still* do.

While we change back into civvies, Bran and I get a text from Rosie inviting us to come over to her house for dinner.

"Oh, yes, please." Brandon says, then texts that exact reply.

On the drive over, he pushes his BMW ten miles over the speed limit because he hasn't eaten since breakfast. With all of their late-night comic-creator sessions, Mr. Sanchez has become Bran's favorite cook—a fact he'll never divulge to his mom.

We feast on homemade tamales courtesy of Mr. Sanchez. I'm tempted enough to split a chicken and corn with Brandon. My taste buds tingle as I savor the moist corn masa and juicy meat. I'd forgotten the pure joy of eating just for pleasure.

The dinner conversation is chill with nary a word about boxing, which is exactly what I need right now. Bran and I talk comic books with Mr. Sanchez, a huge Deadpool fan. Rosie joins in, mostly because she loves Ryan Reynolds. Or more accurately, she loves Ryan Reynolds's abs. Hell, who doesn't? And so dinner becomes the first official meeting of the Ryan Reynolds's Abs Tribute Society, also known as RRATS.

Rosie interjects half a dozen times with what becomes the group's official slogan: "Woo-hoo! Ryan Reynolds's abs!" So we name her Commissioner of Abs Spirit.

As everyone, aside from me, gorges themselves on a dessert of flan and vanilla bean ice cream, I ask, "So do I get a sneak peek at the zombie epic to end all zombie epics?"

"No can do, B," Rosie replies. "For that, you'll have to come to the big unveiling on Sunday."

"Boo. Hiss."

"But we do have something else fairly awesome to show you." She rises and leads Bran and me to her bedroom.

Whenever I visit Rosie's room, I'm always reminded how devoted she is to her craft. Art supplies occupy every square foot of the tiny space. Paint bottles and tubes—both oils and acrylics—line her shelves. Paintings and pastel drawings of her own creation, mostly of people from the neighborhood, decorate the walls: the hefty mailman making his rounds, the elderly lady observing the comings and goings from her stoop, as well as Mr. Sanchez preparing a dish in the kitchen. Each piece brings out the vibrancy and immediacy of its subject more than any photograph could. Damn, my girl is talented.

On her study desk sits a tray of markers of various colors and sizes. I snag a red, a green, and a thick black one. I pull the cap off the black; the tip is nearly an inch wide. Perfect.

"Hey, can I borrow these? Got a couple art projects of my own."

She frowns. "Uh, sure, I got plenty."

"Salamat po," I say, thanking her in Tagalog. I pocket the markers.

In the corner, an easel holds Rosie's latest work: a charcoal drawing of Vicki and me sparring in the ring. I lean over for a closer view of the details. Rosie's even taken care to show the sweat glistening on our gloves.

"Oh, damn. This is amazing, Rosie."

"Thanks, but it's for Vicki. She requested a Rosie Sanchez original. Paid gig and everything." She motions to her bed. "This over here . . . this is for you."

Laid out on the bed is a black T-shirt. On the front, air-brushed in red-blue-and-yellow block letters, are my initials, B.A., linked like a sports team's logo. The colors of the Philippine flag blend together like a graffiti art piece.

"Oh, wow. This is straight fire, Rosie. This is the Human Torch going full-on supernova."

"Ay, peep the back." She flips the shirt over. At the top it reads, BOBBY "THE TSUNAMI" AGBAYANI. The Philippine flag graces the middle part, but the red and blue have been replaced by the rainbow colors of the LGBTQ+ flag. The effect is graphically stunning.

"I . . . I can't believe you did this." I wrap her up in a bear hug, lifting her from the floor.

Brandon shuffles his feet. "Hey, I picked the flag colors."

"Figured you did," I say. Grinning, I pull Bran into a group hug. For once, none of us offer up a snarky remark, and we embrace each other like only the best of friends are allowed.

"I'm also making Team Agbayani shirts for all of us," Rosie says. "Even Luke and Vicki."

Bran pecks me on the cheek. "You know we got your back all the way, right? We're going to be cheering you on every second. I'll even be in your corner manning the spit bucket."

Rosie grimaces. "Yeah, I'll just be cheering you on."

"Good enough." A tear forms, but I wipe it before it can fall. Bran and Rosie are my fam, my kaibigan. For a fleeting moment, I pity Rex. I doubt he has anyone who cares about him the way these two amazing individuals care about me. They've got my back. Maybe tomorrow night Rex will beat me bloody, but in this moment, I am invincible.

ROUND 26
The Day of the Fight

My dad, Joseph Angeles Agbayani, passed away on a scorching August afternoon, the heat doing nothing to ease his suffering. He was in and out of consciousness, but I still read to him his favorite X-Men story from his childhood collection: *God Loves, Man Kills.* His eyes were alert as I described the ending battle.

The last coherent words he spoke to me were "I'm ready . . . I am." To this day, I don't believe he'd given up. He was just ready to move on past the pain and uncertainty to whatever came next in this great adventure.

Today is my what-comes-next—only I'm not sure I'm ready.

I sit in classroom after classroom, staring at the jabbering teeth and tongues up front, and retain nothing. People speak to me; I look through them. Whether they offer support or spit hate, I barely notice. The whole day, I manage to avoid being in Rex's presence, but he's always with me. Like a wart.

Time to remove it.

The buzz on campus is palpable. Rosie says even the faculty is talking about the fight, pulling for me. Win or lose, practically everyone I know will be there to witness it. No pressure.

After school, Rosie and I catch a ride with Bran over to the Jab Gym. They both sport their Team Agbayani shirts, and I'm in my custom-made "Tsunami" one. I feel almost like a super-hero breaking in a new costume for the first time, with all the uncertainty that comes with it.

We arrive a little after four. Luke's closed the gym in preparation for the fight, which is scheduled to pop off at six. Brandon and Rosie help a few regulars set up dozens of chairs around the main ring while Luke and I get ready in the locker room. Rex and his crew take the women's side, which I'm sure has the misogynists in them thrilled.

"Mind if I do your wraps?" Luke asks. "Was sort of a tradition with me and my boy."

"Sure." I sit on the bench, and he pulls up a folding chair. "Wrap away."

He exhales slowly, unrolls the cloth, and sets to the task. "Okay, remember now, he's gonna try to take you out early with a bunch of haymakers. Let him tire himself out trying. You're too fast for him. You're gonna slip and counter, slip and counter, just like Man—" He nearly mentions He Who Must Not Be Named but catches himself and coughs. "Uh . . . and always, *always* keep your guard up."

He reviews more strategy, taking me through each step of our game plan, his tone confident and reassuring. If Luke believes in me, maybe I have a chance. Maybe I can actually win this. When he tucks in the final strap, he asks, "How's that feel now?"

The wraps are tighter, crisper than I could ever manage. "Good," I say, throwing a playful combination in his direction.

"Oh, you think you can take me on, youngblood?" He

throws a quick one-two of his own. "Aw, yeah, old-timer still got some skills."

"Yeah, you do." I swallow and lick my lips. "Hey, Luke. Thanks for all this. I, well . . . none of this would be happening without you."

"No, kid, thank *you*." He pounds my fist with his own.

Rosie marches in, her game face on. "Yo, old-timer. You ready?"

Luke's joints crack as he takes his time rising. "Let's do it."

"What?" I say. "Where you guys going?"

Rosie pounds her fist into her hand. "Gotta supervise the opposition. I don't trust that punk to not slip something in his gloves."

"Ah. Smart." Good old Rosie. I guess sometimes her paranoia does come in handy.

"Loosen up with some shadowboxing." Luke follows her out. "We'll strap the gloves on when I get back."

When they're gone, I get in some throws at the mirror. No more thought, no anger, no fear. Just muscle memory and movement.

"Who knew this place could hold so many?" Bran practically skips in. "Listen to that crowd. The gym is jumping."

I close my eyes, and the buzz from the gym floor surges through me, powers me.

Bran approaches as I finish up a final combo. "Looking good, B. Staying hydrated?"

"Right." I take a sip from my water bottle. "Did Rex bring my bike?"

"Surprisingly, yes. It's right against the ring post. Jerk actually followed through."

A double knock comes at the back exit.

Bran knits his brow, motions for me to stay put, and inches up to the metal door. He peers into the peephole. "It's Jorge," he tells me. "Hey, man, what's up?" Bran asks him through the door. "What do you need?"

"Gotta talk to your boy" comes the muffled reply. "It's important, güey. Concerns Rex. He up to something real shady."

"Sounds urgent," Bran says to me. "You should probably hear him out."

What could Jorge possibly have to tell me, especially so close to the fight? I don't need any distractions, but if Rex is about to pull something underhanded . . . "Yeah, you're right. Let him in."

The clang of metal jolts me to attention as Brandon pulls back the bolt and swings open the heavy door. Sunlight pours in, throwing Jorge's shadow across the floor. He limps into the room, revealing a battered visage. Purple and blue frame his swollen eyes, and red accents his cracked lips. My face burns hot.

"What happened?" I pull a chair out at the table and he falls into it. "Rex do this?"

He winces. "Dude's loco. Him and Eddie. Punk asses jumped me after school. Heard I been talking to you."

I take a seat at the table beside him. "This is so messed up." As if I needed any more motivation to put a hurt on Rex.

"You said he was up to something?" Brandon asks.

Tears well up in Jorge's eyes, and his breaths turn rapid. "I . . . I can't . . . can't do this."

I squeeze his shoulder. "Hey, it's okay. In about ten minutes, Rex is gonna answer for what he's done to you, along with all the other crap he's pulled. I promise you."

Jorge dabs at the tears with his sleeve and winces on contact. "All right, then."

He holds out his fist, and I stick mine out to bump it. He grabs my forearm with one hand and with the other, he pulls out his balisong. A flick of his wrist whips the knife open. Before I can react, Jorge slams the blade down on my left palm, stabs through the wrap, puncturing skin. Blood squirts from the wound. I cry out and spring up from the chair.

"Bobby!" Brandon dashes between us and shoves Jorge aside. "Back off!" he screams. He quickly scans the room, pulls my towel off the bench, and wraps my blood-soaked hand.

Pain shoots out from my throbbing palm. My pulse thumps like a jungle drum.

"I'm sorry!" Jorge says from the corner, whimpering. "Rex. Eddie. They made me. They wouldn't let up." The knife clatters to the floor, and he grabs the back of his head with both hands. His face morphs into a mask of horror and regret. "I can't take another beatdown. I can't." He dashes out the exit.

"Jorge!" I scream, but he's gone.

The door slams shut like a guillotine. Luke and Rosie bolt into the room.

Rosie flinches when she sees my blood-soaked palm. "What the hell happened?"

"Jorge," Brandon says. "Rex put him up to it."

"I knew that pendejo was shady! I knew it!"

Not wasting time, Luke peels back the drenched towel and examines my hand. I wince. The wound is deep and about an inch wide. I try to make a fist, but my fingers barely curl before the pain stops me.

He rewraps the towel, tightening the pressure. "This . . . this is bad."

My eyes well up. "No, Luke. Don't."

"You can't fight like this. You can't protect yourself."

"No! I can't back out now. Not with everyone out there waiting!"

Bran touches my shoulder. "B, we need to get you to the hospital."

"Brandon, please!" I shout. He takes a step back. "Luke, come on, I can hold him off with my jab."

"And your left? Forget about punching, you can't even lift it. Listen, kid, I've never said anything like this before 'cause I ain't never seen someone like *you* before, but you are straight-up gifted. A natural. You learned moves in a couple weeks some fighters can't do after years in the ring. You . . . you can't let this punk jeopardize that. *I* can't let you." He drops his gaze. "I gotta call it off."

"I still got my right hook. Please just patch me up. I can do this!"

"No, you can't. You gotta listen to me. My job is to protect you, Ray!" Luke stiffens at his slip, his cheeks flash deep purple. My own turn warm as well.

I want to tell him I'm not his son, and my real dad is long

226

gone. All I can depend on is myself. I don't even have Manny in my corner anymore. If I ever did. I open my mouth, but the words stall, dying like my chances of ever settling the score with Rex.

Luke turns away. The rumble from the crowd grows louder in his silence. His shoulders drop. "I'm sorry."

As he rises, I grab on to him with my good hand, but he pulls away. "Luke, don't! Luke!"

Rosie crouches down to my eye level. "Bobby, this completely sucks, yeah, but he's right." Her words are just white noise blending in with the buzz of the crowd.

Luke trudges out, and Rosie follows on his heels. A minute later, his muffled voice crackles over the sound system, his words barely intelligible from the back. He attempts to explain what happened, even accuses Rex of foul play, but a cacophony of boos follows. The crowd chants Rex's name. Each time is a thunderclap to my psyche. The uproar mocks my hard work and preparation—which apparently were all for nothing.

Brandon sits beside me and brings me under his arm. I lean into him. "Come on, B. Let's get you out of here." He pulls me up.

I don't resist.

ROUND 27

Bran speeds through Friday-night traffic en route to the nearest urgent care, a few miles over in Chinatown. He blasts his horn, dodging a VW Bug that nearly clips us. I should be the one dodging. Dodging, bobbing, punching. Maybe even winning.

Hell, forget about winning. I'd have to get into the ring first, and I couldn't even do that. Right now I'd settle for landing a few decent jabs before suffering a devastating knockout. At least then I could say I showed up, gave it an honest try, lost with dignity, blah, blah.

But now I'm just a quitter. A punch line. *Gay guy walks into a boxing gym . . .*

I'm not just a joke, I'm gullible as hell. Did Rex plan this from the beginning? Get his lackey to gain my trust then spring his trap when I'm focused on the fight? How could I have fallen for Jorge's act?

No. No way he can be that good of an actor. He was genuinely distraught about stabbing me. Well, good for him. His remorse does my throbbing hand and ruined reputation a lot of good.

While Bran and I sit in the waiting room, neither of us brings up how I'm going to pay for this. We both know that I'm flat broke with no insurance, and he'll have to cover it. I'm just glad he doesn't mention it.

I try to remember the last time I was treated in an actual hospital. Probably when Dad took me to the ER after I broke my arm falling off a jungle gym. Thoughts of him loosen the knots in my shoulders and stomach and for a moment keep my mind off the night's spectacular humiliation, which will haunt me and my children long after I depart this evil, duplicitous world.

Beside me, Bran sniffles and wipes his nose with his jacket sleeve. Wait, is he crying?

"This is my fault," he says.

"What?"

"I shouldn't have let Jorge inside. Shouldn't have pushed you to trust him. Rosie . . . she was right. God, I'm so stupid sometimes!"

For a long moment, I say nothing. *Has Bran influenced me that much?* Maybe, but there are worse people to emulate. Okay, so he might be a little naive. But he has an open heart, and if he's helped me become more trusting, that has to be a positive. With my good hand, I squeeze his arm. "You're not the one who cut me, okay? This ain't on you."

"I guess." He shrugs and slouches back in his seat.

"Hey, I don't blame you, okay? At all."

Bran manages a hint of a smile. "Okay."

Nearly an hour passes before we're finally brought to an examination room. The room is, of course, spotless and carries the strong scent of disinfectant, which reminds me of my cleaning supplies at the Jab Gym—which then reminds me about Rex. I crumple the paper covering the examination table. By the time the doctor arrives, I've ripped off half of it.

The doctor enters, a fit, bespectacled Indian woman who looks young enough that the ink on her medical school diploma could still be drying. She introduces herself as Dr. Varma and gets right down to examining my hand. She decides the first order of business is to numb the pain with an injection of a drug she calls lidocaine. I like her already.

"So how'd you manage this bit of nastiness?" Doc Varma asks as she cleans my wound with sterile water from a needle.

I try to think of an answer that doesn't involve ambush by stabbing.

"Oh, he was slicing a tomato," Brandon says, avoiding eye contact with her. "It's our anniversary, and he was making me lasagna."

"Ah. Well then, happy anniversary to you both," the doc says, smiling. "So tell me, do you always cook with boxing straps on?" She nods to my right hand, still wrapped.

Bran looks away and doesn't elaborate on his not-so-well-thought-out cooking tale.

"Yeah, it, uh, beats pot holders." I shut my eyes, hoping she'll drop the interrogation.

"I see." She takes the hint and sutures the wound in silence.

After I've been cleared to leave, at the checkout desk, my gaze clings to the floor as Bran hands over his credit card and pays for the visit. I don't bother protesting. I need to get over him having money. Right now I'm damn fortunate that he does.

"Thanks," I say to him.

"Don't worry about it."

On the drive home, Brandon asks me for the millionth time if I'm okay, and I respond for the millionth time with a nod. What's the point of words? Words only lead to tears. And I'm tired of crying.

Brandon pulls up to my complex and keeps the engine humming.

"Gonna need some time, okay?" It's the first sentence I've uttered since the hospital. Without waiting for a reply, I exit the car and dash through the complex gate.

Light seeps out from the bottom crack of our door. Mom is home. I slip into the hallway and shoot for my room, but she calls out to me. Her voice and the tangy aroma of chicken adobo lead me into the kitchen.

"Hi. How was work?" She spoons rice from the cooker into a bowl. "Hungry?" She plops a drumstick in, tops it off with a scoop of sauce, and hands me the bowl.

I take it with my right hand, making sure I keep my bandaged one hidden in my hoodie pocket. "Thanks."

We eat together, the first meal we've shared since this whole drama unraveled—the drama I've completely kept from her. The food is tasty, but does little to comfort me, and it only makes the guilt tear away at me more. I want to tell her everything, vomit it all out like a demon being exorcised. But I can't. Rex, the beatdown, my locker, Jorge, the botched fight, Dad's bike—it's all too much. And she can't help me, anyway.

Tears spill out. I swipe at them with my sleeve, but one escapes and trickles down over my chin.

"Bobby? What's wrong?"

"Nothing. I'm okay." I wipe my nose. "Hey, you remember when we walked all the way to Lake Street Park? That time we got a free Thanksgiving turkey? From uh ... Manny Pacquiao?" It's the first time I've said his full name since the news broke. I can barely sputter it out; my enunciation leaves something to be desired.

"Oh, wow. Feels like forever and a week." She brings her cup to her mouth and sips as she reflects. "I remember you were all smiles playing with the other kids. And your laugh ... like a melody. You were so happy that day."

"Well, yeah, we got us a big honking turkey and met the champ of the world." Tears stream over my cheeks, and I don't try to hide them. "Great day. Perfect day."

Mom squeezes my arm. "I heard what Pacquiao said, dear. I'm so sorry." She rises and wraps her arms around me. "You know, just because someone's famous doesn't mean they're talking sense. You don't pay attention to any of that tanga bullshit. You are *my* champion, anak. Hear me?"

"Okay." I hold on to her like I'm nine years old again. "It's just hard to believe Manny actually believes those things, y'know? I ... I looked up to him so much and now ..."

"And you can still admire him for what he's accomplished and all the good he's done. Doesn't mean you have to agree with him or like everything about him. Everyone has their faults, Bobby. Everyone has contradictions."

"Yeah, I guess so."

She seems to make sense, but I'm not so sure. I don't know if I can ever forgive Manny or look past what he said. Does he even care about all the people he's hurt with his words? Is he sorry? I wish I knew.

I remember what he said to Oscar De La Hoya after their lopsided fight: *You're still my idol.*

Is Manny still mine?

I spend Saturday morning writing tanagas, which I haven't done in far too long. Strictly pen and paper, no texts. The words and rhymes tumble out of me four lines and twenty-eight syllables at a time, and I start to feel like myself again. Punching something isn't the only way I can get my aggression out.

The poems are, admittedly, far from my best. They mostly consist of twenty-eight syllables of various revenge scenarios I want to unleash upon Rex, as well as some good old-fashioned shit-talking.

> *Christians are kind, are they not?*
> *But in hell, your soul will rot*
> *You will not escape the void*
> *Go pop another steroid*

One poem is slightly repetitive:

> *Die, Rex, die! Painfully, please!*
> *Die, Rex, die! Painfully, please!*
> *Die, Rex, die! Painfully, please!*
> *Die, Rex, die! Painfully, please!*

I won't be posting that one on Instagram.

Mom has a rare morning off, so she whips us up some ube puto cake for breakfast. It's the first ube treat I've had in weeks, and every bite is a drool parade in my mouth. *I will never forsake you again, sweet purple yam.*

Brandon texts to check up on me and ask if I'm going to the Jab Gym this weekend; he started working back at the comic shop, so Luke needs the help.

I reply, I don't know. I don't think so.

After the embarrassment of "the fight that didn't happen," I can't see myself ever stepping back in the Jab Gym. The idea of pushing a broom around while real fighters train will only serve to remind me that I couldn't step inside the ring when it mattered most. No, thank you.

Plus, I know Luke was only looking out for me, but he should've let me at least try to fight. The worst that could've happened was I'd lose. Now I'll never know.

Bran texts back, All right. See you tomorrow?

Crap. Tomorrow the comic book contest winners will be announced at the Villain's Lair. I nearly forgot, what with my hand getting skewered and me being publicly humiliated. I reply, Of course. I'll be there.

On Sunday afternoon, I jog to the Villain's Lair. Not how I was hoping to get around after Friday, but I'm used to it. Plus the run helps me clear my head somewhat. I have a half mile to go when Bran texts me: Announcing results soon. Still coming? I text back and quicken my pace.

When I enter the shop, it's filled to capacity with aspiring comic book creators and their supporters. The sight reminds me of how packed the Jab Gym was on the night of the fight that never was. How many of these people were there and are now judging me?

To add to my lovely anxiety, Bran's parents stand at the back of the room. They both read through what I assume to be Bran and Rosie's comic book entry. The more Mrs. Elpusan reads, the more her smile beams wider. Mr. Elpusan, on the other hand, has a constipated look of disapproval—the one he usually reserves for me.

Mrs. Elpusan spots me and waves, motioning for me to come over. I wave back but move away from them. I'll play nice for the sake of Bran and his big moment, but the last person I want to converse with is Mr. You're Just a Phase Stick up His Ass.

Near the cashier counter, Bran and Rosie chat with some fans while Mr. Sanchez looks on proudly. I wade through the crowd over to their side and wait until they're finished talking.

"There he is!" Mr. Sanchez says to me. I wave at him.

Rosie goes in for a hug, making sure not to bump my injured hand. "Yeah, thanks for coming, B."

"Of course. Least I could do after you guys have been so amazing to me."

Before Bran can speak, his boss, Larry, quiets the gathering. "First I want to thank all our contestants who created such stellar work. Y'all are some comic book–creating superstars. Okay, let's get to the winners!"

I whisper to Bran, "Good luck."

He smiles and slips his hand into my good one. I let him. Nobody's paying attention to us, and the crowd is too compact for anyone to notice anyway. Larry announces the third-place winner to boisterous applause and holds up a vampire comic with lurid cover art.

Bran's mouth falls open. "So much gore. It . . . it's gorgeous."

"Down, boy," Rosie says with a smirk.

The contestant, a Black girl rocking a Blade T-shirt, acknowledges the cheers with a raised hand.

Larry clears his throat and waits for quiet. "And second prize goes to the Lair's very own Brandon Elpusan and his partner, Rosie Sanchez, for *Zombie Slayer Squad*!"

Rosie shrieks and wraps Bran in a bear hug. After all their fighting, them coming together like this is beautiful. My eyes get a bit misty. I hang back, not wanting to intrude on their well-earned moment. Rosie has other ideas; she pulls me into a group hug, and all three of us jump around and holler in celebration.

After Larry announces first place—a superhero/steampunk mash-up—Rosie leads Bran and me over to a shelf where the competing comics are displayed.

"Check it out, B!" Rosie says. Printed copies of my friends' original comic are stacked high for customers to purchase. She takes one from the pile and hands it to me.

The artwork and coloring are dynamic and expressive, almost too beautiful for the lurid genre. Rosie really outdid herself. Splashed across the top of the cover in oozing green letters, the title reads, ZOMBIE SLAYER SQUAD! Below it, a familiar Latina woman with orange hair takes on a horde of zombies.

"Hey, is that your mom?" I ask Rosie.

"Yep, and she's a badass zombie-slaying vegetarian! Take that, ya meat-eating freaks!"

I chuckle. "Nice. This is amazing, guys." I can't remember Rosie ever smiling so much. Her mom would be so proud of her. I squeeze Bran's arm and mouth, *Thank you.*

"That's not all. Look who makes a cameo." Bran opens the book near the middle and points at a character—who looks conspicuously like me—fighting off zombies in what looks to be a derelict boxing gym. Entrails are aplenty, hanging from zombie midsections and even draping from the ring ropes. Looks like Bran won that particular creative impasse.

"Wow. You guys didn't have to do this."

Bran shrugs. "Well, you did say no comic book heroes look like us, so . . ."

"Yeah," Rosie says, patting my back. "The world could use more queer Filipino boxer-slash-zombie-hunters."

My friends mean well, and the gesture is flattering, but after Friday night, I definitely don't deserve it. "This is great, but I'm no hero." I hand the comic to Bran. Unlike Rosie, I couldn't do right by my dad. The fact that his bike is forever lost to me still hurts badly.

"Bobby, come on—" Bran starts, but he's cut off by a customer asking him to sign his comic.

I slip away and wander through the shop, glancing at the comics lining the shelves—mostly out of habit. My skin turns clammy, and I flinch as I brush against customer after customer. My breaths quicken to gasps. I stumble toward the back area, slide behind the counter, and escape into the storage room.

Dozens of white boxes stuffed with old comic books line the shelves from floor to ceiling, reminding me of a blank canvas. Appropriate, since I feel like a bit of a blank right now.

I move to the break table—where Bran and I shared our first kiss.

Before Bran, I rarely visited the Lair. Browsing the comics racks isn't much fun when you have no cash to actually buy anything. But when he invited me to read old issues in the storeroom, I came back. At first, I didn't catch on that he just wanted to get me alone to kiss me. Two visits later, I let him.

My breath slows to normal. Despite being slightly claustrophobic, the storage room has always been a place of refuge for me. Usually, I'd take out a few comics and read, but this time I sit and just be.

A knock sounds at the door, and Bran enters. "Hey, you okay?"

I shrug. He sits down beside me, and we're quiet for a moment.

"Sorry," I say, "I know this is a big day for you. I'm really happy for you guys. And I love what you did. I just don't think I deserve it. I mean—"

"Shh, don't stress over it." With a strong, soothing touch, he squeezes my shoulders in a circular motion.

"Um, what are you doing?"

"I owe you a massage."

The tension in my neck and shoulders slowly melts away. "Oh, damn. There it is."

"Hey, you're really not going back to the Jab Gym?"

"So I can clean up after all the regulars while they clown me for punking out? I don't think so."

"Come on, your hand was gushing blood. You couldn't fight."

"I doubt anyone else sees it that way."

"Well, who cares what anyone else thinks? I thought the point of training was so you can defend yourself?"

He means well, and his argument makes sense, but I'm not in the mood for logic. "Look, after all that went down, the Jab Gym is the last place I want to be, okay?"

He studies me. The disappointment in his eyes makes me look away. "Yeah. Yeah, I get it."

"I need to get going." I rise, reenter the main store, and navigate through the crowd toward the front entrance.

"Bobby, wait up!" Bran calls from behind me. I ignore him and exit the store.

On the sidewalk, Bran's parents are huddled off to the side. Mr. Elpusan grips his son's comic book in one hand while gesturing with the other. "This is just a waste of the boy's talent!" he exclaims. "Bad enough he has to write these silly comics, but he has to fill them with all this bakla nonsense!"

"Tama na. Stop this now," Mrs. Elpusan snaps, scowling at her husband.

Brandon comes up to my side. He must have followed me out. "Dad?"

Mr. Elpusan's body freezes in place. He turns around, his cheeks and earlobes flashing hot crimson. Bran's head drops low, and he strides away from his father.

My gaze meets Mr. Elpusan's, this man who all this time was masking his bigotry while singling me out as "a phase." I throw him a smirk. "Guess the real phase was you pretending not to be a homophobic bully. *Sir.*"

I chase after Brandon and come up even with him. He wipes away a falling tear. I lace my fingers with his. No words are spoken. I squeeze his palm softly, and we walk through the streets of Silver Lake, hand in hand.

Monday arrives too quickly. The long walk of shame to first period is peppered with trolls testing my last nerve. Shouts of "Pussied out!" and "Faggot fail!" split my ears and make my skin burn. When I arrive in class, I notice my fists are clenched. Both of them.

Eric starts in on me as soon as I take my seat.

"Hey, pare. Why'd you punk out at the fight? Man, I hauled my ass all the way over to Echo Park to support."

"Uh, thanks? And I didn't punk out. Rex was the one who got shook and resorted to bullshit shady tactics."

"Yeah, sure, bruh. Whatever." He leans forward and hovers at my ear. "Yo, you do the home—"

"Do your own damn homework," I say. "And stop crowding me. Your meth breath is singeing my nose hairs."

Before he can get past his shock and think of a comeback, Mrs. Jennings tells the class to open our textbooks to chapter seven. She lectures on matrices. Five minutes in, I'm one of the few still listening. The lesson is a welcome distraction. I lose myself in the cold logic of math where, unlike my hell-on-Earth life, everything makes sense and the answers come when you work toward a solution. For the past couple weeks, I've let school slide. That needs to change right now.

At lunch, I hide out behind the gymnasium away from the hecklers and haters. Maybe this will be my new hangout for the rest of the year. It's more private than the library, there's a nice shade, plus plenty of nonjudgmental ants to keep me company.

My phone buzzes, shattering the quiet and giving me a jolt. It's a text from Rosie, asking where I am. I ignore it. She'll just bring up the fight that never was, and I do not want to talk about it. Even if it's all I can think about.

I let loose a drawn-out sigh and pull out *Alpha Flight* #106 from my bag. It feels like a million years ago since Bran gave it to me on our anniversary; hard to believe it's only been a few weeks. I read through it, careful not to crease the spine. Even though the '90s art and writing haven't aged well and parts of the story are problematic, I still cherish it. When Brandon first gave me the comic, I thought he was trying to not-so-subtly hint that I should come out. What he really meant was when I did take that step, he'd have my back. And he totally did. Even if I didn't so much as come out of the closet as I was dragged out of it—by whom, I'll probably never know.

My remaining classes plod along even as I try to lose myself in the work. Despite my best efforts, a pointed smirk from a random guy is all it takes for me to lose focus. When the final bell rings, I stay in my seat as the classroom empties. *How in the hell am I going to make it through the rest of the school year?*

Finally, I trudge into the hallway to find Rosie waiting for me. "Follow me," she says with furrowed brow and marches off toward the exit. Knowing better than to question her when she has that look, I do as she says.

"What's up?" I ask as we exit the gate and approach the traffic-swamped parking lot.

"See for yourself."

The blare of a familiar horn draws my attention. Brandon pulls up to the curb in his BMW—with Luke in the passenger side. Luke waves meekly at me.

Bran actually brought him to school of all places. I am so not ready to deal with this, especially here. I whirl on my heel and slip back through the school gate.

"Bobby, wait!" Rosie says, running up to my side. "Come on, just hear the old guy out."

I ignore her, take a detour through the soccer field, and trample through the weed-strewn grass.

"Ay, lookee here," an all-too-familiar voice calls. "Queer boy's back."

Déjà vu and dread envelop me like a heavy fog. Rex, Eddie, and Jorge sit on the bleachers, almost as if they'd never left after the beatdown that started it all.

"What's up, bakla bitch?" Rex says. "We gonna finish this?"

ROUND 28

Rex lounges on a bottom bleacher, his dingy Converse resting atop the seat of Dad's bike. Eddie sits beside him, shuffling a deck of cards. Jorge crouches on the top bleacher, bruises still marring his eyes and mouth. I shoot him a glare. His gaze drops to the ground. The smart thing to do would be to turn back to the parking lot immediately.

"Let's go, Bobby." Rosie tugs on my arm, but I don't budge.

"Ay, let me take him, Rex." Eddie rises from the bleachers. "I can handle the lil bitch."

"Sit down, Eddie," Rex says.

"I want my bike. Now." My voice shakes, just like my legs and my arms—hell, my whole body.

Eddie ignores his brother and marches up to me. "Then you probably should've showed Friday instead of punking out like a little bitch, bitch."

"Shut up, Eddie," I say.

"Yeah, right. What're you gonna do, faggot?"

In two quick strides, I rush Eddie and nail him with a right hook to his big mouth. He falls to the grass, dazed but not out.

"Oh, *dayam*," Rosie crows. "You got punked!" She turns to me. "You were right. That was so much sweeter than pepper spray. Do it again!"

I pounce on Eddie and pin him to the ground with my knee. "You ever call me that fucking word again, I'll make you eat your teeth. You'll be crapping them out your bony ass for a month. Understand?"

Eddie's eyes bulge.

Rex stalks toward me, hands clenched. "Get your bitch ass away from my brother."

I ignore him and cock my good fist at Eddie. "Do. You. Understand?"

"Okay, okay!" he says, whimpering.

I stand to meet Rex. My bandaged hand still stings, but I force it into a fist, raise my guard, and crouch into a fighting stance. Rex walks right into my jab. I tag him twice on the nose. He stumbles back and smiles.

"Not bad, pare." Rex touches the bridge of his nose. "But you should've followed up with the left. Something wrong with it?"

"You should know. You're the one who sicced Jorge on me."

My knuckles throb, a reminder that I'm fighting without gloves for the first time. And there won't be any bell or ref to save me, either. I stretch my fingers and clench my teeth to stave off the pain.

Rex grabs at my stitched-up hand. I flinch, and he drives a fist right into my gut. I collapse to one knee, and he kicks me hard to the grass. The brothers swarm over me, kicking me in the side, each blow like a dagger strike. I cover up, protecting my face.

"Stop!" Rosie screams. "Leave him alone!"

Through their flailing legs, I glimpse Jorge approaching, a new balisong blade in his grip. *No. Not again.*

"Get off him!" Jorge shouts at Rex and Eddie, jabbing the knife at them. "Back off!"

"What the hell?" Rex sidesteps the blade.

"It ain't gonna go down like this, hear me?" Jorge says. The knife quivers in his hand, but he keeps it trained on them.

Rex shakes his head. "You're making a big mistake, pare. Ain't no take-backs here."

"Don't want none. And I ain't your pare no more. You're gonna fight him fair or not at all."

Rex eyes the knife, probably wondering if he could grab it from Jorge without getting sliced.

"Ay, whatever. What I wanted, anyway." He raises his hands and retreats a few steps. "Get up then, punk," he says to me. "Let's do this."

And then Brandon runs up to my side. "You okay?"

I cough a couple times, catch my breath, and nod.

"Come on. On your feet, youngblood." Luke reaches down, and he and Brandon help me stand.

"Why'd you help me?" I ask Jorge.

"Can't let you end up like my tío. He would've never forgiven me."

His intervention doesn't exactly make up for him slicing my hand open, but I'm grateful for the assist. He flips the balisong closed, pockets it, and steps back.

"Can you do this?" Luke asks.

My side feels like a slab of raw meat, but I push the pain out of my mind. "Yeah. Yeah."

"Attaboy." Luke pulls me close. "Okay now, just like in the ring. Let him come at you. Wait for his throw, slip it, then

245

counter. Remember, the punk has zero technique, relies on roundhouses and barely has a jab. He ain't in your class. You show him that. Now, how's your left?"

I manage not to wince as I flex my hand. "Okay, I guess. Still hurts."

"Then use it sparingly. But when you do, make it count."

"Come on." Rex lifts his guard up. "We doin' this or what?"

A crowd of about a dozen students has formed a loose circle around us, with more filtering in from the parking lot. Predictably, a few of them pull out their phones and start recording. Great—if I get my ass kicked again, this time it'll be preserved online for the world to see forever.

Charlotte Wilkes yells, "Stomp that little bitch, Rex!"

"Keep talking and you're the one's gonna get stomped," Rosie shouts at her. "Oh, yeah, we got next, girl!" Brandon restrains her from rushing Charlotte. Too bad. I wouldn't mind seeing that fight.

On the balls of my feet, I circle Rex. He tries to mirror me, but he's slow, flat footed. Luke's voice repeats in my head: *You got crap footwork, you got a crap fighter.* Rex lunges with a big right. I sidestep it and sting him with a double jab, followed by a tentative left that glances his chin. Pain rips through my hand. The stitches shift.

"Thought you had some pop, bruh." Rex beckons with his fist. "Come on, bring that weak shit."

He flails with his jab and grazes my ear. I rotate away, counter with a jab, and unleash the left, my full weight behind it. The blow explodes against his nose, and blood pours out over his lips. We both cry out. Blood covers my hand, but it's not Rex's. The stitches have broken, and the red has soaked through the bandage. I try making a fist, but my hand throbs at the slightest movement. Hopefully it's not permanently damaged, but I can't worry about that now.

Before I can shake off the pain, Rex recovers. He connects with a gut punch and launches a roundhouse that caves in my cheek and drops me. My head buzzes. Or is that the crowd cheering? Hot liquid spreads over my tongue. I spit out a wad of blood.

"Two punches?" Rex shouts. "That's all it takes? Get up, queer boy. I got more for you."

Luke crouches at my side. "Easy, easy. That's enough, Bobby. You've done enough. I gotta call it."

He's right. I'm a busted up, one-handed fighter. But it'll take more than that to make me quit. Not after everything I've had to endure to get here. "I have to do this."

He squeezes my shoulder. "Then end it now or I will."

"You got this, B." Brandon hooks my arms, lifting me to my feet. His eyes meet mine. "Hey, what's your motto?"

"Self-preservation, supposedly." I smirk, and it shoots a wave of pain through me.

"Uh-uh. You have a new motto now: kick that homophobic wannabe gangster's ass."

I nod and exhale.

Before I can take a step, Rex charges and throws a quick combo. I dodge the first blow; the second tags my ribs and rattles my core. I grunt, biting back the pain. But I take advantage of the close quarters and hit him with a quick jab and jerk his head back with an uppercut.

Rex snaps off a hook that I duck under. I answer with one of my own that rips into his eye and staggers him. His breaths come fast. But mine are steady—thanks to my daily jogs and Luke's marathon training sessions. Rex glances around at the crowd. He's probably never been hit this hard in front of so many people, especially not by someone as small as me.

I can't take much more, either. And Rex seems to know it. "You got some fight in you—I'll give you that," he says. "But your bakla ass is still gonna burn in hell."

He's trying to goad me into making a mistake, but I'm not falling for it. I land a pair of rapid-fire jabs, feint with my left, and unleash a crushing right hook. I put everything I have into it. My fist smashes his jaw, the crack echoing like a kulin-tang gong strike. His eyes roll up, and he topples over, arms flailing. He hits the dirt, and his body twitches twice before going still.

The onlookers gawk in silence. Hell, even I can't believe it.

I stand over Rex, my breaths slowing. "I don't believe in hell, but if I end up in it, I'll kick your homophobic ass there too."

"Woo-hoo! Go, B!" Rosie shouts, leaping to my side. "You, my friend, are a tsunami of boxing badassery!"

Brandon and Luke join in. They hug me and slap me on the back, making me cry out. "Easy!"

Some of the crowd cheers me on, but most disperse while grumbling the usual gay slurs. No surprise there. Queer-haters aren't going to change their queer-hating ways just because I won a fight with a bully. I couldn't care less. They only make my win that much sweeter.

Luke beams at me. "You threw like a champ, my friend."

"Thanks to you, Coach."

I stagger past Rex's inert body toward my bike, only to be blocked by Eddie standing guard over it.

"You ain't touching this." Eddie folds his arms. "Deal was only if you win on Friday. It ain't Friday no more."

Seriously? Read the damn field; it's over. If I weren't so battered and spent, I'd reacquaint his face with my fist. I don't even have enough energy for a snarky remark.

Thankfully, I don't need it. Brandon strides up to Eddie, coming within a half foot from his nose. "Dude, you better step aside or you're going to be tongue kissing the ground like your bro over there."

Eddie glances at Rex lying facedown on the ground, barely starting to come to. He shrinks under Bran's glare and moves aside.

With my good hand, I retrieve my bike. I check it for scratches, squeeze the tires, and surprisingly, thankfully, find it's still in solid condition. As I guide it off the field, my thoughts turn to Dad. He kept fighting until the very end. How could I do any less?

"Hey, B." I stop, grab Brandon's hand, and squeeze. "Mahal kita."

I did it. I told Bran I love him. Somehow it feels like the real victory of the day. His eyes go wide, but he doesn't say it back. He doesn't need to.

We sink into a deep kiss. I barely mind the sting of my bruised lips. It's the most public kiss we've ever shared, but I couldn't care less about anyone watching. Hell, take a picture and post it for all I care. I revel in the kiss. I own it. In this moment, there is only us.

ROUND 29

Mom stares at me, her eyes filling up with tears, bottom lip quivering. "So, you've been . . . busy."

"Yeah." I look away and exhale fully. It's a couple of days after the fight, and I finally came clean to her about everything. There were just too many bruises to hide, too many half truths to keep straight, too much guilt to manage. We sit in our cramped living room, and I brace myself for the yelling. I flinch when it comes—only it's not directed at me.

Mom springs up from the couch. "I want to speak to that principal! He'd better give that piece of basura a year's worth of detention! I want him eating his meals and bunking in there!"

"Well, that's probably not gonna happen, seeing as Rex was expelled."

"Oh." She sits back down, suddenly deflated. "Well, okay, then."

"I was dealt two weeks of detention."

"Not bad, considering." Mom slumps against the couch. "Why didn't you tell me about any of this? I want to know what's going on with you. I'm supposed to be here for you."

"That's just it, Mom. How can you be here for me when you're never here? You're always working. And the few hours you're not, you're passed out on the couch."

She bristles at my words. "I have to work, Bobby. If I'm not waiting tables, we don't eat and we're living in some alleyway begging for change."

An image of the 101 overpass squatters flashes in my mind. "I get it. I know. I just—I miss you."

She smirks. "You mean you miss my home cooking."

"Heck yeah! I miss rice and pancit! And ube! I've been eating nothing but eggs and protein shakes for the past two weeks. Must have noodles!"

A giggle escapes her lips, and it's contagious; I join her.

"Next time, tell me what's happening with you, okay?" she says, wrapping me in a hug, and for the first time in a long while, I feel safe. "You know I love you, anak, yeah?"

"I know, Mom."

"Good. You're grounded for a month."

"A whole month? Seriously?" With everything I kept from her, I guess it could be worse. "Fine." I rise and head to my room.

"One more thing. This fight. Did you win?"

"Yeah. Kicked his queer-bashing ass big time."

Mom grins so wide, I can almost see her molars. "Okay, make it a week."

Sweet. Looks like I'm finally on a winning streak.

My week on lockdown crawls by without much happening. It's actually boring. But I'll take boring over life-in-peril drama every time. I use the time to catch up on schoolwork and do extra credit for Mrs. Cisneros. I manage to bring my grade up to a respectable B.

I also have a talk with her about Rex and Eddie's home situation and the abuse their father has been inflicting on them. She promises me she will notify Child Protective Services. The brothers may not be my favorite people, but the cycle of violence they're trapped in must end.

A knock at the front door interrupts the Saturday-morning quiet. I pull it open, and Brandon stands there, sporting workout gear and a clean shave. His defined brown arms pour out of a sleeveless shirt. He smiles, and it's like the rays of the sun washing over me. *Damn, he's beautiful.* My pogi guy.

"Hey." I peck him on the cheek and hand him a homemade card.

"What's this?"

"Just something that's way overdue. Happy very belated Valentine's Day. Drew it myself—with no help from Rosie whatsoever."

On the cover, an admittedly crude drawing of a zombie holds up a blood-soaked human heart. Red oozes from its severed arteries, just the way Bran likes it. A caption in slimy green letters reads, YOU'LL ALWAYS HAVE MY HEART.

Bran blinks and bites his lip. *Wow, is he tearing up?* "This is the most beautiful thing anyone's ever given me."

Mom bursts into the foyer. "Brandon! There's my future son-in-law!"

Oh, God. "Mom!"

"Hi, Auntie. Kumusta ka."

"I made breakfast. Come. Eat."

"We're in training, Mom. We gotta head out."

She saunters to the kitchen, ignoring my protest. "You like eggs with banana ketchup, Brandon?"

Bran skips after her. "Do I?!"

I have no choice but to follow, but I'm not mad. Mom lays out a spread of fried rice, chicken tocino, and scrambled eggs. It smells and tastes like Filipino breakfast heaven. Bran and I eat our fill but go easy on the rice. We give ourselves a half hour to digest and head out.

"You need to visit more," Mom says to Brandon as she follows us to the foyer.

As soon as we're outside, I peck Bran on the mouth. "Sure you're up for this?"

He grins at me. "As sure as we're Pinoy and awesome."

We jog through the still-sleeping neighborhood on my usual route up Alvarado. I slow my pace to stay even with Bran, who's already winded.

Since the fight, most kids at Westlake are smart enough now not to spout their hate around me, but that doesn't mean they don't still spread it. Eventually, other versions of Rex will come along to test me.

Let them.

Brandon and I jog around a corner, and a block later we reach our destination. Perfect timing since he's due for a breather. We enter the deserted grounds of Unidad Park and take in the expansive, vivid colors of the Filipino history mural. So many heroes and an infinite number of stories. Today I'm concerned with only one hero, and one story: Manny, and my own.

I march over to the edge of the mural where the portrait of Emmanuel Dapidran "Pacman" Pacquiao stands proudly, ready for another battle in the ring.

Brandon joins me.

I pull Rosie's extra-thick marker from my pocket, crouch down to the bottom of the mural below Manny's nameplate, and set to work on the tanaga. My handwriting isn't elegant like Rosie's, and the surface isn't the smoothest, but I do my best.

> *Manny, you drove me to win*
> *You helped me to become strong*
> *But I still know you are wrong*
> *How can true love be a sin?*

Bran reads the lines and squeezes my hand.

"Oh, almost forgot to sign it." I lean back over and write at the bottom, B + B.

Grinning, he pecks me on the cheek. We exit the park and head toward the Jab Gym. Despite the slower pace, we make it in decent time.

As we enter the redbrick building, I recall Manny's words to Oscar De La Hoya after besting him: "You're still my idol." Ever since Manny spouted his homophobic statements, these words have occupied space in my mind. Is Manny still *my* idol? Maybe a small part of me believes so, but I can do without heroes who refuse to see past their own narrow perspectives.

Besides, heroes are supposed to lift people up, not tear them down.

Vicki works the heavy bag while Rosie sketches her on an art pad. I wave at them. Vicki winks back and throws a vicious hook. "There are my guys," Rosie says, smiling.

Luke meets us in front of the counter and tosses me a pair of sparring gloves. "So, youngblood, whatcha think about setting up a real fight? Only this time in the ring with a bona fide trained fighter."

"Seriously?"

"Serious as a heart attack. Told you, you're a natural. Question is, you ready to really get to work?"

I don't even hesitate. "I am."

ACKNOWLEDGMENTS

Like the struggles faced by my protagonist, Bobby Agbayani, getting *Chasing Pacquiao* published has been the fight of my life. Bi erasure and the policing of sexual identities have no place in publishing. Thank you to the LGBTQ+, Filipino, and writing communities for speaking out for me when I needed it most. This book would not exist without you.

Salamat to my fearless agent, Jim McCarthy, who championed my work and kept me believing through every setback. You are the Luke to my Bobby. Thank you to everyone at Dystel, Goderich & Bourret LLC.

A big thank-you to my editor, Jenny Bak, who pushed me to write with more precision. The book is much better because of your thoughtful input. You helped me achieve my dream of becoming a published, professional author, and I will always be grateful.

Salamat to my copyeditor, Cassie Gutman; my production editors, Krista Ahlberg, Sola Akinlana, and Marinda Valenti; and my proofreader, Alicia Lea, for fixing my abundance of grammatical errors and giving the work more clarity.

Salamat to Betsy Cola for your gorgeous cover illustration. Having a queer Filipino teen on the cover is a huge deal. You are helping queer Filipinos feel seen! Thank you to Kelley Brady and Theresa Evangelista for the striking cover design. You made it all come together.

Thank you to everyone at Viking Books and Penguin Random House who had a hand in creating this book.

Salamat po to the marketing team at Penguin Random House: Felicity Vallence, James Akinaka, Christina Colangelo, Bri Lockhart, and Shannon Spann.

All my love to my amazing family, Marifi and Alex. You two are my life and the reason I'm able to dream for a living. Marifi, thank you for believing in me and loving me throughout this challenging journey.

A big plate of ube Oreos to my fellow Bi-venger Becky Albertalli. You are a great mentor to me and an even better friend.

Thanks to Mom and Dad for always encouraging my creative talents. Love to the Pulido, Kreachbaum, Lagmay, Ogata, and Skiles families.

Salamat to Becky Albertalli, Erin Entrada-Kelly, Randy Ribay, Jose Antonio Vargas, and Julian Winters for your wonderful author blurbs. I'm inspired by your work and honored by your support.

A huge thank-you to the following in the book community: Jade Adia and Emma Ohland for being the best agent sibs. Sharing our debut journeys together has helped keep me motivated and grounded. Rebecca Christiansen for writing your timely article on bi erasure. Emery Lee for just being awesome. Mark O'Brien for your helpful edits early on. Jess Owens (and Nigel!) for showing me love on Book CommuniTEA. Beth Phelan and DVpit for helping me and many other underrepresented authors find representation. Mae Respicio for your helpful advice and giving my son a Filipino hero named Alex to root for. Steven Salvatore and Jacob Demlow for inviting me to take part in Pride Book Fest before I was even published. Jhoanna Belfer and Bel Canto Books for keeping Filipino and BIPOC authors on store shelves. Cathy Serafica Deleon, Pamela Delupio, and the Long Beach City Library for supporting Asian authors with amazing book festivals. Salamat to all my friends and supporters on social media.

Thank you for your help with research: William Aguila for sharing your thoughts. Matt Encina, Belinda Rodriguez Encina, and Glendale Fighting Club for showing me how to throw a punch. Anika Walch for being my first reader.

Maraming salamat po to Eliseo Art Silva for your iconic Filipino history mural, which has been a true inspiration to me.

Salamat to Kayla Rozales for designing and maintaining my author website. I appreciate your talent and support.

Thank you to my dearest friends: Logan Steele, for helping me with my decision to come out. Stefanie Jacinto Deo, my Cancer twin and lovable text bud. Christina Kreachbaum, the one cousin who truly gets me. Christine Liwag Dixon, for being a badass who inspires me. Michael Magtanong, for reminding me that my voice is important. Anna Liu, for believing in my talent.

Thanks to my friends for your support: Ping Aguiluz, Leah Cadavona, Mark Dimalanta, Debbie Blanco Glenny, Tad Mukai, Mur Frianeza Rios, and the rest of the Jah Gang. Anna Alvez, Steve Bermundo, Melissa Cabrera, Hope Furugen, Maria Rabuy Inciong, Jeanette Makhlouf, Maritza Roño Refuerzo, Jimmy Rivera, Jeff Rodrigo, Jassamine Teen, Michelle Topaz, Marivic Agbin Walch, David Yoneshige, and the Avatar Refuge. (Long live the legend 6tacky!)

Salamat to ube, the greatest dessert ever!

Finally, thank you to my readers for picking up my first novel. If you are queer—whether you're out or in the closet—your identity matters and it is worth fighting for.